The Diary of a

Serial Killer's Daughter

The Diary of a Serial Killer's Daughter

By L.A. Detwiler

Other books by L.A. Detwiler
The Widow Next Door
The One Who Got Away

To my husband

"Words have no power to impress the mind without the exquisite horror of their reality." – Edgar Allan Poe

Prologue

There is something severely wrong with the child.
There is something severely wrong with me, in truth.
The way I see it now, I have two options.
I leave with her and never come back.
I kill us both.
Either way, I think it's safe to say this.
Things will never be the same.

Part I

2009

7 years old

September 1, 2009
6:47 p.m.
Dear Diary,
Last night was a weird night. I saw Daddy doing some strange things in the garage.

I will tell you about it, Diary. Daddy gave you to me so I could get my feelings out. He said it will be just for me and I can write anything I want in here. The doctor we see told him I need to let things out that are bottled up. Daddy told me over and over this is safe. No one will see.

I like having you to talk to. My teacher always says *Ruby, you are a good writer.* She told Daddy I'm advanced at writing, beyond my years. That makes me proud. I even wrote a poem for Grandma, and she put it on the fridge when I was staying with her. Writing is the only time I feel good about myself. Talking isn't so easy. The words always come out jumbled-y. So you will be my friend. I will tell you my secret. Just please don't tell. I don't want Daddy being mad.

Here's what happened.

Daddy tucked me in after reading *Goodnight Moon* like we always do. He kissed my cheek and said Goodnight, Ruby. I love you. I nodded like I always do. He pulled on the lamp to turn out the light. I heard him close my door.

Later I woke up. It was dark. I hit the button on my watch. Daddy gave it to me when I turned five. I love telling time, so he bought it for me. I'm lucky to have such a nice Daddy, I know. It helps me keep track of time because I'm not so good at it. Like when my teacher says finish in one minute. It's hard for me. But mostly I just like looking at the numbers, saying them out loud. I never take it off. Sometimes I like to watch each number change over and over, right in a row, like magic. Perfect. It never stops. It just keeps changing, one right after the other. I like that. I especially like when there's a seven on the watch. I don't know why. I guess seven is my lucky number.

It was 1:04 in the morning. I sat up and looked out the window. I heard a noise outside. That's when I saw it. The garage light was on. Why was Daddy in the garage? It was late. Really late. Daddy always told me never go in the garage. *It's dangerous, Ruby. Don't go in there. Ever.* I was worried. What was Daddy doing?

I knew he would be mad if he found out I snuck there. He would be angry if I was around the garage. The dangerous garage. But I put on my favorite yellow rain boots and tiptoed real quiet down the stairs.

Daddy's truck was in the driveway. I heard noises from the garage. Was he building something? Daddy builds for his job. Maybe he was working hard on a surprise.

I didn't want to ruin it. I crept so quietly like the cat I once saw in the woods, the one with the ear with a weird edge. Its ear was all chewed up, like a big bite was taken out of it. I crept quiet, quiet, low, low. Careful Ruby.

I snuck to the back of the garage. When I was playing out there once I saw a hole in the wall of the garage near the ground. Daddy didn't know it was there or he would have fixed it. I liked the hole, though. It gave me a peek.

Real quiet, I got down and looked in. I didn't want Daddy to see me. I was curious. Curious was on our word list this week at school. C-u-r-i-o-u-s. I can spell it.

Curiosity killed the cat. My grandma said that once. I think that's stupid. That's not what kills cats. Grandma is weird sometimes. She makes me brush my hair and says Daddy isn't doing a good enough job. I get mad at her a lot.

Real quiet I got down and looked through the hole. Daddy had a saw. There was lots of red, splattered about. All around. So much red.

I saw a big spot of red on the floor. It oozed out, quickly joining with other red splotches. It was like watercolors that you put too much water in and they were leaking out over the edge, making a mess.

I stared and stared and watched and watched as Daddy did something with the girl he had in there. I saw her long black hair. It looked pretty. Silky. I scratched my own neck, my hair up in its ponytail. I hate hair on my neck. That woman had a lot of hair. Did it bother her? Who was she?

I didn't know, but I watched. I watched Daddy work and work. I watched him for a long time. Sometimes, Daddy would move and I got a glimpse of his face from the side. Daddy looked happy. Usually, Daddy's face is serious. I didn't know why he was happy. I was glad.

I worry that Daddy is lonely. It's just me and Daddy. Sometimes Grandma when she stops by. She's Daddy's mom. He says she is lonely since Grandpa died. She worries about us, too, since Mama died. But I think she comes around too much. Hovers. That was a word I learned this week too.

Daddy says he is happy with me. He always says he only needs me, just him and Ruby against the world. Sometimes I still think he *is* lonely. I heard Grandma say that once.

But Diary, he looked happy with all of the red.

I watched some more, amazed as a tool cut, cut, cut. It was so pretty, the way it chopped down.

My legs started to hurt. I looked at my watch. 3:05 a.m. Had I really been out there so long? Didn't Daddy need to sleep?

I yawned. I needed to go to bed. Daddy would be in at 7:07 to wake me up. I love sevens. Times that end in sevens are the best, so I make Daddy get me up at exactly that time. He made sure his clock is set exactly to my watch so they match.

I knew I needed to sleep last night even though I was so curious about Daddy's work in the garage. I crept back quiet, quiet, quiet to the house, careful not to open the door too loud. I went to bed, though, tucking myself back in. I thought about all that red, red, red.

Daddy made me cinnamon and sugar toast this morning before school. He looked tired but happy. I wanted to ask him about the garage, about the lady. I didn't. I know Daddy is careful of the garage. He doesn't like me asking questions about it. I can ask him about lots of things. But not the garage. And not Mama, either. Those are no-question zones. I still ask them—I can't help it. But he just gets all weird about it.

I wonder if Daddy needs some space from me. I am difficult. I worry about how difficult I am. The teachers say it when they think I'm not listening. The kids say I'm weird. I don't know. It makes me so sad. I wish I had friends, but people are hard. I feel bad, bad, bad because I am so difficult. There are too many confusing things about people.

Just Daddy. Just Ruby and Daddy against the world. That's all I need.

School passed by quickly because all I could think about was the red, red, red. So pretty. Red. Red everywhere. I kept picturing that one perfect splotch running in the middle of the concrete floor. I wonder if Daddy will go back to the garage tonight.

Well, Diary, that's all for now. I will see you tomorrow at the same time, 6:47 p.m. Daddy sits down to get ready for his favorite show that starts at 7, so it's a perfect time to write.

I will have to let you know tomorrow if Daddy goes back to the garage.

Ruby

September 2, 2009
6:47 p.m.
Dear Diary,

I wrote a lot yesterday. I like writing though. My teachers always say how much I write. How I'm good at writing. I like it. It's easy. I wish I could write instead of talking forever. I hate it when teachers and Grandma try to make me talk.

Daddy read me *Goodnight Moon* again last night, but he was tired. He was not excited with the voices like the night before. He tucked me in and kissed me and said I love you. And then I sat up and waited. I waited and watched. I was tired. I didn't sleep though. My insides were buzzing. It was exciting.

But there was no light in the garage. There was nothing. I think I fell asleep because then Daddy was waking me up and it was time for school.

I wanted to see more of the garage.

It made me think. Does Daddy go to the garage a lot? Is that lady still in there?

I remember a few times when I was younger, maybe five, when I would hear Daddy's truck late, late, late. But I just ignored it. I was too young. But not now. I'm older. I can figure it out.

I like that Daddy has a game. A secret game. I hope I can learn the rules soon.

This will have to be our secret, Diary. I don't want Daddy knowing I saw some of his game. He might be embarrassed. And I won't tell Grandma. No way. She came over today and brought us raisin cookies and salads to eat because she said Daddy doesn't feed me right. I hate raisins and I hate salads. Sometimes I hate Grandma. So I won't tell her. I won't tell anyone.

Ruby, we all need privacy. You have your Diary for privacy. That is what he says.

So I think, Diary, that I should give Daddy privacy. His garage is like his diary, I guess. I won't tell a soul. I love him. He takes such good care of me. I owe him this.

Sometimes at school the kids talk about their moms. About the snacks they make and about how they wait to hug them when they get off the bus.

I wonder what my mom was like. There is only one picture of her out in the house. Well, only one picture Daddy knows about. It's on the fireplace downstairs now. She has red hair, just like me. Daddy doesn't like to talk about her. It makes him sad, I think. She died when I was really young. I don't remember her.

But when the kids talk about hugs and things like that, I'm sort of glad I don't have a mom. I hate hugs. I don't like being touched. It's an icky feeling. I hate it hate it hate it. Daddy never hugs me. He knows I don't like it. And he's okay with that. We love each other but we don't need to hug.

I'm glad I don't have a mom to hug me. Daddy does just fine without hugs.
Stay Safe,
Ruby

September 7, 2009
6:57 p.m.
Dear Diary,

Today was Monday, so I had school. Back to being around people.

The weekend was nice. Daddy made me breakfast. Waffles on Saturday. Waffles are always Saturday. We had bacon and eggs Sunday. Bacon and eggs are always Sunday. Mostly, we played outside. Daddy helped me ride my bike. We're working on riding faster and getting rid of the training wheels.

When I was riding on the lane I came to a stop by the garage. The door was shut. I couldn't help but think about that lady. I wanted to sneak around to the back and look through the hole. I got closer but Daddy yelled.

"Ruby, no garage. It's not safe. You know the rule."

"Sorry, Daddy," I'd said. I do know the rule. Ever since I can remember, that was Daddy's rule. No garage. I can use the shed that is on the other side of the house. That's where bike lives. But no garage.

Daddy doesn't have many rules. Just ones to keep me safe.

Don't touch the stove.

Don't talk to strangers. That's not a problem. I hate talking.

Don't wander away from him.

Look both ways before crossing a street.

Don't go near the garage

Those are the main rules. I make up some of the other rules for us. Like what times we eat and what time we do things. But I like time. Daddy knows that. He lets me be in charge of time.

So I didn't go near the garage. I didn't want to make Daddy mad. Once, when I was little, I wandered in the door of the garage and Daddy got really angry at me. It's one of the few times he's yelled at me. It scared me so much, I cried.

Now, Daddy is more careful about the lock on the door. It's always locked. But he still warns me, just in case. I don't think Daddy would be happy that I looked in there and saw that lady. It's his secret. We all have secrets.

Like what I write in you.

But this past weekend, it was just me and Daddy. I wrote some poems for on the fridge. Daddy said they were really good. One was about a rabbit. One was just about red. I didn't tell Daddy I was thinking of the red in the garage when I wrote it.

So much red. So pretty. Red, red, red. Just like my hair. Just like apples.

I like red. It might be my favorite now. Maybe Daddy will get me red rainboots for my birthday. It's in December, Diary. Just like Christmas. I was a Christmas-time baby.

Daddy is quiet sometimes. This weekend was a quiet weekend. But he was calm. Peaceful even. I like it when Daddy is quiet because I like quiet. It makes me happy.

We sit on the porch a lot out front. The garage is out back. We sit and look into the forest around us, the trees, the lane. We don't have neighbors. There are no children around to play with. Sometimes the kids at school talk about playing with their neighbors, the kids who live in town near the school. It doesn't make me sad, though. I like it out here. In nature. In quiet. Town is too loud. School is too loud. And kids call me weird and annoy me. I only go to school because Daddy says I have to. Because he has work. And I need to go to school because it is my job.

I try to do a good job. It is hard.

The kids are loud and yell and I hate it. And the teachers try to make me talk and I don't like talking, not in front of the group.

Ruby, look at me when I talk to you, they say.

Ruby, stop slapping your hands on the desk.

Ruby, stop scratching your neck and pay attention.

Ruby, stop lighting up your watch. It's science time.

Ruby, Ruby, Ruby.

I'm the one who is always in trouble. The other kids are loud, but I'm in trouble.

Last year, the school had a lady who would follow me everywhere. To help me, they said. Help me adjust. I hated that lady. She talked a lot and tried to make me talk. She talked about me right in front of me like I was stupid.

I'm not stupid. Just different, Daddy always says. *Different is fine, Ruby. Different is good.* But sometimes it doesn't feel good. School doesn't seem to think different is good. The other kids don't think different is good.

Daddy made them get rid of that lady. I was in the meeting when he said I didn't need some aide. I was just fine without her. He wouldn't have me treated like that. *Ruby is smart and fine on her own. She's just different. She doesn't like to talk to people. But she's smart, and she will learn at her own pace.*

But I know that's not true. I'm not fine on my own. I had squeezed Daddy's hand in that meeting.

I'm fine with Daddy. He makes everything better. He knows what I need. He knows I'm different . . . and he's okay with that. I love him. He's the best.

I hate school. Hate, hate, hate.

So weekends are my favorite. Just Ruby and Daddy.

That's how it should be.

Goodnight Diary. Stay Safe (Daddy always tells me to stay safe. I like that.)

Ruby

September 10, 2009
6:57 p.m.
Dear Diary,

I was late to school today. It was Daddy's fault. But I'm not mad. I'm never mad at him. He tries so hard.

Last night, after *Goodnight Moon,* I stared at the ceiling. I wasn't tired. My brain was doing that spinny, wild thing. I was thinking about all sorts of things that happened, my brain jumping, jumping, jumping all around. The air was too hot and the blanket too scratchy. And then I heard a cricket out my window that wouldn't stop. I pounded my head, just a little, to make it stop. It never stops.

So I lay there for a long while. I heard Daddy's footsteps downstairs and the door creak. He was being quiet, but I could hear him. I heard the truck. I looked at my watch. It was 11:00 p.m. On a school night. He was leaving on a school night. Where was he going?

I sighed. Maybe he needed more time in the garage.

And that got me wondering if the lady was still in the garage, her black hair spread out behind her. I wanted to see her again. I wanted to see so badly.

I knew Daddy wouldn't want me out of the house alone, but I couldn't help it. I got that image in my head and I couldn't stop myself. I needed to see.

So I crept down the stairs and out back. I snuck to the spot behind the garage with the hole and peered in. But I was surprised. The black-haired lady was gone. Her white face, her eyes staring. Gone. All the red was gone too. Everything was back in its place.

Saws and tools hung in their spots. I smiled and got goosebumps on my arms. I loved how orderly it was. A board with tools in a row, everything in line. A table sat in the middle of the garage, the floor clean. Not a dot of red. Not a dot of dirt. Clean, clean, clean.

I made myself small, small, small, and waited. Maybe Daddy went to get the black-haired lady and bring her back for the game. I yawned and yawned but fought to stay awake. I needed to stay awake. I counted. I checked my watch over and over.

Finally, at 12:38 a.m., he came back. The truck rattled down the lane. The headlights went out, and the door opened. I heard Daddy grunt as I peeked through the hole. He was carrying something.

A lady. This one had red hair. Red like me.

I almost squealed. Red, red, red. Red like me, Ruby. So pretty.

The lady was sleeping. Her neck looked funny, her eyes bulgy like a frog. Daddy sat her on the table, and I watched. She was naked. I closed my eyes. We're not supposed to show those parts to anyone, that's what Daddy always said. Maybe the rules were different for grownups. I'd have to ask him sometime.

I opened my eyes and watched as Daddy grinned. He went to the wall and pulled off some rope. What was he doing? Was this a game?

After a long time, I watched him hang that lady up from the ceiling. She dangled like the tire swing at school, swaying back and forth. Was Daddy making a swing? I watched with my mouth open.

He took out a camera. My favorite, the instant camera. I like it because it comes out black and then poof—there's a me on it. Grandma says it's a relic. I don't know what that means, but it sounds like a bad thing.

He snapped a picture, and I wondered what he would do with it. Would he hang it up in the house? I didn't see one of the black-haired lady. Then, after that, he stood, staring at her. For a moment, he didn't look so happy. He looked like he wanted to cry. I wanted to run over and ask what was wrong, but I stayed in my spot.

A long, long, long time later, he pulled her down. It seemed weird to hang her up only to pull her down. He put her on the table, the one the black-haired lady was on. The smile came back as he went to the tools. He took a saw and then another. Two saws. Wow.

He walked to the table and touched her face. He was so close I thought he might kiss her. I've never seen him so happy. Well, once, I think he was happy. There's a picture of him with Mama I saw and he looked happy. He was wearing a suit. She was wearing a white lacy dress and they were on a beach. Daddy looked happy then.

I stared. The saw cut. Then there was red. So much red. My heart beat faster. I loved seeing the red puddling underneath the table. How would he clean it all up? I wanted to see the process. How did he get it clean?

I watched and watched as he worked and worked. Small bits of something were falling to the ground. It was like art class, except all the paint was red. Maybe I would have to try that in school, I thought. Painting with just red. Maybe I could make Daddy a picture out of red paint. He could put it in the garage.

Daddy worked and worked, and I wanted to stay. But I could tell he was getting tired. It looked like hard work. And I knew he'd go to sleep and I couldn't be outside when he went in. So I had to leave.

I hoped I'd get to see the rest sometime. I needed to see the rest. How he cleaned up.

I wanted to know how he got it so clean.

2:41 a.m. I went to bed.

And then, the next thing I knew, Daddy was in my room.

"We're late. Let's go," he said gruffly. My eyes opened. I looked at my watch. How had I slept in? I never slept in. Daddy never slept in.

I was mad. We were off schedule. *We were off schedule!* The day was ruined.

Daddy looked tired. I thought of the lady. She must have kept him late.

I wanted to tell Daddy to save his garage game for weekends, that we can't be off schedule. But I didn't. Secrets and all. Privacy. Rules. He would be mad that I was near the garage. I didn't want him to think I was breaking the rules. I never break rules Daddy sets, not on purpose. Not if I can help it—sometimes I can't.

I hadn't gone in, I hadn't. I'd just looked. He'd never said I couldn't look. But I didn't want him to think I was breaking rules.

I made it through the day. Daddy had driven me to school and then went off to work. He didn't tell me to stay safe when he dropped me off. That upset me. My whole day was bad. He always said stay safe.

But at least he got me to school. And I *was* safe. That was good. I drew a picture of a lady with red markers. All red. The teacher said it was interesting as her eyebrows crinkled. I don't think she meant it. Some of the other kids laughed. I ripped it up. I didn't want Daddy to have a picture that wasn't good, and I was mad that he hadn't said stay safe. It was his fault the picture was bad.

But it's okay. I know he's a good Daddy, after all. He knows the bus is too loud for me and it makes me upset, so he drives me every day. Even if it means he is going to be late for work like today.

Diary, I like telling you what happens. Maybe I'll get some red pens for next time I write. I think it would look so good in red. Don't you?

Stay Safe,

Ruby

September 16, 2009
6:57 p.m.
Dear Diary,

Mama didn't follow rules. Daddy doesn't like to talk about her but when he does, he says she didn't follow rules. He says she was a free spirit. I don't know that that means exactly, but I don't like people who don't follow rules. I bet I wouldn't have liked her.

I will follow the rules. I don't want to go where she is. Some kid from school's hamster died and his mom told him it went to hamster heaven. I asked Daddy what heaven was. He sighed and said Ruby, some things are too hard to explain. I don't think he believes in this hamster heaven.

I don't know where Mama is, if she is in hamster heaven or somewhere else. I don't remember her. Daddy said she had pretty hair. My hair is red. Red red red. Red like apples my teacher says. Red like strawberries, Grandma always says.

I hate strawberries. Grandma doesn't know that. She doesn't know much of anything, in truth.

My hair is red like the licorice Daddy likes and red crayons and my backpack. I like red. It's my favorite color. Daddy's too. He said so yesterday when I told him I love the color red and asked for those red rainboots. He said maybe he could take me shopping for some if I wanted. I hate shopping. Too many people. But he said if I want them, I should really try them on and make sure they are good. So I guess I have to go to the store. I hate when shoes are too tight or too loose. Daddy says I'm picky, which is fine. He says it's perfectly good to know what you like. So I guess this weekend we'll look for boots. Daddy will hold my hand or say something to calm me if I'm upset. He never gets mad when I have one of my fits, as the teachers call them. He is nice and makes me feel better.

Stay Safe,
Ruby

September 18, 2009
6:57 p.m.
Dear Diary,

Daddy used to have a picture of Mama in his room, one besides just the one on the fireplace. I took it from his room when he threw it once. It was in March. I was scared but when he went outside to take a walk, I took it and hid it under my bed. I think he knows I took it. But maybe he's glad I took it from his room. I think it makes him angry. I'm not sure why. I look at it sometimes. I look at the red hair like me. She was pretty, Mama was. I miss her some days when I think about her. I don't know her but I miss her even though she probably would've given me hugs and I hate hugs and maybe I would not like her much. It's weird to miss someone you don't know, but it's kind of like when I miss Santa Claus after Christmas. I've never met him, but I miss him.

I asked once what she was like, just a little bit ago. Daddy said girls who are seven shouldn't ask so many questions. He said it's Mama's fault I'm so curious. I guess at least I learned that. Curious. I never realized I'm curious. I like the idea of being curious. It sounds good.

But curiosity did not kill a cat, as my stupid Grandma says. She came over today. She was asking Daddy questions about me. If I've been to the doctor. To the therapist. If he's making me try new foods. She is nosy. Nosy, nosy. Daddy gets annoyed. I can tell. Grandma needs a hobby. I don't think he likes her coming around. I don't either. But I also don't like when I have to stay with her. Sometimes, Daddy has me stay with her in the evenings. I wonder what he's doing then. He just says he's going out. Whatever that means.

Some of the things Grandma says are so dumb. They make no sense. Like about early birds catching worms and about breaking legs when I have a speech at school. I don't know why she does that.

I like that Daddy knows I'm smart even though I don't talk to people much. My teacher said I am smart but also bad and stubborn. She thinks I'm bad and stubborn because I'm quiet. And because I always remind her of the time, like when we're almost late for recess or lunch. I just want her to know that we are not on time. You'd think she'd be happy that someone is helping her stay on schedule. Someone needs to watch the minutes turn over, and I am nice enough to take the job on so she can focus on the loud, really bad kids.

After Daddy said I was smart, Daddy said Mama liked rubies. I don't know what rubies are. Daddy said they are reddish like my hair, which is why I'm called Ruby. Ruby like my hair.

Ruby Marlowe.

Marlowe with an "e" at the end. It's a hard name to spell. I used to get it wrong sometimes. My teacher got mad when it was wrong and shouted "e" like she was an animal. I saw a monkey on the TV once. It made noises like that. The teacher didn't like when I made monkey noises out loud at her. I was just trying to show what she sounded like. The kids started calling me monkey girl. I missed recess and snack.

I hate recess, and snack was gross peanut butter. Sticky, sticky. I hate sticky. So I didn't care.

Daddy was mad when he found out I got in trouble. *You need to follow the rules,* Daddy said. He wants me to follow the rules. *Sorry, Daddy, I'll try and do better next time,* I said.

My hand hurts now, Diary. I'm going to go now and watch TV with Daddy. That show is on tonight with people sending in videos that are supposed to be funny. I laugh sometimes, but not at the stupid videos. I laugh because sometimes they stir memories in me, like the one of Daddy and the ice cream cone and the dog at the fair. That's a funny one. But Daddy thinks I laugh at the show. He says it's good to laugh, so we watch it together.

Daddy doesn't usually laugh, though. He just grins and lets out a bit of a coughing sound.

Stay Safe,
Ruby

September 20, 2009
6:58 p.m.
Dear Diary,

It rained today. I got to play outside in my new red rainboots. Bright, bright red, my favorite color. Daddy watched from the porch as I splashed out front in a big puddle. Mud went everywhere. Daddy didn't care. He smiled and smoked his cigarettes while I jumped.

I usually don't like water. Rain is okay and puddles, but not the bathtub. Water scares me. It always has. Daddy has to sit by me when I'm in the tub, and he only can put a little tiny bit of water. He says I've always been like this. But puddles and rain are okay. Fun, even.

Smoking is bad for lungs. I tell Daddy that. He should not smoke. We learned at school it is harmful. There are thousands of chemicals and it is addicting and it can kill you. Second-hand smoke is bad, too, but I'm not worried about me. I'm worried about Daddy. I don't want something bad to happen to him. What would I do without him?

He told me old habits die hard. That saying doesn't quite make sense to me, but I still don't think he should smoke.

I splashed and splashed in the puddles. I jumped super high, higher than ever. It made me very happy to jump. My new red boots make puddle hopping a true blast.

Shopping for them was tough. The sales guy tried to touch my feet and I got very mad. I stomped and stomped and cried in the corner. I didn't want to cry, but sometimes emotions just burst out of me like the volcano our teacher made in science class. They just erupt and I can't stop them. Some mother with her kids called me a brat, which made me even sadder and I cried harder. Daddy called her a bad word. We went home the first time without boots. But eventually Daddy convinced me to go back. He always helps me see things in a better light. It took a few trips for me to decide on the right pair and the right size. But I finally got them just perfect.

Daddy helped me try on the boots, and once they were on, I nodded. They felt so good and they were red, my favorite color. But you know that.

I haven't wanted to take them off. I even wore them to bed last night. Daddy didn't mind.

So I spent the day jumping in puddles and having so much fun in my boots, testing them out in every type of puddle. I didn't tell Daddy, but when I splash, splash, splashed, I pretended it was the puddles in the garage, the red puddles.

Can you imagine, Diary? How fun it would be to jump in the red puddles in my red boots? It would be so pretty. But then it might be harder to clean. I hope Daddy goes back to the garage soon so I can see him clean. I want to see what he does. How he does it.

I'm tired from splashing. I might go to bed early tonight. I don't know. I don't ever go to bed early but I'm sleepy.

Stay Safe,
Ruby

September 25, 2009
6:57 p.m.
Dear Diary,

Today was a good day at school.

The teacher had us write poetry. Most kids hated writing poetry, but I loved it. And the teacher noticed my poem. She said it was very interesting. She was worried the bunny was hurt. I told her how once, when I was younger, we found a baby bunny in our yard. It *was* hurt. Daddy helped it. Still, it didn't live. I was sad but couldn't stop staring at its stiff yet floppy body. Daddy said that happens sometimes, that all things die. Like Mama? I had asked. He didn't answer.

My teacher smiled at me today. She said poetry is a way to show feelings. She said the poem was good. She said I did a wonderful job. This time, I think I believed her.

We had to have rhyming words in it. I like rhyming. Rhyming is like cat and hat. Jump and bump. Caboose and noose.

I made the last one up. I don't know where I heard the word noose. I'll have to ask my teacher what it is. But caboose is a train. Daddy and I went on a train once, a couple of years ago I think. I don't remember why. Writing the poem was easy. I showed it to Daddy. He liked it too. He put it on the fridge.

He asked why the bunny was hurt.

I said I didn't know. It just came to me. I don't think he remembers the bunny from a while ago. When did that happen?

Here is my poem Diary. I hope you like it. Maybe I will write more poems tonight instead of watching TV. Daddy said it would be okay to break the routine. I get nervous when the schedule is different, but he told me to work on my poetry if it made me happy. He said we all need an outlet to express ourselves.

So maybe I will write more. But here is that poem.

Stay Safe,
Ruby

Little bunny in the flowers.
He rests for hours.
White as a cloud.
He isn't loud.

Soft like a shirt.
The bunny is hurt.

October 2, 2009
6:57 p.m.
Dear Diary,

Daddy has been really tired lately. We get home from work and school and eat dinner and do homework. And sometimes after I'm done writing, I go out to the living room and he's asleep already.

I worry about him. He has been quieter than usual. Last night, he was too tired to read *Goodnight Moon*. It made me sad and mad at the same time. I read it to myself, but it wasn't the same.

Sometimes Daddy gets in these moods, these weird little funks, as Grandma likes to say. He pulls away. It usually happens in October. I don't know why. Grandma told me October is hard for Daddy and to be patient and good. I asked her why but she just shriveled up her weird looking face. The wrinkles got deeper and she shook her head and told me not to ask that question.

October is hard, but sometimes March is bad for Daddy, too. The picture, the one that was in his room that I stole, the one of Daddy and Mama . . . it has a date on it. March 12th. I wonder why that date is important. I want to ask him but I am afraid. He seems upset and I don't want to bug him. I hate it when people ask me questions when I'm upset. So I've tried to be quiet and good and follow the rules as I always do.

I wonder if Daddy gets lonely. I sometimes do at school when the kids are mean and won't talk to me. But at home, it's okay. I like it just me and him. I don't like talking to other people anyway because it's really hard and they get confused and I get mad. But Daddy isn't like me. He doesn't mind talking to people. At least when we grocery shop or go to the Post Office or to the hardware store for supplies, he talks to people. He smiles at them and asks how they are. Everyone in town seem to like him. But Daddy never really has anyone over. Not except the ladies in the garage.

He used to have a guy from work who came over sometimes. His name was Pete. He would come over on Fridays and drink a beer with Daddy and they would watch TV. But then Pete stopped coming over. I don't know what happened or why. I should ask Daddy.

So now it is just me and Daddy, all the time. When Grandma isn't butting her big butt in.

I like that it's mostly just us. I wonder if Daddy gets sad though. I wonder if that is why he gets moody in October. I wonder if he misses Mama. I wonder so many things.

Maybe Daddy is just really tired. He's said that a lot this week. His job keeps him busy. Daddy builds things. He works in construction and he has built a lot of things in town. He helped build the church and some houses and even a big mall. He says he was always good at building things.

Sometimes, I like to look in the bed of Daddy's truck and look at all the tools he keeps in there. Shovels and axes and all sorts of things. Daddy says you can never be too prepared. That you never know when you might need to build something.

I like that Daddy is good with tools. It makes me proud.

I think tomorrow maybe I'll ask Daddy to help me build something. Maybe a birdhouse. I like to watch the birds sometimes. That would be good. Maybe Daddy wouldn't be so sad if I take his mind off of things.

Stay Safe,
Ruby

October 7, 2009
6:57 p.m.
Dear Diary,
Yesterday was a bad, bad day.

Daddy's been having a hard time. He's moody. He forgets things like our schedule and our dinner foods and to get milk at the store. He tucked me in bed early even though he knows how much I hate being off schedule. He rushed through *Goodnight Moon.* I noticed when he held the book, his hands were shaking.

"You okay, Daddy?" I asked.

He nodded, but he didn't look at me. "I'm fine, Ruby. Just fine."

But he wasn't. I could tell.

He tucked me in, and I tried really hard to fall asleep. To not worry. I was feeling okay—until it started to storm. Really storm. Crashes boomed through the house and lightening blinked in the sky. I'm terrified of lightening. I hate it. Even more than that, though, I hate the loud booms of the thunder. It startles me every time and it makes my head spin and hurt.

I snuck out of my room and down the stairs to find Daddy. He always rubs my back when it's storming. Why didn't he come up to sit with me? When I tiptoed into his room, he wasn't there. Empty. I looked out the window. His truck was gone. How did I miss it? The thunder was loud, the rain crashing into the house. It pinged like popcorn on the roof. When I realized it, I was panicked. It was terrifying, the storm booming and banging and hurting my head. I dashed back to my room and flicked on the lamp. Then I rocked back and forth on my bed. Back and forth. Back and forth.

The storm passed, the lightening stopped. But I was still scared. Where did Daddy go? Why did he leave? Tears fell. After a long time, I heard the truck pull up. I peeked out my window. Daddy was home. He was getting out of the truck parked by the garage. He was rushing, frantic. I thought about going down, my tears drying now. I wanted to see if he brought another lady to play with in the garage. But I was mad. I was still so angry that he left. As if he could sense me, he turned and saw the light on in my room. I froze. Now Daddy would be mad. But I was mad too.

Daddy ran in the house. I heard the door slam. Up the stairs he came, his feet pounding on each step. I sat on my bed rocking. Rocking.

"Ruby? Are you okay? I'm sorry, I'm sorry." His voice was calm, but I could tell he was nervous.

I rocked. I didn't answer. Tears fell. I wanted to explain, but the words got all tripped up and I just cried harder and louder.

"Ruby, dammit, answer me. Are you okay?"

I rocked and rocked, my head hitting against the wall and rattling the picture above it.

"Storm." I choked out the single word.

Daddy knelt down in front of me. I looked down. His hands were dirty. Why were they so dirty?

"I'm sorry, Honey. I am." He softened now, sighing. I felt the anger melt a little bit as I looked at his boots, staring at the floor. "I had to go out. I tried to get home as soon as the storm started. I did."

"Why?" I wanted to ask why he left, but only that one word came out. Daddy knew me, though. He knew what I meant.

He cleared his throat. There was a long moment. "There was an emergency. The storm knocked down a tree, and one of the guys from work needed some help. I didn't want to wake you."

I rocked. That didn't make sense. Daddy didn't leave when the storm started. He was already gone when it started storming. Still, I didn't want to ask. I didn't want to make Daddy upset. I could tell he felt bad enough.

"Ruby?"

He sat beside me but didn't touch me.

"Okay." I replied. It was better now. Daddy was back. Nothing else mattered.

"I'll sit with you until you fall asleep," he said. "I promise I'm not leaving."

I lay back down, thinking about the storm that had passed and about Daddy leaving and about how I was glad he was home. I lay for a long time as Daddy sat beside me. He seemed calmer now. More peaceful. I didn't understand. I closed my eyes and pretended to drift off, feeling much more at ease. After a long while, I heard him turn out my lamp and walk out of my room and down the thirteen creaky steps.

But he didn't go to his room. I counted his footsteps. There weren't enough. He was in the kitchen. I heard the back-door crack open, the opening of it alerting me to the truth. He didn't keep his promise. It was still raining but softer now. I didn't get up and look out the window, though. I didn't want Daddy to be mad. I didn't want him to know that I knew the truth. He was going to the garage. He must have to clean, I had thought, as I drifted to sleep.

When I woke up this morning, Daddy was already in the kitchen. His eyes were dark, and his face stubbly. But he was smiling, making breakfast for us. He was happier. I don't know what it is, but the garage makes him smile more. Maybe he should go in there more often. Why does he wait so long? Maybe last night fixed Daddy. I'm still mad he left during the storm. It scares me to be alone. Maybe some time he'll let me go with him. I wish he would.

I don't think so. I don't think Daddy wants me knowing what goes on out there.

It'll be our secret, Diary. Our little secret that we know what Daddy does out there. Secrets. Secrets. Secrets. We all have secrets. My teacher says not to keep secrets. Grandma says secrets don't make friends. Either way you look at it, it seems like secrets are bad.

But I don't like my teacher, and Grandma is horrible, too. I think secrets can be fun, and I don't have any friends except Daddy. Daddy and I both have secrets . . . and no one knows them but me. I just giggled a little bit at the thought. It feels good to know something others don't. I like knowing more than they do. I like the secrets I get to keep.

Stay Safe,
Ruby

October 28, 2009
6:57 p.m.
Dear Diary,
I finally did it. I finally got to see it all.

Well, not all. I got to see the ending part. I got to see how he cleans. And it was so pretty. I loved it. I wished I could help. I have it memorized so I could tell you, Diary. I wish you could have seen it.

I knew Daddy was going to go out when he tucked me in. He had on his boots, the ones he had on the other night when it stormed. He was also shaking when he read to me. I know when his hands shake when he reads, it's a garage night—or at least close to one. I almost asked him to go along. I asked if I had to go to bed.

"Stick to the schedule, Ruby. You don't want to be off schedule," he said. He looked surprised I was asking. I nodded. I wanted to go with him, but he was right. Schedules are important. And I could tell he had a schedule of his own, one he didn't want me to know about. But I know all about the schedules he keeps, don't I, Diary?

I waited and waited. I almost fell asleep. I let my mind dance over memories of me and Daddy to keep myself from falling asleep. Finally, I heard his truck pull in. I heard him click open the truck, but I stayed quiet. I didn't want Daddy getting mad that I wasn't sleeping. I heard him moving around the garage. Good thing no one is around to hear it. I don't think Daddy wants anyone to see him working. It's private. Good thing we live far away from everyone and Grandma doesn't like to drive at night. We are alone, just the way Daddy needs it. That makes me glad.

After a while, I couldn't wait anymore. I needed to see him clean. I imagined the red, swirling puddles of it all about. I imagined how clean it would be when he was done, everything in its place. I wanted to be a part of that, to know how he did it. I couldn't wait anymore.

I was very quiet like a mouse when I snuck out. Not like the stupid one in the book we're reading in school, but an actual, quiet mouse. Except I didn't even squeak, not at all. I was silent, silent, silent like a sneaky shadow or a gentle breeze that barely moves the flowers. I needed to make sure I didn't get caught. I didn't know what Daddy would do if he saw me. So slowly, quietly, I crept downstairs. I edged out the door and around the house, the back side. I counted my steps, careful and calm. The hard part would be getting to the back of the garage. I had to sneak. I snuck along the ground, low and quiet, fast fast fast. I made it to the back, clinking of metal telling me Daddy wasn't done yet.

I got to my spot behind the garage, to my little hole that lets me peek. Daddy's back was to me, but when he moved to put stuff away, I got to see the lady.

Black hair. Short. She laid on the table Daddy had, quiet quiet quiet. I wondered if she was trying to not make Daddy mad, too. It looked like part of her was on the floor. But once my eyes saw the red, all the red, I didn't notice anything else.

I watched Daddy for a long time, the way he worked so carefully. The way he soaked up the red as the smell of bleach spread. Bleach everywhere. He worked for so long, bagging things up.

After a long long time, when my eyes were heavy, he took the black bags outside. I heard the wheelbarrow move that is beside the garage. I looked at my watch. It was 3:45 a.m. So late. I crept along the side of the garage. He was driving, but not down the driveway towards the road. He was pushing the red wheelbarrow into the woods on the dirt path we sometimes walk on. Where was he going? I wanted to follow him. I wanted to see how he finished the cleaning. But I knew I had to get back to my room. He would maybe be done soon, and I couldn't have him finding me. I looked one more time at the spotless floor, at the clean, clean, clean. Not a spot to be seen. That rhymed. My teacher would be proud.

No one would know that lady was here, I suspected. The red was only in my memory now, like a treasure of my very own. I thought of this lady's splotches, how they were oddly shaped and swirled compared to last time. I loved how you never knew what the puddles would look like. It was like a painting on the floor, different every single time. And I felt like Daddy wanted it that way. I smiled. I could keep a secret. I was good at sneaking and at keeping secrets. I barely talked to anyone except Daddy, and if he didn't want to talk about his garage game, then neither would I.

I dashed back in the house, thinking about all of the red going away, about how good Daddy was with that rag and that bucket and those bags. His garage was perfect, beautiful. All the tools were lined right back up. It's like that lady was never there. Clean and pure and perfect.

Last night, after I tucked myself in and fell asleep, I had dreams, Diary. I don't remember much about them, but I know they were of red. I could smell and taste and hear all the red.

This morning, Daddy was in a good mood.

His garage game went well. I'm happy for him.

Stay Safe,

Ruby

Little cat
With soft white hair
With no care
Do you dare
You are rare
Your ear has a tear
Red everywhere.

~Ruby

Part II

2010

8 years old

June 11, 2010
6:57 p.m.
Dear Diary,
It happened again last night.

It's been so long. I'd almost thought Daddy was done with his game in the garage because he hasn't been out there in so long. Or I haven't seen him if he was. Of course Mrs. Lansberry, my teacher, gives us so much homework this year. I am always so tired. Maybe I missed Daddy's game—but I don't think so. It's like something switched off in Daddy, like he didn't need the garage anymore.

And then suddenly he did.

I hate that Mrs. Lansberry gives us homework. I have better things to do than write stupid sentences with the horrible, dumb words she picks for us. But maybe I'm just angry because I don't like Mrs. Lansberry, period. Just like last year's teacher, Mrs. Lansberry thinks I'm an odd kid because I never talk and I don't have friends. But she doesn't know about you, Diary. You're my friend. You and Daddy. I talk plenty—just not out loud.

School is almost done for the summer. That will mean I have to go to day camp while Daddy works. It's at the YMCA. Daddy says it will be good because there's a pool and fun things to do, but I think he might be stretching the truth. I think he just hopes maybe I'll make friends and teachers like Mrs. Lansberry won't think I'm so odd then. I understand why Daddy would want that.

It will be a nice change from school. It's better than school because we don't get grades and the stupid teachers aren't there. But it's also not better because the kids are even louder there. At least I won't have homework. Or speeches. And at least this year, Daddy isn't making me stay with Grandma. Two years ago, before Daddy found the day camp, I spent the summer with her, and it was terrible. She asks tons of questions about Daddy. It makes me mad. I don't want her butting in between us. She needs a hobby besides knitting me scratchy, ugly sweaters. Daddy made me wear one once to her house, and she was so proud. When I got home, I cut it with scissors. Daddy didn't yell. He laughed. He agreed with me when I said the sweater was ugly. I think Grandma makes him mad sometimes too.

Last night, I was drifting off to sleep after *Green Eggs and Ham*. Daddy bought it for me for Christmas. He thought maybe it would be good to try something new, even though I don't like new things. But I like the green eggs and the ham. I asked Daddy if we could try green eggs. He smiled and said yes. I don't know if I'll like them, they have to be cooked just right. No slimy texture. Yuck.

As I was falling asleep, I heard Daddy slink downstairs and close the front door. My heart beat wildly. I peeked out and saw his truck pulling away. I couldn't believe it.

He must be playing the game again, I realized. It had been so long, but I still hadn't forgotten. For so, so long, I've waited to hear him go out, to see him working in that garage. It's been hard to be patient, to not ask him about it. I've missed it, in truth. All that red, so pretty I can almost taste it, feel it, hear it.

I hurriedly shoved my feet into my red boots—Daddy also bought me a new pair of those last month. The old ones were tight. My feet are growing, growing. I walked downstairs and outside and went to my spot, the familiar little peeping spot in the back of the garage. It had been so long.

Daddy came back a long, long time later—it was 2:09 a.m., my watch told me— and he carried her in. She was wearing a pretty red dress, her long blonde hair pulled up into a ponytail. It looked a little frizzy, like it wasn't quite perfect anymore. It bothered me. Her dress was pretty. I almost squealed out loud. I loved red. Did she know how perfectly it would match the splotches on the ground? It's like she must have known. Just like before, he put a rope around her neck. The same rope. He has it tucked in a drawer in his toolbox. He strung her right up in the same spot and took her picture with the camera. Wow. Maybe Daddy wants to be an artist and this is his way of capturing the moment? If I were him, I'd rather take a picture of the red splotches. They're prettier.

If I could, I would also take a picture of his face when they're strung up. He always looks for a long time, really sad but also happy somehow.

After a long time of staring, he took her down and put the rope away. He carried her across the garage. I saw him place her on the table, pull out the tools, and start working on her. Once, Daddy was watching a doctor show on TV. They were doing surgery. It looked like Daddy was doing that. Maybe he was a doctor once. I should ask him.

There was blood running down her head and into her hair, coloring her ponytail. I noticed when Daddy went over to get his tools. Everything was the same. He carried out the game perfectly. I won't bore you with the same details even though I love replaying them in my head, even when I'm at school. But here's the exciting part—I got to see what happens after. Like after, after. The whole thing.

I was scared because I knew Daddy would be mad if he saw me. But I couldn't help it. When Daddy finally was done and loaded her into the wheelbarrow at 4:32 a.m., I crept behind. The wheelbarrow is a rusty red color, not shiny like I like. Daddy loaded it up with the bags and then started wheeling it away, past the garage and into the woods. His muscles bulged as he pushed the wheelbarrow. There's a little trail. It's bumpy, but I know where it goes. We walked there sometimes when I was younger. Daddy likes the field at the end of the path. It isn't too far back, but it's a beautiful little clearing. The grass grows high, past my waist. The field is peaceful, and I always liked picking wildflowers there. One time, we even found a lost dog out there, a big, brindle dog. It looked like the dog in the book series I love to read at the library. They're called *Henry & Mudge* books, but this dog was speckly unlike Mudge. Daddy said he was called a mastiff. Daddy had leaped between us when it came near me, though, and the dog ran back into the woods. It was scary, but I liked how big the dog was. I asked Daddy if we could get one, but he said he was too busy to take care of a dog. Maybe the dog could've helped him, but maybe not. But the field was always so beautiful. Peaceful, serene, and quiet other than the time the mastiff was there. Just how I like it.

I didn't know it was where he finished the game. That changes so much, but also it changes nothing. It's still beautiful, I suppose.

Last night, I got to see him work in the field. I knew I should go back in to the house, but I couldn't help it. I wanted to see it all. The moon was shining down, and it was so magical looking. It was chilly and the air bit my cheeks. I had to wait for a while, give Daddy a head start so he didn't see me. It was so hard to wait because I wanted to walk with him. I love the trail on a regular day, but at night, it was even more exciting. More quiet.

I waited for what felt like forever, Daddy pushing the wheelbarrow down the path. It bumped along, and I watched from around the garage, wondering if the bags would fly out. They didn't. Daddy walked slow. It seemed like he knew exactly where he was going.

When it was safe for me to come out, I crept along the trail. My feet wanted to kick the dirt, but I didn't. I didn't want Daddy to hear me. I didn't think he would like me following him. I was tired when I finally got to the clearing. I had to creep behind trees so he wouldn't see me. I leaned on the scratchy tree, watching him work in the middle of the field. It was too dark to see the prettiness of the wildflowers. I wished I could see them better.

Stay quiet, I told myself. I hugged up to the tree, squinting to see Daddy in the dark. I wished he had a light out there. I wanted to see better. He was in the corner of the field, a shovel in his hand. Digging, digging, digging. What was he doing? Was it a treasure hunt? I almost ran to him but stopped myself. This was his game. His alone. I had to just watch.

It was dark, dark, dark even with the moon, so it was hard to see. I wished I could be closer to learn, to watch. After a long time, Daddy pulled the bags out of the wheelbarrow and plunked them in the Earth. I was amazed. I wanted to watch more. But I knew I had to beat Daddy back. I took one final look at Daddy, smiled at how hard he was working, and ran back to the house.

I was in my room for a long time. I peeked out the window. He was back in the garage. I heard him come into the house much later.

It was 6:02 a.m. What a long night. Soon it would be time to get up. We would both have a long day. At least it was Friday and the last day of school.

The kids would be loud though. I hated the loud. At least I had the fun night in the woods to think about.

All day at school while the kids played stupid games and screamed about summer, I doodled on a piece of paper. I drew the tree that Daddy was by when he worked in the field. I drew its tall, leafy branches.

I drew it in red. Red like the woman's hair from the blood. Dazzling. Beautiful. Daddy is an artist in all ways. I don't know how I didn't see it before.

Stay Safe, Diary, and happy summer,
Ruby

June 14, 2010
6:57 p.m.
Dear Diary,
Summer camp started today. It was terrible.

The kids were loud. We made paintings. I got in trouble. I hope they don't call Daddy.

They told us to paint nature. I like nature. It's peaceful and pretty and the birds never chirp too loud. Well, once there was this bird outside my window driving me crazy. Daddy called it a woodpecker. He said it was visiting. But I hated that bird. Usually, though, nature is pretty and peaceful and I like it. I like it way better than the peopley part of the world.

The camp counsellors took us outside to some picnic area. The other kids painted sunshine and rainbows and pink grass and purple clouds. It was so dumb. That's not what the world looks like.

I tried to go to my happy place, to watching Daddy. So I, of course, made my painting red. Red like my boots. I drew a tree in red, one of the trees from the field to be exact and decided to put that bunny under it from long ago. Then I put a red puddle around the bunny, just like Daddy puts around the women in the garage. When I was done, I was proud. I liked my little painting. But the boy next to me started shrieking.

"What's that? Oh my God, look at her! She painted a murdered rabbit!" he screamed.

The other kids came over. I started scratching my arm, and then my neck. I scratched and scratched. I couldn't stop. I didn't want them crowding around.

They started screaming over my painting and calling me a weirdo. I covered my ears, squeezed my eyes shut. I tried with all my power to disappear. They were so upset. Finally, I felt a hand on my shoulder. I jumped, pulling away, even more anxious.

"Ruby, it's okay. But we don't paint things like this, okay?"

I looked at the ground as the girl with a brown braid tried to comfort me and explained things about dead bunnies and killing and wrong. I shook my head. Did they know anything? This wasn't wrong. It was pretty. Pretty like the garage. Pretty like Daddy. I didn't understand why no one could see that. It was just one more thing to make me not fit in. But that was okay.

For the rest of the day, the kids pointed and called me rabbit killer. Some stayed away. That made me sad but also a little happy. It was better to be alone than to be making people upset. If it made them stay away, I'd paint dead rabbits all day. Why were they so upset, though, Diary? Dead isn't so bad. It's peaceful. And Daddy gets happy when the girls are dead—is that what they are? Dead?

But when Daddy picked me up and I looked out the window, I started to worry. The kids thought the dead rabbit was wrong. Did that make what Daddy was doing wrong, too? Was he doing something bad?

No. I was mad at myself for even thinking it. Daddy wouldn't do something wrong. Daddy was nice. He fed me and bought me red boots and read to me. He helped a little baby bird just last weekend who had a broken leg. Bad dads didn't do that.

I heard kids talking sometimes at school about their dads hitting and punching walls. Daddy didn't do that.

Those kids were just dumb.

I looked over at Daddy and smiled.

Everything is okay now. As much as I hate to admit it, Grandma is right. We all have bad days. We just have to learn to cope with them. Although Grandma's bad days usually involve losing at Bingo or her neighbor Cindy coming over to gossip—she hates Cindy. Of course, Grandma hates a lot of things. I'm pretty sure she hates me. It's okay. I hate her, too. She came over tonight to make sure things were okay at camp. She offered to watch me if Daddy thought camp was too stressful.

Thankfully, Daddy said no. He loves me too much to torture me with another summer at Grandma's. Plus, he's been trying to distance us from her. I guess it's because she's so annoying. Her voice is like a whining mosquito in your ear that you just can't ever kill.

I'll make it through camp, even if I hate it. Because that's what Daddy would want.

Stay Safe,
Ruby

June 21, 2010
6:57 p.m.
Dear Diary,

I've made a deal with the camp counsellors. I write poetry in the corner, alone, and they let me. I don't have to play any of the annoying games or do any of the sports. I get to just be alone with my words.

I did do one of the activities today in art. They made bracelets. Friendship bracelets, the girl with brown braids said. There was pink and red and orange and green string and beads.

But my eyes caught sight of the red. Perfect, bright red.

I made two bracelets, no beads. Just red, one for Daddy and one for me. Our favorite colors. I put mine on right away.

The counsellors were happy I made bracelets but they seemed even happier when I went back to writing in my corner after it was done. I think they worry after my painting. At least if they're nervous about me, they leave me alone. I like that. I'm happy, sitting and writing instead of playing basketball or making birdhouses or whatever the kids do. I like just sitting in the quiet. It's nice. I don't have to worry about scratching my neck too much or if the kids are going to think I'm weird or if I want to count out the time out loud. I can do it all and no one is upset or making fun of me.

There's another little girl who sits by me sometimes. I don't know her but I like her because we don't talk when she sits with me. She sits and draws. Sometimes she hums, which bugs me a little bit especially since it's always off tune. But I tell myself to ignore it like Daddy and me talk about sometimes. We all have to endure annoyances sometimes. That's what he tells me. I wonder if I ever annoy Daddy.

So camp is going okay. It's fine. I write. It's good like that.

Daddy told me once that Mama liked poetry. She did English in college. Mama must have been smart to go to college. Daddy didn't go. He said that she liked some man named Shakespeare. I asked Daddy how to spell the word so I could get it right in here. Daddy says I'm too young to read Shakespeare. I'll have to see if they have him in the library when school starts again. It would be neat to read the books Mama liked.

I don't want to ask Daddy to go to the library because he seems busy. I've noticed he's been in the garage a lot. Even during the day on the weekends, no ladies or anything. He just goes in there and cleans and organizes. He tells me to play in the yard, not to come in. I wonder what he's doing in there. I saw him bring a couple new tools in once. Sometimes, he just paces in there, back and forth. Back and forth, wringing his hands. Once I even heard him slam his fists on the table. I kept my head down and kept drawing with my chalk. I didn't want to make him mad.

Tonight, Daddy is watching TV downstairs. He's watching a Western. I like those.

He seemed upset at dinner. Usually, once he plays the game in the garage, he's happy for a long time. A long, long time. But not this time. Maybe the game didn't end right. I don't know. But his hands were shaking last night when he read *Green Eggs and Ham.* And Sam's voice just wasn't as happy.

I'm worried. I hope he can win the game so he can be happy. Maybe he'll go out again tonight. It would be good to see him happy again. I'll let you know tomorrow.

But Diary, he did love the friendship bracelet. He said it was his favorite color when he put it on. You already know that, though. It's my favorite, too. But at least now we have matching bracelets in our favorite colors so even when he's working and I'm at dumb camp, we can remember each other. I like that. I'm never taking mine off.

Stay Safe,
Ruby

June 22, 2010
6:57 p.m.
There was red last night.
Lots of red.
Her hair was even red.
It made me look at my hair.

Would Daddy ever put me in the game? I imagined myself swinging from the rope, dangling and staring as Daddy took my picture. I wondered what it would be like to look up at the garage ceiling while Daddy worked, my eyes bulgy and my neck purple like hers. Her red hair was short in a bob. I liked that it wasn't touching her neck. I wonder if she hated hair on her neck like me. I bet she did.

He worked hard, smiling and peaceful, but the saw seemed angrier than usual. It bit into her faster and harder and there was more red spraying every which way. It took him longer to clean up. He was a little sloppy. I wanted to tell him a couple of times that he wasn't doing it right. But I reminded myself it was a secret, he didn't know I was out there.

He dropped a rag when he was heading to finish the game in the field. He pushed the wheelbarrow away. I waited until he was gone. I picked up the rag. It smelled bleachy, but it was stained. Red, red, red. I could barely contain my smile.

What should I do? Daddy never dropped the rag. It seemed wrong to leave it there. Stealing is bad, I know. But I wanted to help Daddy, and I finally had my chance. I snatched it off the ground, looking left and right as if someone might see me. Which was silly because there's no one out here on our lane to see. We're out here all alone, just the way we like it. That's what Daddy always says when Grandma says we should move in town so I can be by the normal kids. Whatever normal means.

I wanted to take the rag with me to my room and put it in the perfect hiding place. With you of course. Right with you. I bet you like red, after all. But I was too scared Daddy might find it there. I had to think fast, so I put it in the next best spot.

The shed. Where my bike lives. I snuck over to the shed, creeping along like a quiet little cat. I searched behind the shed, trying to think of where to hide the rag so Daddy didn't find it. I didn't want him feeling bad about making a mistake. We all make mistakes.

I found a rock, a big rock behind the shed. I folded up the rag real small and covered it with the rock. Behind the shed there are tall weeds. It's overgrown. Daddy doesn't bother cutting weeds back there because it's right along the trees. Perfect. A perfect spot for the rag. Not as perfect as with you, Diary. Of course not. But it will have to do.

The rag would be like a soft blanket for you if you could have it. It could keep you company—maybe someday. But for now, it's keeping rock company. And it will keep the red memories alive.

Stay Safe,
Ruby

Back and forth,
Back and forth,
He marches in anger.

It's not red.
He's not smiling.
It's not right.

The sun is out,
But he doesn't notice.
The lightening bug burns me.
I want to twist its neck.
Will it scream?

Part III

2012

10 years old

March 6, 2012
6:57 p.m.
Dear Diary,

I think Daddy's upset again, just like he used to get a couple of years ago. It's been so long since I've seen him in the garage. I've been pretty sure he was done with that. I thought maybe he'd won his game or the switch in him turned off completely. The past couple of years have been—ordinary. Quiet. Good. However, things seem to have changed. Things aren't so quiet and good and peaceful with him anymore.

Something's sparked the game in him again. I can feel it, can sense that he's different. Just like the last time he was different. I don't understand what triggers the game or what keeps it at bay. It must be one of the things that only grownups understand, like love and grocery shopping and bills.

All I know is, I think things are changing.

For one thing, I notice his hands are shaking again. It's not a little bit of a shake like when someone gives a speech and is nervous or when my teacher claims she has caffeine withdrawal and needs more coffee—ew, coffee. I hate the smell of coffee. Thank goodness Daddy doesn't drink it.

These are wild shakes. It seems like he can't control them or doesn't notice. I wonder if it's like me with my neck, when I scratch, scratch, scratch until it bleeds but don't even realize it happens.

We still read together every night. I can read by myself, but sometimes the sentences are so long and hard to focus on. I pay attention better when Daddy reads. Plus, I like the routine of Daddy reading to me. We're in the second book in the *Harry Potter* series. Daddy says he doesn't really like wizards and fantasy, but he reads it with me anyway. I think he truly does like it because sometimes, he keeps reading past the chapter's end. I like the spells. I memorize them and at school I shout them out. The kids laugh at me, and the teacher yells. I try to stop, but I can't sometimes. They just comes out because they just fit.

Last night, when we were reading, I noticed Daddy's hands were shaking wildly when he was reading. And there's something else, something I didn't notice when I was young. He rubs his ring finger on his left hand a lot. There's a pained look on his face when he does.

He told me more about Mama last week. He talks about her more lately. Maybe because I'm older, or maybe it's because time has passed. Grandma says enough time has gone that he could move on. Grandma's always pushing, pushing, pushing. Like how she insisted on taking me shopping last weekend for appropriate clothing for a young lady. She tried to get me to buy a lacy dress. It's like she's trying to make me hate her.

Daddy isn't completely comfortable talking about Mama, though. He still gets clammy, cold when I mention her or ask a question. Still, it's progress because at least now I get some answers. Just a few tiny snippets here and there. It feels good to get to know my Mama, even just a little bit. It's weird to think she lived in this house and spent time with me—but I don't even know her at all.

I think she might be why he's sad sometimes. I still see the tattooed wedding ring on his finger, the way he rubs it with a faraway look. Mama must have hurt him badly. It makes me angry at her. Who could hurt Daddy? And how could I have ever loved a person who would hurt him? It makes me not want to miss her or be sad that she's not here.

Someone at school lost their mom a few weeks ago. Her name is Anna. She's been crying a lot. I hate it when people cry. Mrs. Hollenberry told me I should talk to her, maybe because she knows I lost my mom when I was young. But I don't want to talk to Anna.

I told Daddy about it at dinner. Usually, I like when we sit in silence at the table. I eat my chicken tenders and fries, just like every night. Dad eats pizza or eggs or whatever he feels like making himself. Sometimes he eats cereal. But tonight, I told him about Anna and her mother and the car accident.

Dad stiffened. It was a long moment of him slowly chewing on his scrambled eggs before he said, "The world's unfair, sometimes, Ruby."

I wanted to ask what he meant, what rules the world isn't following. But I knew he was talking about Mama. I wonder if Mama died in a car accident like Anna's Mom. I've never asked.

I know some things about Mama even though I don't remember her. I know:

She died when I was 2.

She had red hair.

She loved poetry, especially Shakespeare.

Her favorite food was Chinese food, which I've never tried.

She wanted a cat in the worst way, but I'm allergic to cats so she couldn't have one.

Her favorite color was blue. Not red. That's unfortunate (vocabulary word. I can spell it perfectly. Easy).

Looking back at the list, I know six things. Six things about Mama. I wonder if that's normal. How many things do other kids know about their moms?

It's okay. Don't feel sorry for me. People are complicated, but paper and pen are not. Daddy is not.

I worry about him, though. I can sense he is agitated. I wonder what about. I keep thinking that maybe I did something wrong. Last week, I dropped a glass and it shattered everywhere. But Daddy just helped clean it up, said not to dwell on it. I did think about it, though. All night. All the next day. I cried a few times, and my teacher didn't understand. But Daddy did clean it up and I realized that you couldn't even tell it happened. He's so good at cleaning.

A part of me is sort of hoping, I guess, that he continues the garage work. I miss watching him there. For so long now, I've had to rely on rereading my Diary entries to get that rush. It never quite compares, though, to witnessing it live. It's not as passionate and thrilling.

Daddy in the garage was exciting, peaceful. Methodical. Just how I like it. It was more interesting than any other show I could've ever watched.

The other night when I'd gone to bed, I heard Daddy watching a show on television. I crept down the steps real quiet, peeking in. The show had lots of blood, lots of red. There was a man holding a saw. I blinked. Was it Daddy? Daddy just shook his head at the screen, not knowing I was there. Like he was judging the guy. Maybe that's what stirred it all in Daddy again. Maybe he realized he is so much better at the red, at the saw, at the game.

I don't blame him for thinking that. I watched the show for a minute. The guy had it all wrong. The red doesn't splash like that. I know what it splatters like, and Daddy sure as heck knows what it splatters like.

I'm going to go down and watch television with Daddy now while I work on my scarf. The school librarian gave me a book on knitting, so Daddy took me out to buy yarn. Not scratchy yarn, yuck. Soft, soft, soft yarn, like a bunny's fur. I'm going to make Daddy a scarf. Maybe if he has to go into the garage this winter, it'll keep him warm.

I picked white yarn. The red specks would look so good on it, wouldn't they?

Stay Safe,

Ruby

March 13, 2012
6:57 p.m.
Dear Diary,

I wish I didn't have to go to school. I wish I could stay home or help Daddy at work or just stay home and write. It must be wonderful to be a writer because you could just stay in, away from everyone. People reading your words can't see the faces you make or the way your hand twitches or how you stop to scratch your neck. They just see the true you, what you want to say. Maybe someday that's what I'll do.

Today was a really bad day at school. Worse than ever. Some of the girls in my class, Clarissa, Sarah, and Chloe, have been very mean to me. I don't know why all of a sudden they've noticed me. They know I don't like to talk to anyone. They know I'm different. They usually just leave me alone. But for some reason, it's become apparent that they really don't like me.

Yesterday, in art class, I was working on my painting. I was making a picture of our house using red. All red. Just how I like it.

"What a freak," Clarissa said as she passed by. "Is that period blood?"

The girls snickered.

"No. It's paint," I replied because what else could I say? We'd just learned about periods at school. The school nurse had the talk with us while the boys played outside. I'd doodled on my desk trying not to make eye contact while the girls in the class had laughed and whispered. I tried to think about what the appropriate response would be to her question. I decided I should reassure Clarissa that no, it wasn't period blood. I hadn't had my period, in fact.

"I heard you're a Daddy's girl," Chloe said. She has long, long black hair that reaches way down her back. It reminds me of the shiny black hair of the lady Daddy once had in the garage. I imagined what it would look like with streaks of red paint in it, but I stopped myself.

"Yes," I replied as I worked on the door of the house. My neck itched, but I tried to fight the urge to scratch it with red paint on my hands. The teacher, Mrs. Cartwright, was busy helping a table of girls in the other corner work on their perfect flower paintings. She didn't notice the three around me.

Clarissa laughed, leaning in. "Just how close are you, huh? I mean, you don't seem to talk to anyone else and I always see him drop you off in the morning. Kind of weird that you don't have any friends. Daddy's girl, huh?"

"Yes. I love Daddy."

"She loves Daddy," Clarissa repeated. I didn't know why she was repeating me.

"Daddy's girl. Daddy's girl. Do you sleep in his bed with him?" she asked, adjusting her too tight top and hiking up her skirt. It made me uncomfortable. "Does Daddy touch you? Huh?"

The other girls were giggling wildly.

"No. Daddy knows I don't like touched."

Sarah, the girl with short, short brown hair snorted. "So he just looks then, huh? Or maybe you touch him? My Mama says your Daddy always was a weirdo."

I didn't quite understand what she meant, so I just kept painting. Anger started to surge though. They didn't know Daddy, not like me. It made me upset they would say mean things about him. And how did Sarah's mom know who he was?

"What's with all the red anyway?" Chloe added in, as if she had to be a part of the fun too.

"I love red. It's mine and Daddy's favorite."

"What a freak. Truly. Hey, Joey, come here," Clarissa said to the boy nearby. "Look at this. I think Ruby's painting with period blood. Pass it on."

Joey laughed, and I felt my face burn.

"It's not, it's just paint," I screamed. Ignoring the paint on my hands, I reached up to scratch my neck.

"Oh, I think it's blood," he said, laughing as he ran over to tell another boy.

Stupid kids. Stupid kids. Stupid kids. The room was swirling, so loud. I needed to leave. I pounded my fist, anger surging within and ready to explode. Why were they so loud? The girls laughed in the circle around me, and it was like a pounding in my brain. It screeched through my head, over and over, and I couldn't hear anything else. Couldn't even hear myself think. I was losing myself to them. I covered my ears.

"Stop, stop, stop," I shouted, squeezing my eyes shut and wanting to disappear. I wished I had a wand, a real spell. I wished I could make myself disappear. The girls were chanting something in my ear, quietly. I shoved past them to run out of the room.

I heard Clarissa shriek as she tumbled to the ground, but I didn't stop to ask any more questions. I ran straight out of the room, down the hall, away, away, away. I wanted to go home.

The principal found me on the playground, tucked away behind the building in my favorite corner with the purple flowers. I picked them once to bring home. The kids laughed and said they were nothing but weeds, but I loved them.

I sat, gently banging my head against the brick of the school building. Thud. Thud. Thud. Smash away the craziness. Smash away the noise.

Quiet.

Peace.

Just like I liked it.

And then the principal ruined it all wish his graying moustache and his weird haircut, his choking voice. He yelled at me and ruined the quiet. He made me go back inside.

Daddy got called in.

They told him I shoved a girl, that the kids said I was saying weird things about the picture I was painting.

"No, no, no," I said, my hands trembling. I didn't want to tell them the truth. I didn't want to talk to them. I wanted to go home.

"Come on, Ruby," Daddy had said after some angry exchanges between him and the principal. I got to go home. Daddy didn't look angry, just worried.

I felt bad for making him upset, but I was glad I got to leave that awful place with those terrible kids. Daddy didn't talk to me about it on the way home. He let me sit in quiet. He knew me like that. He made me dinner, and he talked about his day and about the weather while I pushed the food in circles on my plate. After a long time, when the pounding in my brain had mostly quieted, he finally spoke.

"Ruby, we have to talk about today. What happened?" he asked calmly, his voice deep and reassuring.

I looked up at him, staring at the dimples on his face. I liked those dimples. Fun little marks on his face. I wished I had dimples.

"The kids were mean. I didn't push her. I didn't. I know the rules." I wanted someone to believe me. I hadn't meant to hurt her. I hadn't.

"I know. I believe you. Were they giving you a hard time, Ruby?"

"No. I wasn't having a hard time. Painting is easy."

"Okay, Ruby," he said, and I noticed he was tapping his hands on the table.

"I didn't use period blood. I didn't," I said matter-of-factly.

Daddy sighed.

"Ruby, kids are going to say mean things. That's how they are. You're going to just have to learn to toughen up, okay? To not let it get to you."

"Okay, Daddy," I said before excusing myself to go on the porch, to sit outside and to just be in the quiet.

It was a bad day today. But Daddy made it better.

There's something, though, I didn't tell Daddy, Diary. Something I didn't tell anyone. But I'll tell you.

When the girls were talking about Daddy, it made me really mad. I don't know why. I just don't like that they talked about him like they know him. I don't like it at all. And when Clarissa wouldn't leave me be, when her voice was grating in my head, when she was shrieking in my ear, something bubbled inside of me. It burned in my chest, in my belly, everywhere.

I didn't push her on purpose, not really. I didn't mean to hurt her.

But here's the thing. I think maybe I wanted to. I think maybe I wanted to shove her down on the table and add her red to my painting.

Is that what Daddy does in the garage? Are those ladies he brings there Clarissas? Are they grating on his nerves? I haven't really thought about that. Who they are. Who the women of his garage are. I wish I could ask him. But Daddy gets nervous when I'm even near the garage. I don't know why. He's beautiful in there.

I just think that like me and the incident at school, Daddy doesn't want to talk about it. I can't talk about it. I need to do that for Daddy, just like he does for me.

Maybe Daddy and I aren't so different. Maybe that's why he understands me so well. I like thinking that. It makes me feel okay with being so alone at school—because I'm not really alone. I have him. Daddy and Ruby. That's all we need in the world.

Stay Safe,

Ruby

March 20, 2012
6:57 p.m.
Dear Diary,
It was a big night last night.

Daddy returned to the garage. I thought maybe he was done with it all. How long has it been? A couple of years? I think I was eight last time. At least the last time I saw him in there.

But he's not done. I found out last night. I heard him pulling out in his truck an hour or so after I fell asleep. I always hear when the truck starts. He doesn't realize how sensitive to noise I am. I hear every sound, every creak. It's hard to sleep most nights because of it. It feels like when the truck pulls out, it's inside my brain.

Last night, I was glad. My heart was racing. I couldn't believe it. I hadn't realized how much I'd missed watching him in there, seeing his work. The memories were still strong but experiencing the thrill in real time is just so much better. I climbed out of bed, tucked my feet into my boots, and crept down the stairs. I waved hello to Bubbles III—Daddy let me get a new fish and then another new fish when they kept dying. I won Bubbles I at a carnival game. I hate the carnival in town, but last summer, it was good because I won Bubbles. Daddy said I had a good arm. I was proud he noticed.

I walked out back, the grass crunching beneath my feet. It was a bit chilly out, spring not quite breaking through yet. I blew out and smiled as my breath floated upward in a smoky, hazy cloud. It looked like I was smoking, like how Daddy does sometimes when he gets a cigar and puffs it out on the front porch.

I found my old spot, just as it was the last time. The same hole. But things were different. I had to crouch lower now. I was bigger. It wasn't as comfortable. I wished I had a better view. I realized I wouldn't be able to see as much as I'd like from here. Too bad I couldn't make a better spot. Or be in the garage with Daddy.

But I know better than to ask.

A couple of days ago, the sun was shining on Sunday. I was playing in the driveway, hopscotch I'd drawn. I skipped the pebble too hard. It hit the garage. I went to get it, crouching down by the door and then slowly standing up. I peeked in the window.

"Get away from there," Daddy yelled.

"I didn't go in," I replied, my lip quivering. I hated it when Daddy yelled.

He scowled. "Stay away from there, do you understand? It's dangerous in there."

I wanted to tell Daddy I knew it wasn't dangerous—it was breath-taking. I wanted to tell him all the details I remembered. The way the blood pooled. The way he cleaned it, so perfectly and completely. The way their long hair cascaded over the back of the table while he worked. But I didn't. The way his hands shook, the look on his face. It scared me a little. I've never been scared of Daddy, never felt like he would hurt me. But something about the way he stared when I got near the garage, it sent a shiver through me. I think maybe, just maybe, there's a tiny sliver of a chance Daddy would hurt me if he knew I was here. I think it's possible.

I shoved away the thought. How could I even consider that? He wouldn't hurt me. He wouldn't. Daddy would *never* do anything to hurt me. I believed it with every single cell in my body—didn't I?

Something told me, though, I needed to be careful. I needed to make sure I didn't make him mad when it came to the garage. I silently crouched in the chilly night air, waiting and waiting. And waiting some more.

12:36 a.m. Early for Daddy's work. He pulled up in his clunky truck, and he carried her in. I peeked through as he walked through the garage door, plopping the lady on the table before rushing back to lock the door. I got a good view of her then. Her long, wavy black hair cascading down towards the floor.

It was black. Black like Chloe's from school. It seemed like Daddy's favorite was black-haired women. I grinned at the thought. I thought about the red from my painting and how good she would look with red all over her. If only Daddy could bring Chloe here.

I watched, remembering how beautiful the elegant dance was, how perfect Daddy was. He was so careful, following the same steps as always. It was almost exactly how I'd remembered it from the last time. The rope wrapped around her neck. The dangling, swaying motion of her body. The photograph. The solemn moment as Daddy studied her, shaking the photo carefully to reveal the image forever captured. The moment of peace and joy on Daddy's face, the excitement in his movements. Then the body put on the table. Gloves on his hands. Pulling down each tool from its spot. Standing in just the right places, using the same outlet, using the same downward strokes to complete the task. Stepping around the pools of blood. Smiling as he walked around the table. Bagging up of the parts, each one going into the black garbage bags in a specific order and then into the trustworthy wheelbarrow.

The tidying up. The cleaning, cleaning, cleaning. The smell of bleach wafting through the air, tiny bits escaping through the hole nearby. The tools all in their spot. The gorgeous red painting on the floor wiped away. I was the only viewer of the masterpiece, the only one to remember Daddy's brushstrokes. I studied like it was my job.

I could help you, Daddy. I'd be a good worker.

Maybe someday, I could help. I'd give anything to be around him when he was like this. This side of Daddy was foreign to the side he showed the world. I enjoyed being privy to it, like a majestic spot in the middle of the rainforest undiscovered by human eyes. Daddy was an unknown enigma walking around town. No one knew exactly how skilled he was—no one but me.

I longed to follow him when he loaded the bags into his truck, but I knew I needed to get back in the house. I was cold, my fingers almost frozen. Wandering inside the house once he was out of sight, I thought about the lady.

Daddy had killed her.

I didn't know that when I was young. I didn't understand. But I do now.

He killed her.

Killing is wrong. That's what my teacher said. That's what anyone says, really.

We'd learned about killing in history class and in some of the stories we read in English. Killing was an evil thing to do, and there was no coming back from dead. Staying alive was the main goal and getting killed was bad.

You had to be careful. It was like careful was the favorite word in the adult world.

Careful crossing the street so you don't get killed.

Careful talking to strangers. You could get killed.

Drugs could kill you and alcohol, so you had to be careful about peer pressure. Drinking cleaners and driving without your seatbelt could get you killed. Putting too much information online could lead a predator to your house and get you killed. Grandma is always telling me that strangers could steal me and kill me. She's always paranoid about that, grabbing my hand in public places so no one can snatch me, telling me to be careful around strange men. I'd rather be snatched than to have to feel her dry, cracked skin touching mine.

Everyone talks about killing and how to avoid it, and how the answer is to just be careful. Careful, careful, everywhere. Even Daddy tells me to be careful and to watch when I cross the road and to not wander too far when I take a walk in the woods.

But no one talks about what happens when your Daddy kills someone. No one talks about that kind of dead, or how to be careful around that situation. Why? Do other kids' Daddys do this, too? And if killing is wrong, why does Daddy make it seem so right? So pretty? Daddy would never do something wrong. Would he? They must have been bad people.

I sit here now, thinking about it all, Diary. It's so much more complicated than when I was little and didn't understand. I *do* understand, sort of. Daddy is killing people, women. He's hiding them. But I also know that Daddy's a good man. He's a good Daddy. And the killing game in the garage makes him so happy. Ecstatic even—vocab word.

How could it be wrong?

I don't care what anyone says. Drugs and alcohol and strangers and cars can kill you, and that's bad. But Daddy's not bad. I love him. I'll protect him. I'll keep him safe.

Always. It's the least I can do.

I'm off to watch television with Daddy, Diary. I'll talk to you later.

Stay Safe,

Ruby

They say black is the color of death.
Swirling all around,
The grim reaper's cloak waiting to snatch you up.
Black like forever when you die.

But I think death is red.
Red like strawberries on the lips
On a hot summer day. Red like the
Mermaid's hair floating in the sea.
Red like apples and hearts and the lollipop
I ate as a child.

Red like
the warm puddles
in June.

Part IV

2013

11 years old

September 19, 2013
7:57 p.m.
Dear Diary,

I'm still bothered by the time difference. I know it's been a couple of weeks, but I still want to write 6:57 p.m. It doesn't feel right. Not. At. All.

But Daddy says chess club has been good for me. He likes that it gets me around the other kids more. He thinks it will help me be more social. I don't think he realizes that's not exactly true. Really, I just sit and quietly play. I don't speak to anyone. But it's fun beating them. I do like getting to figure out the best moves. It's all about knowing the rules and having the smarts to put the moves together. I don't think it's that hard, but the other kids seem to think it is. It makes me feel good to win, even if they complain that a weird kid beat them. I hate that word. But I've grown used to it. Apparently kids think quiet means weird. If only they knew.

Daddy taught me chess over the summer. His grandfather taught Daddy when he was young. Said it would keep him out of trouble. I don't know if it did or not. Daddy doesn't talk about when he was growing up very much. Neither does Grandma. I know, though, that Daddy had a brother named Dwayne. He died before I was born. Daddy won't say what happened. Grandma has a picture of Daddy and Dwayne in her house, but when I ask about him, Grandma shakes her head and changes the subject to quilting or raisin-filled cookies or something dumb like that.

There are so many secrets, I'm realizing. There's so much stuff Daddy doesn't like to talk about.

For wanting me to be social and interact, Daddy is sort of clammy about a lot of his own life. Sure, he's chatty and can hold a conversation with anyone we come across. He doesn't shy away from people out in public like I do. He isn't afraid to talk and laugh and chat about all sorts of things—but not everything. The past parts of him and the real parts of him—those things stay secret. But that's okay. I get it. Everyone thinks you have to talk, talk, talk. You should tell everyone everything you are thinking and feeling all the time. I hate talking. Sometimes thinking is better. That's why I like chess.

But chess club is after school and it throws our schedule off by a whole hour. I almost quit because of that. I was getting antsy. I was doing that thing with my hands, almost how Daddy's hands shake when he's getting angry

58

inside. I couldn't stop scratching my neck, so much so that it was bleeding. I was getting upset a lot and just feeling frustrated.

"Ruby," Daddy finally said to me. "You're getting older. You need to be flexible. The world isn't perfectly black and white all the time. It doesn't fit with your schedule. You're going to have to figure that out."

Daddy says he wants me to be successful when I go to the junior high school next year. He says he wants me to start blossoming and finding my way. Whatever that means.

I just want to keep writing, keep spending time with Daddy, and survive school. I wish I could just quit and be home schooled like Victoria Alders. She was a girl in my class last year who stopped coming because she had anxiety and actually had a meltdown in school. Worse than the ones I've had. I felt bad for her because I understand why she did that—but I also am jealous because now she is homeschooled and doesn't have to come anymore. Daddy says he wouldn't feel good about teaching me everything. He says we need to let it to the experts. Plus, Daddy has to work. I thought about trying to have a meltdown to beat Victoria, but I couldn't do that to Daddy. He would be so upset, and what would he do? I'd probably get stuck with Grandma teaching me all day. That would lead to a real, true meltdown. Even going to school is better than being with her.

Mrs. Vickers, my teacher this year, is old, old, old. Her craggy face is always shrivelled. I do like, though, that she sticks to the rules. She yells meanly when the kids get too loud. She likes quiet. And even though Mrs. Vickers doesn't really seem to like me, I like her. She likes peace and calm, so she's okay in my book.

We finished the book we're reading in English class, *The Giver.* A lot of the kids were angry about it, about how they kill people in the eerie little society. They kill babies if they're twins. They kill you when you get too old. One girl in class cried. It made me nervous. I know I cry a lot when I'm frustrated, but I just don't know how to handle it when someone else is crying. It makes me really uncomfortable and aggravated, like I want to run out of the room. Sometimes I do.

I wanted to raise my hand and say that killing isn't always bad when we were discussing the book. Sometimes it's the best option. Sometimes it can be okay. I thought of the garage and Daddy and how expertly he executed it. I wondered what he would think of the book.

"Daddy, have you read *The Giver*?" I asked him at dinner tonight. Chicken nuggets and fries, my favorite.

"Yeah, I think so. A long time ago."

"What did you think? Of the killing?"

He looked up from his plate. "I don't know, Ruby. That's a tough question. I think that world in the book was very different than ours, and maybe we'd have to think of it on their terms. I don't think there's a single right answer."

"Because not everything's black and white?"

He smirked. "That's right."

But I noticed his hands were a little unsteady as he forked the steak he cooked for himself into his mouth. I wish we could talk more. He's the one person I want to talk more to. I want to know so many things, but he clams up.

Sometimes I wonder if I really know Daddy at all, and that hurts.

Stay Safe,

Ruby

September 23, 2013
7:57 p.m.
Dear Diary,

Today at school, Daddy had to come in. We had a special meeting. It's basically a meeting because the school thinks I need special help because of some of my differences. Daddy says it's all a money game, that I don't need help. That I do just fine. But he wants me to have the best chance, so he swallows his pride and goes along with it. Just in case it might help me. Personally, I think I do fine and get along and don't cause too much trouble most of the time. Not like some of the kids. I don't know why they focus on me when kids like Randy and Josh and Margaret are always throwing true tantrums and being super mean. And of course, Clarissa is always being nasty and telling lies. Those are the kids who need meetings, not the quiet ones.

Daddy tries his best, though, to be nice at the school even though I get the sense he didn't like it when he went. He listens to their ideas and tries to be openminded, as he tells me. But he isn't openminded to everything. He makes sure to put the principal and the other people at the meeting in their place if they say something he doesn't like. Watching him at the meeting, it makes me realize what he must have been like when he was my age.

Strong. Powerful.

I wonder if I could be that way if I needed to be.

While they talked about transition plans and behaviour modification plans, I sunk into myself like I often do. I thought about yesterday, how Chloe and Sarah and Clarissa have been lurking again. They're in different classes than me, but they still find ways to get to me. To harass me at recess. To have the kids chant things around me on the playground.

I don't know why they picked me, but it makes me angry.

They call me stupid and dunce and all sorts of synonyms. The thing is, their vocabulary is weak. I want to shout out dozens of better words they could use—I like synonyms. I don't shout them out, though, even when I want to. I just let them think they're so smart.

I notice now that when they bother me, I wring my hands. Over and over. Sometimes, I imagine what it would feel like to have their tiny, twiggy necks between my fingers, to crunch and squeeze until they were gasping, until they couldn't talk. Until they're quiet.

Stay Safe,

Ruby

October 8, 2013
7:57 p.m.
Dear Diary.
He came home empty-handed last night. And he caught me awake, like that one time when I was younger. I know now that I can never, ever tell him I know what happens in there.

Maybe what Daddy is doing is wrong—because why is he so mad about it?

I'll start from the beginning. I jolted awake when I heard his truck leave. I couldn't believe it. It's been so long. So, so long. I, of course, got myself out of bed. I knew that I had plenty of time, that there was no rush. It was 10:57 p.m. I knew I had at least an hour until I had to be positioned to watch. I was in the mood for a good cleaning, after all. I could almost see the blood swirling with the bleach, the puddles disappearing. So satisfying.

I decided to read for a while to pass the time. I picked up the first book in the *Harry Potter* series—the first is always the best, after all. I read the words I had memorized, languishing in the tranquillity of it. I was getting ready to go downstairs, to head to my spot, when the truck came squealing in, practically crashing to a stop. Something was wrong. I tossed down the book, leaning to look out the window.

Daddy got out of the truck and rushed towards the house. He was empty-handed. Where was the woman? Why wasn't he going in the garage? He looked up, saw my light, and my heart stopped.

"Ruby," he bellowed when he barged through the door downstairs, flinging it open with such force that I heard it smash against the wall. I was rocking on my bed, scared that I was caught. I hated being caught breaking the rules. My fingers were doing the wringing thing, and I couldn't stop it. I squeezed my eyes shut, knowing from the tone I was in trouble. *I didn't do anything, Daddy. I didn't. I love you.*

"Ruby," he yelled again, stomping up the steps. He looked red and flushed, out of sorts. Sweat was beading on his forehead. He was a fit man. Why was he so exhausted?

"Ruby, what the fuck are you doing up? Huh?" he yelled as he stormed in my room.

"I . . . I heard you leave . . ." I murmured, staring at the flooring, tracing patterns in the carpet with my big toe.

He came forward, grabbing my arms. "Listen, okay? This is important. I didn't leave. Okay? I didn't leave tonight."

There was panic in his voice, something I've never seen. He's always cool and calm and collected.

"What's wrong?" I asked, confused, still staring at the carpet as my toe danced over the fuzzy texture.

"Ruby, listen. Do you love me?"

"Of course, Daddy."

"Then do this for me. Repeat it. I never left. Okay? I was here the whole time."

"But that's a lie," I said. I shook my head as anger surged within.

"Dammit, Ruby, get your head out of your ass. This is important. What the hell were you doing up anyway? Snooping around? What I do is my business, you hear? You need to stay out of it. You got it?"

His hands squeezed my arms. They started to hurt.

"Yes, Daddy," I replied. "You were here."

My bottom lip quivered. I tried to hold it together. Daddy let go, sinking to the floor, burying his head in his hands.

"Shit, I'm sorry. Ruby, I'm sorry." Now Daddy looked like he might cry too.

"What's wrong, Daddy?"

He looked up at me. For a moment, I thought maybe he would tell me something. Maybe he'd let me in. *I know all about it, you can tell me,* I tried to convey with my eyes. My eyes, however, rarely reveal the true inner workings of my mind, of my feelings. They betray me all the time.

"Nothing for you to worry about. I'm okay, Ruby. I'm okay. It'll all be okay. All that matters is you. Fuck me, how could I be so stupid? You're all that matters."

It felt like he was talking to himself, forgetting I was in the room, just like so many others often do. Sometimes it's like I'm wearing an invisibility spell, even if I don't want to. Tears welled at the thought.

"Ruby?" he asked after we sat in quiet, sweet, sweet quiet, for a long moment.

"Yeah, Daddy?"

"Have you ever stayed up other nights?" His face was pale.

I looked at him. I didn't lie. Not ever. Not to Daddy. Not to anyone. But especially not to Daddy. However, my mouth wouldn't move. It was like it was pasted shut, my dry throat constricted and my tongue uncooperative. I couldn't say the words that were the truth. I saw how angry he was when I was looking out the window. What would he do if I told him yes? It might break him. I hated seeing him upset.

My teachers have said before that sometimes white lies are okay. Sometimes white lies save relationships, are a kindness. Like when she told me I shouldn't tell Cindy her new haircut was hideous and made her face look fat. My teacher said I could lie about that, that it was a white lie to help Cindy's feelings. I didn't understand. If I were Cindy, I would want to know my hair looked bad and my face fat. But apparently other people don't think like me. I'm different that way, they said, because most people don't want to know the complete truth all the time.

Maybe this was one of those moments when lying could help Daddy. Perhaps it was better to ignore the complete truth, to shield him from it. I would give it a try. I needed to be flexible and try new things, after all. Daddy had said so himself.

I exhaled. "No. I just couldn't sleep, Daddy."

Relief flooded his face as he accepted my words so quickly. Sometimes, I guess we believe the words we want to hear the most.

"Okay. I just . . . I want to make sure you're getting enough sleep. I'm trying to be a good Dad, Ruby. I'm trying." I crossed the room, sat beside him, and nuzzled into him.

"I know. You are a good Dad," I whispered.

And he is. He is such a good dad, I'll do anything for him.

Lie to him.

Lie to others.

I'd do anything to protect him. Anything. And for the first time, Diary, it's become clear that Daddy needs protected. I don't know what happened, but I think maybe he almost got caught tonight. I've seen the news and heard about stories of bad guys getting caught. One boy in our class, Francis, his dad accidentally ran over another man with his car because he was driving too fast. He didn't follow the rules, and now he's in jail. I can't imagine Daddy going away. I can't imagine being without him. Who would take care of me? Who would take care of Daddy?

65

We need each other, plain and simple. There's no other option.

So I need to be careful. I need to watch out for him, no matter what.

I'm not letting some stupid woman or anyone ruin it for Daddy. I'll do whatever I have to do. Rules are so important—but Daddy is more important.

Stay Safe,

Ruby

October 15, 2013
8:57 p.m.
Dear Diary,

Daddy exploded today. It happened at school.

In English class, we were writing poems. It's my favorite, as you know. I love poetry. I took my time and wrote a poem that I felt proud of, that I felt was really good. I was so proud, I decided to let my teacher, Mrs. Vickers, read it to the class. Let me tell you the truth: I never let anyone hear my work. I never volunteer. But I was really feeling like it was a good poem. I was feeling inspired. I wanted to be flexible and try something new.

She started reading it to the class. I thought this might be my chance. Maybe people would see what a good poet I was and leave me alone, stop picking on me. Stop stealing my stuff and putting ketchup on my seat at lunch and calling me gross.

Maybe I could have a friend, someone to sit with at lunch and to share secrets with. Someone to laugh with and to share my poetry with. Being alone at school got tiresome, especially since Daddy wasn't there.

But once Mrs. Vickers got past the first stanza—we learned that's what each paragraph is called—she stopped. My eyes stung. I didn't understand. She got really quiet and said, "I think that's enough for now, Ruby."

The kids laughed, teasing that my poem was so bad, she couldn't finish it. She hushed them and then had Clarissa share her poem. It was a rhyming mess about puppies. So stupid. So terrible. But everyone clapped and Clarissa grinned that devilishly annoying grin. She made sure to turn around and give me a wink. I swore I'd never share again. Ever. Eyes burning, I realized that I would never have a friend. Never. I'd have to be strong, like Daddy said. The world isn't black and white. You have to be strong.

So I wiped away my tears and kept doodling on the paper in front of me. I swore I'd let it go, shake off the hurt. I thought I'd heard the last of the poetry situation. After school, though, when I headed out to wait for Daddy to pick me up, Mrs. Vickers stopped me.

"Ruby. I've called your father. He's coming after school for a meeting with us and the principal."

"Why?" I asked. My heart fluttered.

"You know why."

But I didn't, Diary. I had no idea. I figured it had something to do with the poem. My mind started racing. Maybe, I thought, it was so good that Mrs. Vickers wanted to give me an award. Maybe she would tell Daddy I was a prodigy—vocab word—and that we should look into a writing school for me. Not that I'd ever leave Daddy, of course. I waited patiently. I had to pee, but I squirmed in my seat, doodling on a piece of paper, waiting for Mrs. Vickers to escort me down to the office. How proud Daddy would be.

When we got to the office, though, and I rushed to hug Daddy, the principal didn't look very happy. He didn't look like he was ready to give out an award. But maybe he was just tired.

"Mr. Marlowe, I'm sorry to call you in like this. But we're quite alarmed by Ruby, to be honest. Some of the poetry she is writing is very, well, disturbing for a girl her age. And if she keeps this up, I don't know what we're going to do."

"What are you talking about?" Daddy uttered as the principal handed a piece of paper across to him. Mrs. Vickers sat perched like an eagle in her seat, looking down her shrivelled, twisted nose at me.

I didn't understand. My heart beat wildly. My poem was good. I knew it was—it was probably the best poem I'd written up to that point. Surely Daddy would see that. It *was* good, wasn't it? I hated that Mrs. Vickers and the kids in class had me doubting the one thing that made me feel proud. I hated that they were taking even that away from me.

I tried to calm down, twisting my hands, wringing them and wringing them like they were full of lemonade I could squeeze out. The chair felt itchy, scratchy on my legs. I was wearing shorts because it was hot and I didn't like to be too hot. I wiggled my toes in my red rain boots. It wasn't raining, but they were the only shoes I liked wearing. They were comfortable and they were red. And I could wiggle my toes inside them and no one could see. I wiggled and counted, wiggled and counted. I looked at my watch, lighting it up over and over again. Suddenly, the principal's office felt too small. It felt like it was squishing me, constricting me to the point I could barely breath. I fought the urge to jump out of my seat and run away. I didn't want to leave Daddy.

"I don't see the problem," Daddy said finally after looking across the table. "She's being creative."

"It's dark," Mrs. Vickers murmured, as if she had to get her two-sense in. "Ruby, dear, why did you write this?" she asked then, as if I was on her team instead of Daddy's.

I just shrugged. I wrote it because that's what I wanted to write. I didn't need to defend that to her. She clearly didn't understand poetry.

"Now, there's nothing threatening and there's nothing that seems to suggest self-harm, as our guidance counsellor has noted. There's nothing to warrant a call to CYS at this time, but we're worried about Ruby's mental state. This sort of thing isn't typical for a girl her age, and we worry. Especially with her . . . condition."

Daddy's breathing intensified, his face melting into a look of anger. He stood from his chair, and my heart stopped.

"Ruby, come with me." He reached for my hand, leading me out of the office. "Wait here, okay?" he asked kindly, motioning to a seat in the office.

And then he shut the door.

He wanted to protect me, I think. But the door was too thin and Daddy was too angry.

Like an explosion, Daddy screamed at the principal. Principal should be careful. I wondered what he would look like out flat on the table in the garage. Him and Mrs. Vickers. It almost made me hope for it to happen.

Daddy's voice was barely muffled. I stared straight ahead, listening to him tell the principal and Mrs. Vickers what he thought.

"Listen to me. That girl is amazing at poetry. It's her outlet. I've dealt with your fucking horrible comments about Ruby and your grossly inadequate teachers not understanding her because this is supposed to be an excellent school. It's supposed to give my daughter the best chance at success. But I will not have you threatening to call CYS because she writes poetry that is beyond your fucking imbecilic minds, and I won't have you citing her condition like there's something wrong with her. She doesn't have a fucking condition. She just sees the world differently. She's special. That's what she is."

I beamed that Daddy yelled at the principal like that, even using the words we're not supposed to use in public. Suddenly, the principal didn't seem so scary. I was glad Daddy was on my side, always on my side.

"Mr. Marlowe, I need you to calm down or I'm going to have to call security," the principal said. It was a total power move, but he should've just stayed quiet. With Daddy in the room, there was no way he was gaining the power—especially not with Daddy so angry.

"Call your goddamn security officer for all I care. And I'll call the media and tell them how you're harassing my child. Unbelievable."

"Mr. Marlowe, we know Ruby has been through a lot, with what happened to her mother and all."

"Don't you fucking talk about my wife like that," Daddy barked, and I imagined Mrs. Vickers turning ten shades of pale. They'd overstepped, and she knew it.

The door flew open, the poem in Daddy's hand. "Come on, Ruby, let's go home. We're done here."

I stood from my chair, still wringing my hands. I didn't look in the principal's office, didn't make eye contact with the principal or my teacher. At the door to the main office, Daddy turned.

"You ever give my girl a hard time again, you ever call CYS on me because of her poetry, you're not going to like what happens."

"Is that a threat?" the principal asked, but I could hear the terror in the way his voice was shaking.

"It's a fucking promise." And with that, we left.

Daddy was shaking the whole way home. Raging.

"Sorry, Daddy. I'm sorry," I said, looking out the window, wishing I could take it all back. I hated that I'd caused Daddy this problem, this inconvenience. It was a good poem, though, wasn't it?

"I'm sorry, Ruby. I'm sorry I didn't give you better. We should've went and looked for a different school district. We should've. But I can't move away. I just can't leave our house, you know? I can't leave there. I'm sorry."

He was rambling, talking faster and faster like he did that one night I caught him come home empty handed. Daddy was so upset, he flew through a stop sign. He is the most careful driver. It isn't like him.

"I'm fine there, Daddy," I murmured, and I knew I could be. I could do anything for Daddy.

I knew why we couldn't leave. Daddy murmured on and on about how the house was the last place Mama was alive, and how he couldn't leave. But I knew the truth. Mama's spirit could go anywhere. But the bodies of those ladies couldn't. And if someone found their hiding spot, Daddy could be in major trouble for real. Bigger than if CYS came in.

70

"You keep writing your poems, Ruby. I'm proud of you. They're really good."

I beamed. He was proud. That's all I could ask for. From now on, I didn't need to share them at school. I'd write them for myself, for Daddy sometimes. I didn't need Mrs. Vickers or the stupid kids at school to see them.

"Ruby, just one question, though. What did inspire the poem?" Daddy asked, a look of concern plastered on his face.

I alleviated the thoughts I knew he was thinking. "I don't know, Daddy. It just comes to me. You know red is my favorite color."

He grinned, nodding, as if assured that he was doing all right after all. We'll believe what we want to. It's the thing I keep realizing over and over as I sit on my perch, away from everyone, observing. People will believe the story we sell to them, even if it clearly isn't true.

He took me out to dinner then, the diner at the edge of town that has the best chicken nuggets and fries. Then we went to a movie, which is something we usually don't do because I don't like being in a crowded place, but it thankfully was pretty empty. I think Daddy just was trying to calm himself down.

It didn't work, though. His hands are still trembly. I'm worried about him. I decided to show Daddy I could be flexible, maybe that would calm him. So that's why I'm late writing.

Stay Safe,
Ruby

Fingers, fingers,
All about the room.
Pointing, accusing, shaking at her.

She pulls them off,
One by little one.
Red swirls and pools, all about the skin.

Redness, redness,
Swirling and swooping both without and within
Her eyes dance at the sight.

Eyes, eyes,
All about the room.
Staring, glaring, studying her.

She takes the fork and plucks them out
Watching them explode.
Who is staring at her now with judgemental eyes?

No one. They are all still, all quiet, all redness of their own.

October 16, 2013
7:57 p.m.
Dear Diary,

I thought Daddy would go in the garage after the thing at the school. He didn't.

Even though it's October, when he's moodier than usual, he doesn't go to the garage or go out after he thinks I'm sleeping. I know now that October is when Mama died. I think that's why October is such a tough month for him. I think that's why some years, the game takes place mostly in October. Some years, I think it's so bad that it leaks into other months. But October is always a tough month, garage or not.

Maybe the threat to call CYS scared him. I know what happens when they come in. Bernard, a boy in my class, had CYS called on his family. He doesn't see his mom or dad anymore. He's staying with some family that lives way out in the country. He only has two shirts, and he's always hungry. Daddy doesn't want that to happen.

Even though I hate it when Daddy gets moody, I know it could be so much worse. The one girl at school, Brittany, talks sometimes about how her dad throws things when he's angry. Sometimes she has bruises on her. I know I'm lucky. Daddy's never like that, even when he's got the quaking hands.

I try to be good. I try not to disappoint Daddy. And I've kept writing, like he told me to.

Daddy lets me venture out more now that I'm older. I think sometimes he likes the peace. I tell him I'm going for a walk. I love walking, love being outside in the fresh, quiet air. I feel like a part of something bigger when I'm out there. Watching the clouds roll by, peeking in on a tiny bee in a flower. There's always so much to take in, but my senses don't feel overwhelmed. Somehow, even with all the sights and sounds and smells, they feel just right out there without anyone around.

I don't tell Daddy I often end up in the field, the one in the woods. The one that he frequents, too. There's something magical about being there, something comforting. It's a true comfort to a frazzled spirit on days when things get too hard.

I know I'm not alone, not completely—but the ladies don't talk. It's perfect for writing my poetry. It's quiet and pretty. I wonder if they like it there as much as I do. Sometimes I ask them, but they don't respond.

73

They only sway the grasses, the branches of the trees. I smile as the sun beams down on me. I like their responses.

Stay Safe,

Ruby

November 2, 2013
8:57 p.m.
Dear Diary,

I'm sorry I'm a little late writing today. I never am late, but wow, do I have a story for you today. I was taking a walk after dinner. Daddy was preoccupied. He said he was tired and headed to the couch to watch TV. I don't know why he's so tired. It's Saturday, and we had a lazy day at home. I don't mind, though. I like my quiet time, out in the trees, in the field. I took my other journal just for poetry—I can't risk losing you out there, after all—and headed to my spot.

But on the way, I made an amazing discovery.

A squirrel.

Not just any squirrel. A dead squirrel. It was on its side on the ground, chew marks on it. Its fur was pulled off in pieces, and some pieces of red showed. I dropped my journal, crouching down to examine it. All the red. All the missing fur. It's frozen face.

It was fascinating.

I've seen dead animals before, of course. I've seen the dead birds in the yard or the dead cats on the side of the road when we drive to the grocery store. I've seen dead bugs and dead dogs. I've seen dead women. But I don't remember seeing a dead squirrel, not in that condition.

I wished I had a camera with me, Daddy's camera. I wished I was good at drawing so I could capture it. I stood, staring at it, taking it all in, and the idea came to me. I knew what I would do with it.

I scooped it up on my notebook, it's body a little smelly. I held it tightly on top of the notebook, feeling its matted fur. I've never pet a squirrel. What an experience. So soft.

I walked behind the house, to the other side where the shed is. The shed I'm allowed in. I was really quiet, creeping through the yard with soft feet and gentle movements. I didn't want Daddy seeing me. This was my game now, my secret. And there was no hole in the shed for anyone to see.

I shut the door. It was dark and stuffy, so I cracked open the shed door just a bit. The shed doesn't have a lot of space, not like the garage. And it doesn't have tools. Not like Daddy's. I would have to improvise.

So I put the squirrel in there, resting in the corner by my bike. I would have to find some other things I needed. I would have to creep back inside the house.

I wandered in the backdoor, tiptoeing when I heard Daddy snoring on the sofa. I didn't want him to know. My heart pounded. Is that what he felt like? It was so exciting, like being in a spy movie or something. I felt alive to the core, trying to evade being caught as if my life depended on it. Maybe it did.

I crept upstairs, found the ball of knitting yarn, and cut off a long, long piece. I tiptoed back downstairs, into the office area we have in a spare bedroom. I glanced around until I found it. The camera. Perfect.

If Daddy found me, what would I say? Stupid girl, I thought. He won't find me. I know how to sneak around. I'm a genius at this. Daddy's a master in the garage, and I'm a master at sneaking about. We've both learned skills these past few years, both gotten a lot of practice. I made it outside, Daddy not even rustling. He must've been tired.

Back in the shed with my amazing treasure, I realized how giddy I was. It wasn't the same as Daddy, certainly. I had found the squirrel dead.

But then again, maybe that's what Daddy does? I can't believe I haven't thought of this before. Maybe he finds the women. I've always assumed he kills them, but what if, like the squirrel, he just happens upon them? Maybe when he ventures out, it's like a grand scavenger hunt he's playing until he finds what he's looking for. Where does he find them? Is he helping someone else? Maybe what he's doing is okay after all. I didn't kill the squirrel. It's not my fault I found it.

I took my piece of rope and tied it around the squirrel's neck, just like I've seen Daddy do. I found a nail tacked in the shed wall. I hung up the squirrel. I watched it dangle, dangle. Beautiful. If only there were blood spilling, it would be perfect. After all, I knew how to clean it.

I realized I would have to prop the shed door open more so I got the right lighting. I popped it open more. This was risky. If Daddy woke up and poked his head outside, he would find me. And maybe he would know what I know. Maybe that would make him angry. Maybe he would tie me up too. The risk of being caught, though, made it so much more enthralling. Nothing risked, nothing gained like Grandma always says. She is usually talking about buying an extra Bingo card or playing the lottery. This game of chance is a little bit different. The stakes are higher.

I hurriedly got the camera ready, snapping the picture of the dangling squirrel and then shaking the photo paper. The anticipation almost killed me.

4:45 p.m. I looked at my glowing watch as I shook, waiting for 4:47 p.m. to look at it. Sevens are my favorite, of course. It's the best number. The moment of truth came. The picture was perfect. Beautiful even. Frame-worthy. I wished I could show Daddy. Wouldn't he be proud? But this would be my secret. I would stash it away, just like he does.

I took the squirrel down from the nail and removed the yarn. Holding the body, I wondered what to do next. There was a moment of uncertainty before it hit me.

I knew what to do. I knew exactly what to do.

I wished I had the hedge clippers or a saw or something, but I guessed I didn't need it. Squirrel was small enough to take care of without that. Still, I wanted to see the splatters.

I carried the squirrel to the woods, past the spot I found him. I walked on and on to the field, to my field until I reached my tree. I didn't have a shovel, but I used my hands. Right over the spot I first saw Daddy working. I dug a little in the ground, wishing we had a dog to help me. Wouldn't that be great for Daddy, if he had a dog? The one crossing guard who works at the school has a giant dog named Henry, just like the books we used to read in second grade. He would go to work with her sometimes. He didn't really help, though. He just stood, slobbering in his spot while she directed traffic.

But a dog could really help Daddy. It would lessen his work a lot. I'm sure it would help. Maybe I should ask for a puppy for my birthday. A big mastiff like Henry or like Mudge from the books.

I placed the squirrel in his final resting spot. Now the lady from years ago would have a pet. Wasn't that a great thing? I wondered if squirrels made okay pets. I wasn't sure. I'd have to ask Daddy. I covered my work with dirt and some leaves, smiling at my ingenuity and staring at my photo the whole way home. I tucked it in the journal until I could get back here to you.

But it still took me a while to write. Because I couldn't stop staring. Daddy was still sleeping on the couch—he's really tired. So I just kept looking at the photograph, studying every angle, every shadow, every line. Do you think Daddy does this? Does he get out his photos? Does it give him the same rush?

I thought about how it must be more of a rush if you actually killed the squirrel—or lady—yourself. Imagine that, having a photo of that work. Amazing.

I'm going to store the squirrel's photo with you, Diary. What a collection we're building. I wonder what we'll add next.

Stay Safe,

Ruby

She is a strand blowing in the wind,
Floating, floating, floating,
But going nowhere.
She is nowhere.

Darkness strangles her,
But so does the light.
Where does she belong?
Where does she fit?
One place calls her in,
Molding to her like a second self.
Only one place.
But sometimes that's enough.

Part V

2014

12 years old

September 10, 2014
6:57 p.m.
Dear Diary,

Sometimes I get these dark, dark thoughts swirling in my head and they won't go away. They're like glue in my brain, like pieces of black glitter that someone blew out of their hands and into my soul. They float and flutter around and about, never far.

I think it's seventh grade. It's so much harder.

I'm in a new school building now, the big one at the other end of town. Daddy and I have to get up earlier to make it there on time. He still drives me because the bus is too loud and the kids are so mean. He drives me in the morning, but I have to ride the bus home because Daddy isn't out of work yet. I have to ride the bus to the stop way at the end of the lane and walk the whole way home. I don't mind the walk—it's peaceful. The bus ride, though, is terrible. One bus ride is enough for one day, so thankfully Daddy can at least take me in the morning.

The building sits right across from the papermill in town. I hate the stink of it. The sulphur-laden, burning smell makes me want to vomit every time. The stench seeps into my pores. I can smell it on my backpack even when I come home. It lurks about on my fingers, on my shirt, in the strands of my hair.

The building is enormous, like a puzzle. There are all sorts of hallways that intersect and numbering systems that don't make any logical sense. It's not organized at all, not like Farmer's Heights Elementary with its neat and tidy hallways in perfect lines. It's a chaotic swirl, and the kids run and dash down the hallways, bumping and shoving all which ways.

Daddy got me permission to leave my classes two minutes early so I can get out of the noise, but it doesn't help. The kids tease me for it, and I always feel like I'm missing something, which makes me super nervous.

I have to go to so many classes in a day, and the blaring bell is set too high. I've even emailed the principal to tell him, but he must be busy because he never responded. Every time it sounds, each hair on my head and on my arms stands at attention and I feel tingly in a bad way inside. I squeeze my eyes shut religiously when I hear the grating sound, but it never gets better.

I have so many teachers now, too. None of them seem to understand anything about me. They take points off because I won't talk in class. They always try to have us collaborate—which means working in groups with kids who pick on me and steal my stuff and kick my shins when the teacher isn't looking. Or call me names or make fun of my hair or touch my arm because they know it makes me angry.

There are all new faces now, too, since we're in a bigger school. I hate it. I hate new people. I hate the cafeteria where everyone is corralled like cattle and acts worse than beasts. I hate all the loud shrieking and the announcements and gym class where we're supposed to change into scratchy shirts and shorts and run around and get sweaty.

I hate it. Hate it. Hate it.

I wish I could disappear. I think about what it must be like to be those ladies that Daddy buried in the peaceful, quiet field. Sometimes I think about how nice it would be to sleep there amongst them, the beautiful ladies resting gently underneath the soil. No homework. No scathing remarks from teachers. No rude kids or hair pulling or book dropping. Nothing but peace.

How would I do it? I wonder sometimes.

We had a suicide prevention talk a few weeks ago in our health classes. It was supposed to show us how bad suicide can be and how we can ask for help. But I was fascinated by it all. By the talk of ropes and hangings and pills. By the talk of razor blades on veins. I wonder if Daddy would be interested in it, too.

That's how I would want to go. Razor blades. Blood squirting from my veins, splattering in exquisite patterns, leaving one final masterpiece behind.

And I know Daddy would know how to clean it up just perfectly. I wonder if when we die we can see what happens afterwards, sort of like watching a movie? A lot of the kids at school complain about their parents making them go to church on Sundays, where they learn about heaven and hell and what happens when you die. Daddy never took me to church. I asked him once about it, but he said it's all a bunch of nonsense to raise money. He said no one knows what happens when you die.

But Daddy sort of does. He's watched the life leave all those beautiful women. He's stared them in the eyes, I would imagine, as they left this world. What was that like, to watch another exit this hard life? Did it give you any insight into the next? Sometimes I think about what that must be like, to have that power, to have that control over someone. But I also think about what it would be like to be on the other end, helpless, at someone else's mercy.

I've noticed people don't like to think about death or talk about it. It's okay, though. I don't like to talk about anything with anyone, in truth. It just leads to confusions and miscommunications and more teasing to endure. I rarely talk to anyone at school. I sit alone at lunch, and I try my best to avoid group work. When I'm forced to interact, a simple head shake or nod is usually all I offer. There are new kids now, from other elementary schools, but they've already come to the same conclusion as all the kids who think they know me—I'm weird, dumb, and one to avoid.

Usually I'm fine with being quiet, prefer it even. I'd rather write out my words in you. Sometimes, however, the conversations at school do interest me. In history class once, we talked about medieval torture and punishment. I was all ears. I even answered discussion questions about it. Many of my peers turned to look at me. It was the first they'd probably heard my voice.

They called me a sick freak afterwards for my comments about death and torture and about the artistic beauty of some of the torture devices. The teacher, who is a young guy, looked very uncomfortable. I thought I might get sent to guidance, but I didn't. I was glad.

Still, even with the few good moments—like when we get to write poetry in English class, or when school got cancelled because of a water break—it's all so bleak. I don't feel like I can survive. I don't feel like I can manage to make it through.

Then I look at Daddy.

He's often in a dark mood. More and more lately, he seems troubled. Sometimes, by the look on his face, I think he'd rather go out and sleep with those ladies in the field, too, and find out what happens after we die. But he doesn't. He perseveres. Even when his eyes turn dark and an uncontrollable rage burns within him at the smallest thing, he finds ways to keep on going. He finds ways to tame the anger, the gloom. And when things get really tough, his moods unbearable, he turns to the killing game in the garage. It's his outlet. It's his way to control those dark, dark feelings. Maybe I just need to find a way, too, besides my poetry. It helps, but lately, things are getting harder.

And I can tell you this—my outlet isn't chess club. I quit after Tommy Coinshall cheated. I hate cheaters. I hate it. There's nothing more unforgivable than that.

Stay Safe,

Ruby

September 15, 2014

6:57 p.m.

Dear Diary,

Today was a really bad day again.

Clarissa Thompson is now in my gym class. You know, the one who tortured me all through elementary school? I thought that at least one benefit of being in this godforsaken, confusing building would be that I'd have less interaction with her. But I was wrong.

She doesn't really talk to Sarah and Chloe anymore. I guess she's too cool for them now, her lowcut tops and too short skirts drawing in the eyes of the boys. She prances down the hallways like a giraffe on stilts, her red lips always pouty and her red nails way too long. I like red—but not on her. It almost would make me hate that color if it weren't so perfect.

And now she's in my gym class, my least favorite class anyway.

I always change in the privacy of the bathroom stall in the locker room. I don't want anyone gawking. Today, like every other hellish day that I have to go to gym class, I changed into the horrific shirt and shorts like I have to for my grade and carried my clothes out, getting ready to put them in my locker. 3-12-04, my combination. I chanted it under my breath like I always do, needing to get it on the first try so kids don't make fun of me or call me retarded.

3-12-04.

I was beelining for my locker, trying not to peek at any of the girls or they call me a pervert.

"Oh shit, the retard's in this class? Fucking great. Just want I want. A pervert to spy on me," a nasally, familiar voice bellowed from right beside me as I tucked my clothes into my locker.

I turned to see the face I'd already identified, more bronzed and more angular, but still familiar.

Clarissa Thompson.

I ignored her, scratching my neck as I tried to edge out of the locker room area and to the gym.

"What, too good to say hi to me?" she asked, bumping into me. She was only wearing her bra.

I scratched my neck more, my cheeks burning as her naked flesh bumped against me. I wanted to shove her away, but I knew I'd get in trouble. This couldn't be happening. It couldn't be.

"Still sleeping with your Daddy?" she whispered in my ear, and I spun around, shoving her against the locker so suddenly and forcefully that it even alarmed me.

Clarissa squeaked, stopped in her tracks, as I banged her against it. "Don't talk about Daddy. You hear me?" The voice was animalistic, like it wasn't even my own. My hands were shaking.

Just like Daddy's

"Relax, freak," Clarissa said, shoving me backwards. I headed out of the locker room as I heard the girls murmur about me. I didn't care if I got in trouble. I didn't. She shouldn't be talking about Daddy like that. She didn't even know him.

Gym class was a misery, as usual. Kickball turned into me being the target over and over until Mrs. Carlisle let me sit on the bleachers. I counted the points for the teams, frustrated that Mrs. Carlisle was wrong about the final score.

Back in the locker room, I grabbed my clothes quickly and rushed to the bathroom to change. I wanted to get out of there as fast as possible to avoid Clarissa. But when I returned to my locker to put my uniform away, I stopped to stare at the front of it.

Bright red lipstick that matched Clarissa's lips was smeared all over my locker.

Freak.

One word. The girls were laughing, videoing my reaction on their phones. Tears started to well as I found it hard to breath. I don't know why, but seeing that word in bright red, red like the garage red, I melted. I cracked. It was like all the horrible things she'd said and done to me were swirling into that one word on my locker.

I threw my uniform on the floor and dashed out of the locker room, ignoring Mrs. Carlisle's pleas for me to stop. I dashed out the door on the left, ran through the parking lot, and didn't stop until I was under my second favorite tree by the soccer field.

I stayed there until the security guard came to retrieve me.

I stayed there, clinking my head against the bark, wringing my shaking hands, and thinking about how much I needed Daddy to go back to the garage—maybe with a familiar face.

Stay Safe,

Ruby

September 22, 2014
7:57 p.m.
Dear Diary,
Gym class has gotten worse. Way worse.

Every day is a new dilemma, a new conundrum. With her tight body and charming smile, Clarissa's won over the girls in our locker room. They work together, distracting Mrs. Carlisle while Clarissa makes my life hell.

It started out small, with the nasty messages on my locker, the broken lock, the stolen clothes. It moved to the planting of horrible pictures in my locker of naked girls, of naked men. I needed it to stop.

I tried talking to Mrs. Carlisle, but the words wouldn't come out right and she thought I was just making excuses to get out of gym class. I wrote her a note, but even that came out jumbled as I tried to explain what was happening in a way that made sense. But the other girls, of course, vouched for Clarissa, and there are no cameras in the locker room.

I tried skipping gym class, but that only lasted one day until I got into trouble for that. Now, the security guard personally escorts me from my 2nd period science class straight to the chamber of hell, as I now call the locker room.

The truth is, like with so many things, I'm on my own. I try to grin and bear. I try to be strong, like Daddy told me once. But today, things went way too far.

Today, while Mrs. Carlisle was busy talking to Annie in her office about grades, Clarissa took it to a new level, even for her. When I came back from the bathroom, there was something taped on my locker.

A picture of my mama. It looked like a high school yearbook picture. My mama's smile, her red hair, though . . . it was unmistakable. It was her. Tears welled. I didn't understand. Because above the picture was one word.

Murdered. Written in red lipstick that was also X'd over my mama's face.

"Where did you get this?" I half-whispered.

Clarissa looked over. "Who, me? You think I did that? Please," she said, rolling her eyes that were covered in makeup.

I couldn't stop the rage. I shoved her against the locker, pinning her tightly. "Where did you get it?"

I squeezed, feeling her spindly neck in my hands. She tried to stay calm, but I saw her flinch. I smiled at the glimmer of fear in her eyes. So this was what it felt like to have the upper hand.

"It's not that hard, you know. Your mother went to school here, after all. She was my mother's age. Put it together, retard."

I blinked, letting go of her neck just a bit, easing up on the pressure. I didn't know that Mama went to the same school as me. I had no idea. How could I know, though? Mama was like a censored topic in our house. It made me realize once more that there was so much I didn't know. It hurt that Clarissa knew more about my own mother than me. Which brought me back to the message.

"Why did you write this?" I asked, pointing to the word as I tightened my grip again.

"Use your head. If you'd stop screwing your dad for two seconds, you'd realize the truth about the psycho. My mom says there's no way it was a suicide."

I blinked, staring into the face of the girl I wanted to hurt so badly—but also the girl who told me more than I ever had known.

Suicide? Murder?

I let go of Clarissa, who gave me a bit of a shove. I stepped back, falling to the ground, leaning against the locker. I gently rocked, banging my head over and over.

Was it true?

Did she kill herself?

Or was she murdered?

And could Daddy . . .?

If Daddy did it, then why does he miss her so much?

I wanted to say it was crazy, it was nuts. And when Mrs. Carlisle found me at my locker after the bell, she scooped me up into her arms and told me the girls were horrible liars. I wanted to believe her. I wanted to believe that Clarissa was just a horrendous person who lied. But here's the thing, Diary.

We both know something Mrs. Carlisle and even Clarissa doesn't.

Clarissa might just be mean—but she doesn't know Daddy like I do. She doesn't know about the killing game. She doesn't know how good Daddy is at cleaning up blood. She doesn't know what I do . . . then again, is there more to Daddy than even I can see?

I'm confused, Diary. So confused. I hope I can figure it all out. Because if Mama died like the ladies in the field . . .well, then what? *Then what, indeed.*

Maybe nothing changes.

Maybe everything changes.

Maybe Daddy is even darker than I thought.

Stay Safe,

Ruby

September 23, 2014
1:57 a.m.
Dear Diary,

I don't know what I was thinking. I guess I was thinking about the whole situation with Clarissa, about what she said about Mama. I guess I just wanted answers. But I did something very, very bad today. Very bad.

When Daddy was sleeping, I crept down the stairs, my tools in hand. I'd watched a video once on how to get into a lock with a bobby pin. I knew it was a longshot, truly. But I'd memorized the video in case I ever needed it.

Now, it seemed like a time that skill was worth trying. I was desperate to get in, even if it meant breaking the rules. Sometimes you have to tell white lies to save relationships, and sometimes you have to bend the rules to save yourself.

I felt a sudden urge to be in the garage. Not outside, not looking in. But actually inside. I guess I thought that maybe I could find a clue, a hint about Mama. A ring or a note. Or maybe just a presence. I would feel her presence in there if Daddy put her in the killing game, right? I didn't know. I didn't know at all.

I also thought that maybe I could borrow one of Daddy's tools, a sharp one, to protect myself. Clarissa's games were getting more and more annoying, scarier. I needed to stop her, and nothing else was working. Maybe it was time for a little game of my own. I fiddled with the lock, trying to find the right angle like I'd remembered in the video. Over and over, I jiggled the pin in the lock, trying to get in and praying I was as masterful at sneaking around as I thought. I needed to get in. My hands were shaking, tears falling. But sometimes we believe what we want to—I believed I was masterful at sneaking around. I was wrong.

"What the fuck are you doing?" a voice bellowed from behind me.

I turned, and my heart stopped. I almost shrieked, thought about running. Daddy snatched the pin out of my hand and grabbed my wrist.

"I'm so disappointed in you. What the fuck are you doing?"

Daddy never talked to me like that. He never grabbed my wrist like that. Suddenly, for the first time, I was terrified. Truly terrified—of Daddy. His hands were shaking, after all. He pinned me against the wall of the garage, putting his face right up against mine. He never made me look at him, but this time, his fingers wrapped around my jaw.

91

"Look at me," he demanded. This was how I knew he was mad. This wasn't the Daddy I knew, the kind one who made waffles and drove me to school and bought me new red rainboots every year. This was someone else.

"I'm sorry, I'm sorry, I'm sorry." I chanted the words, over and over. They mingled with the tears cascading down. "I'm sorry."

"What were you doing? You know it's dangerous in there." His voice was a piercing, animalistic cry tinged with the spit frothing in his mouth. He was almost rabid, a belligerence spewing from him that I'd never, ever detected before.

"It's dangerous in there. In school. In gym." My heart pounded so loudly, I swore they could hear it in the next town. My brain swirled, wrapping around memories of gym and Daddy and the picture of Mama and all that had transpired. My head pounded with fear, with memories, and with the knowledge that I'd been a fool.

"What?" he asked, releasing my chin.

"She scares me. Clarissa scares me. She says bad things. I need to protect myself."

"What were you getting from there?"

I wanted to tell him I was getting one of the saws or one of the knives, the ones I saw cut through flesh. But I could tell even though his voice was calming, the dangerous side of Daddy wasn't through yet. I felt for the first time in my life that if I told him what I knew, he might kill me. He might kill me and I would never know what happened to Mama. Sure, the serenity of the field was alluring. But not yet. I needed to find out about Mama first, felt driven to uncover the answers. It was like the urge to wear my red rainboots even when it wasn't raining or the need to scratch my neck—the desire to find the answers was an unwavering siren's song that lured me in and wouldn't let go.

Plus, there was Daddy to think about. Even though I was scared of him in the moment, I also knew without a doubt that I needed to save him. I needed to stick around so I could keep an eye out for him. I wouldn't be able to protect him from Clarissa's comments or the town or the police if he killed me. I needed to stay alive.

"I don't know. But you say it's dangerous in there and I need something dangerous to protect myself." The words flew off my tongue in a semblance of rationality. I was thankful that I could croak out the words, that they didn't get lodged in my throat like they sometimes did.

Daddy pinched the bridge of his nose, allowing me to finally avert my eyes. I heaved in and out, the air filling my lungs. I wanted to dash to the field, to find my tree and sit underneath it, rocking gently in the night air.

"Fuck, Ruby. That's not how we do things. We Marlowes aren't like that, are we?"

Yes, Daddy. You are.

But I shook my head no, the obedient daughter he always knew me to be.

"Fuck. I thought I taught you better."

You did, Daddy. I know how to do lots of things. I know how to clean up dripping puddles of blood. I know what bones sound like hitting concrete. I know what patterns blood makes when the saw cuts in. I know what cuts to make where and how. I know how to make the most of the trash bags.

"It's not your fault," I murmur.

"It's that fucking girl's fault. I'll take care of it."

"No, Daddy. Don't." *Yes, Daddy. Do.*

"Get in the house, Ruby. I'll take care of it tomorrow. But until then, look at me."

I froze, peering up at him, staring at his eyebrows. They had wisps of gray in them. Did he know that? Suddenly, that bothered me.

"If I ever catch you going into my garage or trying to, it's not going to be good. Not good at all. You hear me? It's dangerous, Ruby. It's dangerous having you in there."

I looked at him, wondering if he could see it in my eyes that I knew. That I knew what dangerous, beautiful things happened in there. His eyes didn't give it away. They only betrayed the burning frenzy simmering in his soul, in his chest. It was the first time I'd detected that level of rage focused on me.

"Yes," I assured, the word punchy and terse.

Daddy walked me to the house, up the stairs, and to bed. He tucked me back in, careful to do it just right. He was back to the familiar man I knew instead of the monstrous person who had scared me moments ago.

"I'm sorry, Ruby." The words were breathy and soft, marked by what I assumed was a genuine remorse.

I wanted to ask for what, but I thought maybe I knew. Subconsciously, maybe I've always known.

"Mama had pretty hair," I whispered into the darkness once he turned to leave.

He paused in the doorway, and maybe I was imagining it, but I thought I saw his face crinkle, his forehead scrunch just a bit like when he's deep in thought.

"She did," he agreed. He leaned on the threshold, and I thought he might ask me something else. Instead, he shut the door, leaving me to my thoughts and the whirring sound of the fan for the rest of the night. But I had a story to tell. This story. It felt too momentous to let go.

Daddy got mad at me.

I thought he might kill me.

And now, though, I think Clarissa might be next on his list.

Goodnight, Diary. I need to get some sleep now—if sleep will come.

Stay Safe,

Ruby

October 14, 2014
10:57 p.m.
Dear Diary,

I've never been so pissed at Dad in my life. Never. That's why I'm late writing. So much has happened. I've been stewing in anger and haven't had a chance to write until now. My hands were too shaky to hold the red pen, to scrawl down the words that were crying for escape.

He's in the garage now. He thinks I'm sleeping. I saw him carrying a black-haired lady from his truck. I'm angry that it isn't Clarissa. When he said he would take care of things, he meant the normal way. Going into the school and complaining. The way that doesn't work. It's annoying. I thought for sure he meant he was going to chop up Clarissa. I was anxious to see her blood splatter on the floor.

But that's not what I'm mad about. It's much worse than him letting Clarissa live.

How could he do this?

It's Ruby and Daddy. That's it. That's all we need. He's said it over and over and over. But for the first time ever, he brought home a woman. Into our house. And not to butcher into pieces, not so I could watch the beautiful blood pool and spill and then disappear.

He thinks I need a babysitter. He thinks I need a positive female role model. *I can't believe it.*

Her name is Stacie. Stacie Grenshod. What a disgusting name. What a terrible, horrible name. It reminds me of green and shoddy, two ugly words. I hate green. She is apparently 21 and dropped out of college and needs a job. So Daddy hired her.

It's the dumbest thing I've heard. We don't need her. I cried and fought with him about it when she showed up. He told me that he knows I've been having a hard time and it will be good for me to have a female in my life.

"I have you, Daddy. That's all I need," I stammered through the tears.

"I know. But Ruby, I can't be here all the time. I have things I have to do, places to go sometimes."

"Then take me with you," I urged. I wondered if the places he was referring to had to do with the killing game. But wouldn't having Stacie here complicate things? Isn't it dangerous to have her lurking about? What if she uncovered the game? Daddy is being an idiot.

And I don't need a female influence. I wonder if he found out what happened at school, what the kids said about Mama. I haven't asked him. I don't care. She is gone, always has been. I don't love her. How could I love someone I don't know?

I love Daddy. I want to protect him, not some red-haired woman I feel nothing for.

Daddy has been going out more after dinner. Sometimes, when Daddy is off work, he goes to a bar called Tavern 7. It's a city over from us, about twenty minutes away. I only know this because a few times, we ran into some guys at the grocery store while we were out and they asked if he would be coming over to Tavern 7 anytime soon. I think he used to go when I was at chess club. Maybe that's why he got so frustrated when I quit. I pretended to study the apples while I listened. I pieced together that sometimes, Daddy goes there before garage game days. Sometimes days or weeks before. He also goes there sometimes when I'm at school and he's not working. I thought he was always working. It made me angry to know there were things he kept from me.

Anyways, apparently he met this Stacie woman there a few weeks ago. I'd heard him slip out around ten one night, probably the night he met her. I remember he came back empty-handed. I hate those nights. They get my hopes up for nothing. No cleaning. No blood. No hard work by Daddy.

Today, at 5:03 p.m., according to my watch, there was a knock at the door. And let's be clear—there's almost never a knock at the door.

Startled by the change in procedure, I watched Daddy saunter to the door as I stood in the kitchen, eating my dry cereal. I like crunchy right now. It's the best. Milk makes it way too soggy. And that's when I saw it. The smile. The smile Daddy reserves for two occasions: me, and for the garage. But here was a new occasion. He was smiling at something, or rather, someone else.

The black-haired woman at the door.

Her hair was silky and shiny, gorgeous. Not as pretty as Mama's, of course. Skinny and tan, she had a pointy chin and high cheekbones. Her almond eyes were mysterious and pretty in all the right ways. She looked like a supermodel.

"Hi, I'm so excited. I baked some of those cookies we were talking about the other night, so I brought a batch." Her voice was high-pitched with a scratchy quality that I hated. She spoke too loud and too fast, and I hated the way she looked at Daddy. She was bubbly and perky and dressed like she was going to a princess ball in some flashy dress.

I stared, chewing my cereal and weighing the interaction. Daddy blushed. He never blushes. What was he doing?

"You didn't have to do that." His words came out soft and lilted a bit.

"It's no problem. Hi, Ruby, I'm Stacie. I'm really excited that we're going to get to know each other. Do you want a cookie?" She blinked at me, holding the plate out as she crossed the kitchen like I was some homeless dog she was trying to lure. She clutched the cookies like they were gold treasure. I didn't move, leaning on the counter like a robot, wringing my fingers on my right hand. I kept chewing, crunching louder, like I hadn't heard her. I stared at the floor, not wanting to acknowledge her. Let her think I'm stupid.

"Ruby, please, can you say hi? Stacie is so excited to spend time with you when I have to go away for the evenings for work or meetings." Daddy acted like I was a two-year-old.

I shoved the ceramic bowl on the counter in one quick jerk that startled Stacie, brushed past her, and stormed up the steps. I wouldn't be any part of this. I shut my door but left it open a crack.

"I'm sorry. She's at that difficult age. And her condition doesn't help things."

Tears burned my eyes. Daddy never referred to me as having a condition. He loathed people who did. What was he trying to be? Why was he trying to impress her?

I pulled out the picture of Mama I had stolen from Daddy's room when I was young. I touched her pretty red hair, thought about how different things might've been. I flipped the photo over, looking at the words scrawled. Two words, in Daddy's handwriting.

I'm sorry.

Why was he sorry? I'd always wondered. I'd always been confused as to why those words were on the picture.

But now, I was starting to realize Daddy wasn't perfect. He had a lot to be sorry about. Like bringing Stacie, some strange woman, into our house. Like thinking I needed a babysitter. I sighed, wiping tears from my eyes as I stared at Mama's slender figure in the photograph.

10.08.04.

The date on the photograph. Underneath the *I'm Sorry.* Is that when Mama died? And what happened? I was two, not old enough to know. And Daddy didn't talk about it. It was one of the walled-up things he didn't like to mention.

10.08.04.

The date everything changed for Daddy. What was he like then? What was I like? Were we happy as a family? Would we be happy now if she were still here?

After a while, I heard Daddy leave. I tucked the photograph back, swiped at my eyes, and climbed into bed, pretending I was asleep. Stacie softly knocked on the door.

"Ruby? Ruby, I know you're not sleeping." She walked gently in and sat on my bed.

"Ruby, listen. I'm sorry. I know you don't know me. But I want to get to know you. I know this age is really tough. I want to do what I can to help."

I sat up slowly, turning to look at her as I wrung my hands. I thought for a long, long moment about my words. Then, I did something I rarely do. I raised my chin so I could look into her perfectly lined, shimmery green eyes.

"Then get the fuck away," I said. I used the word we're not supposed to use. Daddy uses it when he's really mad, and it usually works. I like how it punches the air when it leaves a person's mouth. It makes a statement, a look-at-me statement that I never experience otherwise. Stacie looked startled.

"Okay, I'll be downstairs if you need anything. I'll check on you in a while." Her voice was subdued. I'd killed the light in her. That made me happy. Maybe she'd quit. Maybe Daddy would get rid of this nuisance in our home.

Daddy and Ruby. That's all we need. Not a babysitter. Not Grandma. No one.

A few hours later, I heard Daddy's truck. Stacie had checked on me several more times, but I'd given her the same response. I heard them exchange words. Maybe she was quitting. Then, Daddy came upstairs. I sat up.

"Sorry, Daddy," I murmured, realizing he was probably disappointed. The nark certainly told him about my outburst. I was sure a goody-two-shoes like Stacie would be busting to tattle. It would be worth it, though, if it got rid of her. Anxious, I waited for him to tell me that Stacie quit.

"Stacie said you weren't very nice to her."

"Sorry," I said again, picking at my nail.

"Ruby, I know this is hard. It's just—I worry about you. I'm trying to be the best Dad, I am. Sometimes to do that, I need to get out of here and take care of things so I can support our family. I need to take care of you, but I can't always be here. You know? And Stacie seems nice."

"I don't need a babysitter."

"I know Ruby. But please give her a chance. I think she could be good for you. The only other woman in your life is your grandma, and I know she's not always the easiest to handle."

At that, in spite of myself, I laughed, thinking about the time Grandma fell down the stairs when she was watching me. I shook my head.

"Okay, Daddy," I replied. "I love you. Sorry I'm so bad and difficult sometimes."

"And I'm sorry I'm not perfect. I'm sorry sometimes I make bad choices."

"You're perfect to me. You don't do bad things. You do beautiful things," I replied. He looked at me puzzled, and for a moment, I wondered if he knew that I know. I fantasized that he knew, that we could play the game together.

However, dreams don't always come true. Daddy brushed the words and perhaps the inner awareness he had aside. "I'm not perfect. But I'm glad you think so. I love you."

He offered me a fist bump. He knows this is what I prefer to hugs. I smiled. This is what I mean. He's perfect. He knows me. He respects me. Daddy went down for TV time, and so here I am writing in you.

I'm still mad about Stacie. I'm still pissed at Daddy. As I've been writing this, though, I've noticed the anger subsiding. Writing really is good for the soul, just like my teacher said once. Besides, I know I just have to be patient. I know that Stacie won't last.

I hope that eventually, maybe Stacie will end up in the garage, right where she belongs. And oh, what fun that will be to watch. To see those almond-shaped eyes staring blankly ahead as he cuts every perfectly toned, tanned limb to pieces.

I'm sitting at my desk now. Daddy went outside after he thought I was asleep. I peeked out my window to see him opening the back of his truck. He has a cover for it now, so you can't see in. He keeps it locked. So many locked and secured pieces in Daddy's life. He's a man with lots to hide.

He pulled out a bunch of bulking bags before reaching way, way, way to the back. I saw him pull out a woman. A black-haired woman. My heart leaped.

It's long, black hair, from what I can see here. I'm going to head down now. This must be why he had Stacie come over. He must have had to go pretty far to get this lady. Maybe he was worried that he wouldn't be back in time to tuck me in, and he knows I don't like it when I'm completely alone at night.

I'll write more later. I'm going down to watch.

Stay Safe,

Ruby

October 17, 2014
6:57 p.m.
Dear Diary,
When Daddy picked me up at school today, he had a surprise for me. Really, surprise isn't the right word, though.

Torture. Punishment. Hell. Nightmare.

These are words that fit what he had in store for me.

Stacie was coming over again. Apparently, he needed to go out for the night, and he felt like Stacie should come stay with me again. He thought I could give her another chance.

"Hi, Ruby," she said with a smile when I got home and she showed up. She proceeded to babble on and on and on about how she would make chicken nuggets for dinner and the cake I like and how she got me a present and she knows I don't like surprises so she told me it was a clock and . . .

I stared out the kitchen window, trying to drown out her voice. It was hard to ignore the grating squeaks. I thought about the garage and the killing game and how stupid Daddy was being. Even I could see how risky it was to have someone in our home. Why was he suddenly going out so much? And farther away? And earlier? I didn't understand. But I did know one thing. I wanted Stacie gone. She was trouble. She was annoying. And I didn't want her with me.

Nonetheless, Daddy insisted I sit at the table, talk to her. I could see it was important to him. I couldn't risk making him mad at me. It wouldn't be good to push him away from me. If Daddy needed me to make Stacie work, I would try. I would have to let this problem solve itself. Or I'd have to solve it for us. Either way, it would take some patience.

Once Daddy left, Stacie started making me dinner. She hummed songs while I sat on the living room floor, watching her and getting angrier and angrier. Over dinner, I asked Stacie a few questions. She was elated to tell me about her ridiculous life.

Here's what I learned:

She majored in science in college but ran out of money. She wanted to be a researcher.

Her parents both died, and she has no family.

She's 21.

She's planning on travelling the world, place to place. She works odd jobs here and there for now to save money. I guess I'm one of the odd jobs.

She's staying at the motel in town, The Hazelside Inn.

I don't like her.

The last one isn't something I learned, in honesty. It's something that was just reinforced by spending time with her. At least I could say to Daddy that I had, in fact, tried. I had attempted to be civil and flexible and strong and give her a chance. It's not my fault she's such a horrendous woman.

A part of me knows maybe I'm being irrational, that I just am being possessive of Daddy. I don't like sharing him or our home or our routine. I don't like that Daddy doesn't trust me to be alone. I don't like that he trusts her to be in our home, so close to everything going on. I don't like that Daddy's suddenly gone more often. I don't like how she's messing up the routine here.

Overall, Daddy's been distracted now. I'm not sure why. Daddy didn't even notice that I came home with a cut on my arm, for example. Some girl in math class tripped me on my way out, said I was fucking weird. She said she was sick of me staring at her. I wasn't, actually. I was just trying not to look at Mr. Carson, the math teacher. So I was looking at the girl's shoes. They were red Converse, pretty red. My favorite. Daddy usually would notice something like a cut on my arm because he's perceptive. He watches out for me. He didn't, though. Not this time. I hated that.

Everything is different now that Stacie is in the house. She's ruined it all, even if Daddy doesn't realize it. Stacie needs to leave. She needs to pack up her bag and hike out of here to her next spot. No one will miss her, least of all me. And Daddy might think she's good for me, with her glistening skin and cutesy accent. But she's bad for me and him. Only I know who Daddy really is—and I plan on keeping it that way. She doesn't love him like I do. She wouldn't protect him, not like me. She's nothing like me. We don't need her here.

Stay Safe,

Ruby

October 30, 2014
6:57 p.m.
Dear Diary,
I haven't told anyone this.

I used to want a mom. I used to hope and wish for one on my birthday candles, on the stars, every night before bed.

I was younger, probably five or six. I used to daydream about what it would be like if I had one. I used to see the moms in television shows and at the grocery store, and I wondered why I didn't have one. I wondered if I would like having someone to bake me cookies and sit beside me, on the other side of me, when Daddy and I watched TV. Not too close, of course, just a few inches between us so the fabric of our shirts kissed. Someone to fill the other chair at our kitchen table and to help Daddy take me to school. Someone to be in our family.

Things have changed, though. I've grown up, and I've realized that I don't need a mom. I don't even want one.

I know that should make me feel guilty. I don't know exactly how Mama died or why, but I know it makes Daddy upset so it must've been bad. Really bad. It makes me wonder if it was murder like Clarissa said—or something else.

He only talks about her if I ask directly, and even that makes him uncomfortable. He clams up on that one day in March, March 12th, and that one day in October, October 8th. And really the whole month of October. Those are the days I see him drinking heavily. In between the garage days during those months, there are other kinds of days, too. Darker days. Bourbon days. Those are days Daddy buries himself in his room, and I am left by myself. Those are the only days that I feel like Orphan Annie, like I'm on my own.

I'm strong, though. I can handle it. I'm used to being alone, prefer it sometimes. And it makes me feel like I'm helping Daddy.

Anyway, I used to want a mom, but not now. I see my classmates' moms and they're awful. Hugging, kissing, touching. Asking nosy questions. Prancing around in miniskirts that show too much of their flabby, cottage cheese thighs. Hovering around the school like policeman in too much pink.

When I was young, I had a babysitter sometimes, when Grandma was at Bingo or out of town or busy. She was even worse than Stacie, if you can believe that. She was old, though, and Daddy never blushed at her, that's for sure. Mrs. Felton was her name. She was actually one of Grandma's friends—which explains a lot. She had six cats and smelled musty. I always hated the odor in her tiny, cottage-like house, begged her to buy some air freshener. She told me not to be rude. I wasn't being rude, though. I was being honest. There's a big difference.

She would feed me popcorn and cookies and we would watch game shows. It was boring. But the worst part was she talked too much. She thought she could mother me.

"Poor girl, no mom. What a pity." She would say that to me, like I was deficient. I would hope she would take those knitting sticks and knit her lips together instead of the scratchy wool scarves she would make for me and force me to wear.

Even if I *was* lacking something, she couldn't fill that hole. I saw my mother in the pictures, the beautiful red hair that cascaded down her back like a mermaid. Mrs. Felton's hair was wiry and coarse, tight gray curls glued to her head. She was *not* my mother. I told her this repeatedly. She told me I was rude.

She told Grandma I was rude. Grandma smacked my mouth.

She told Daddy I was rude. He just told her I am who I am.

I think that about him, too. He is who he is. And I love him no matter what.

That's why I know I don't need a mom. I have enough love from Daddy. We understand each other. We support each other. We protect each other. I would do anything for him—even lie.

And I never used to lie, Diary. Never. But there's a first time for everything, and I've realized the world isn't black and white like the world in *The Giver*. A big part of living is figuring out when a lie is necessary and when telling the truth is okay.

Stacie was over to babysit again, Daddy insisting he had to go out for work. It makes me think of those days with Mrs. Felton, when I was too young to be alone. How ridiculous that now, at my age, I have a babysitter again.

Daddy slathered on the lies thick, going on and on about some work project and how sorry he was that he had to go out but it was necessary. I saw the way his hands were shaking, though. I don't think it's for work. Still, why is he leaving earlier now? Why isn't he going late at night, when I'm asleep? What's changed?

Over dinner, Stacie was being her normal, annoying self. Chitter-chattering at me and attempting to be all cutesy. I was shoving around chicken nuggets on my plate, contemplating ways to get rid of her for good, to scare her away.

I thought about the crayon drawing I had made yesterday in my room, the one shoved underneath the mattress, waiting for the right time. It was weak, but it was a start. Stacie wasn't ready to babysit someone like me anymore that I was ready to accept someone like her being around. And even though I told myself I'd try hard to make it work, there came a breaking point tonight.

After dinner, I decided to sit on the sofa and watch television. The funny videos show was on. It wasn't the same without Daddy, though. Stacie was chattering on and on and on. I finally yelled at her to stop. She got up and walked across the room.

And guess what she did then, Diary?

She picked up the photograph. Off the fireplace. The one of Mama.

"Pretty hair," she said, staring at Mama like she knew her. Staring like she knew who Mama and Daddy were together or like they mattered to her.

I don't know why, but I just didn't like it. I hated that she was touching the picture. I hated her. I hated that she was looking at Mama's hair, studying her, like she knew something I didn't. Like maybe she knew something about Daddy I didn't. Something in the look in her eye, in the way she perused the photo—it bothered me, severely. My neck got itchy and my hands felt hot. I couldn't help myself, Diary. It just happened.

Before I knew what was happening, I was tackling the unassuming Stacie to the ground. My nails were scratching, and my screams mixed with her yelps as we rolled on the floor. At one point, I felt my teeth biting into her shoulder, gnawing the flesh like a dog with a bone. After a long moment, Stacie managed to scramble away—but not before I tasted a splash of her blood on my tongue, felt the soft, warm flesh melting between my teeth. Panting, I sat on the floor, and stared straight ahead. I didn't say a word.

I know I should've felt guilty. But I didn't. I felt a hunger for revenge, a rage, something dark taking over. Was this how Daddy felt with those ladies? Was there something inexplicable that took over him, too? Stacie backed against the wall in the living room, studying me as if she was afraid. She should've been afraid. She had no idea what I was capable of, what we were capable of. I've never hated someone so much, not even Clarissa or the girls at school. Something in Stacie just made the dark parts come to life within, wicked parts that must've been dormant all this time.

I heard her wander into the kitchen and pull out her cell phone. She called Daddy.

She didn't say another word to me. I sat still, rocking in the corner.

When Daddy got home, I rushed to the door, past a still-shaking and paler Stacie. It took him a long time to return. He must have been far away. Looking at my watch, it took him an hour and a half to get home after Stacie called.

It was a long hour and a half for Stacie, I bet. It flew by for me. I couldn't contain myself. I felt alive and giddy with what I'd accomplished. This would be it, I knew. Stacie was done here, and I couldn't be happier. It was worth the taste of blood in my mouth to get rid of her for good. Even if Daddy was mad, someday he'd see I did a good thing for us. Daddy asked what happened. I didn't speak. Just shook my head, rocking myself with my arms wrapped around me.

"Ruby, go upstairs. I'll be up soon, okay?" he asked, his voice soft.

I went to my room and paced as I listened to Stacie's muffled, sobbing voice. I heard her explain what happened in accurate detail. I heard Daddy apologizing. I wanted to stand still so I didn't have to strain to hear, but I couldn't stop my feet. I literally couldn't stop them from wearing a path in the carpet. I strained my ears, though, thankful my hearing was sensitive.

Daddy sighed when she was done telling her side of things. "I'm so sorry. It's who she is, you know? I should've known she wouldn't react well to change. I thought it might be good for her, but I was wrong. I don't think she can handle it. She's never been an easy child, but I love her. I'm sorry she hurt you. She's never done something like this before."

Stacie sighed. I could tell Daddy's charm was working on her. He had a way with words, no matter what was happening.

"I'm okay. I got some peroxide from the bathroom cabinet. It'll be fine. It just scared me." Her voice was an irritating chirp I wanted to suffocate.

"I appreciate you being so understanding."

"I think it's sweet you're so patient with her. She's definitely difficult. I'm sorry I couldn't make it work." Stacie's voice calmed, the shakiness ebbing.

But in me, emotion quaked. Rage festered instead of relief, threatening to ooze out every single pore. Who did she think she was, talking about me like that? Tears welled. *I'm not difficult. I'm not. I'm not.* The mantra got stuck on repeat, cycling through my head as I tried to rise above it and listen to the rest of the conversation, trying not to hear the words all of my teachers and the kids and the principals use to describe me. *I'm not difficult . . . am I?* The question assaulted my brain with confusion tinged with guilt. I shoved it aside, though. There wasn't time to worry about it. I had bigger concerns. Like what Daddy was going to do to Stacie.

"She's the one who's patient, dealing with just me as her parent. Trust me when I say that I appreciate all you've done for Ruby. Or tried to do," Daddy replied.

Fury surged up again. I wrung out my hands as I listened to Daddy continue on.

"But, well, my focus needs to be Ruby right now. I don't think it's good to bring someone else into her bubble. She's at a difficult age, and I know these next few years will be tough for her. She's going through changes, changes that are tricky for any girl, but especially for Ruby. I need to be here for her, 100%. I just don't think this is going to work, not after tonight. I don't think you babysitting her is a good idea. I'm sorry I promised you a job and now it's not working."

"I agree. I'm so sorry, but I can't do this either. Thank you for the opportunity, though."

I breathed in. I could hardly believe it. I didn't need that drawing from under my mattress, the one with the knives and Stacie and the twisted limbs. I spent all those hours perfecting the curve of her jaw, the color of her eyes, the red of the blood pooling beneath her for nothing.

But I didn't care. The wench was gone, and things could go back to normal. I liked that my teeth helped Daddy see the dangers of having Stacie around. I liked that I freaked her out, even if just for a minute. I liked that Daddy told her it wasn't going to work. I smirked to myself, scratching my neck as I thought about how good it felt to know she was gone for good.

When Daddy came up to my room after she'd gone, he apologized.

"I'm sorry, Ruby. I shouldn't have brought her here. I don't know what I was thinking. But no more. Just you and me, Ruby. Just you and me."

And the garage women. But they were quiet, just like I like them, I thought as he came closer for a fist bump, his cologne wrapping around me. It was too strong. I wanted the non-cologne Daddy back.

I thought about telling Daddy that Stacie had thrown me to the ground, had hurt me. Just to ensure he didn't try anything like this babysitting business again. I decided I didn't need to, though. It sounded like Daddy had learned his lesson.

I did have one question, though. I wondered if Daddy was going to eventually add her to his collection now that he was done using her. Or was that against his rules? How did he pick the women of the garage? So many questions. So much time to figure it out now.

Just Ruby and Daddy.

I know, Diary, that it won't be long now. His hands were shaking when he left me go. The hunger for the killing game is strong, I can see it in his eyes. I can almost smell it on him, if my nose works past the awful cologne. Maybe Stacie stirred something in him, or maybe Stacie was just a distraction from his October self all along.

Stacie's lucky she left when she did, or she would've been painted up by Daddy in red, red, red. Or, who knows, maybe she would've looked amazing in my shed. I picture the squirrel hanging from the ceiling. I wonder if the noose I made could've held her.

If she's smart, she'll leave town and never come back. If she's stupid, she'll stick around, and Daddy will add her to the women in the field. My thirst to watch it all, to live vicariously—one of our vocabulary words this week—through Daddy is pulsing.

Let the game begin again. Thanks for nothing, Stacie.

Stay Safe,

Ruby

November 1, 2014
6:57 p.m.
Dear Diary,
Someone really needs to get rid of the old hag.

Daddy says I can't call her that. But really, someone does. Apparently, Grandma heard about what happened with Stacie. I don't know how. Stacie must have been running her flabby mouth in town the next day, and Grandma has spies everywhere, I swear. That woman knows everyone and everything, even when we don't want her to—which is all the time.

She showed up today with some disgusting healthy salad that I would never eat. She shooed me to my bedroom while she talked to Daddy. Grandma doesn't know I have super hearing. However, she really doesn't know much about me or Daddy at all, even though she thinks she does.

"Honestly, I'm worried. If you need help with Ruby, you should've told me. She's at such an impressionable age. And with her condition . . . "

"Mother, stop. Right now. Ruby's fine. I'm fine. It was just a misunderstanding."

"She bit a woman. That's not a misunderstanding. Where is this violence coming from? I don't understand it. You know, Misty Johannsen, my old neighbor, was at Bingo last week. She said her daughter who has a son with the same tendencies as Ruby, well, she decided it was best to send him to a boarding school where he could be under surveillance. Sometimes it's just for their own good."

A hand slapped the table.

"Shut the hell up. Don't you ever tell me what to do with my daughter. I take good care of her. I do."

I imagined Daddy wringing his hands. I wished he'd wring Grandma's neck.

"I know. I'm not saying that. The girl, she's just different. She needs help. I just worry. Especially since you're doing this alone. And with her mother's tendencies . . ."

"Stop right there. Stop butting in. Stop worrying. We're fine, Mother. I think I can handle my own daughter."

"I'm your mother. It's my job to worry. I know you still miss Caroline, but it's been so many years. Have you ever thought about dating? Trying to find someone? I just worry about you being all alone, doing it all by yourself."

Silence. Then, after a long moment, Daddy's angry voice bellowed. "Don't fucking talk about her like you cared for her."

"I care about you," Grandma replied. "That woman was nothing but trouble from the moment you met her. She wasn't cut out to be a mother, let alone to a daughter . . ."

"Get out," Daddy responded. "I mean it. Don't come into my home saying horrid things about my daughter, your granddaughter. I won't have it, Mother. I dealt with it with Caroline."

"And I was right about her. Look what she left you with. She was weak. She was selfish, the way she ended it all . . ."

Something shattered, causing me to jump. There was a pause, and then finally, footsteps. I heard a door slam, and Grandma's car pulled away. I wanted to feel sad, to feel stressed. But I didn't. I felt happy. Daddy got rid of the horrible woman, at least for today. And I'd learned something important. She hated Mama. Why?

When Daddy came upstairs, I sat quietly.

"Daddy?" I asked after a long moment.

"Yes, Ruby?"

"Did Mama kill herself?" I don't know where the words came from, but I'd been thinking about it a lot, even before Grandma's conversation.

He blinked, looking at me for a long, quiet moment.

"Yes, Baby. It was complicated though."

My chest squeezed at the admittance. I guess I'd known all along but it just felt different hearing verification.

There was a long pause. Daddy looked like he was somewhere else. I interrupted him, though. "Was it my fault?"

Daddy's face went pale. I felt like I'd caught him in something. He averted his eyes, and then paced around the room. He started wringing his hands.

"No, Ruby. It wasn't your fault. Your mama was complicated. Things were complicated."

I didn't respond, but I couldn't help but wonder if Daddy was lying. Why would Grandma say those things?

"Are you going to disappear, too?" I asked, verbalizing for the first time the fear that's always close to my heart.

"Of course not. Of course not," he whispered, looking at me intently. There was something on his face I couldn't read. But bringing up Mama, it upset him. It made him different.

I hope he was telling the truth. I hope he isn't going to go away, too. I can live without Mama. But I couldn't live without him.

Stay Safe,
Ruby

November 5, 2014
3:47 a.m.
Dear Diary,

It feels weird writing in you. It's so late. No wait, correction. It's so early. Hold on, I'm going to light up my watch and double check.

3:48 a.m. now. I'm at my desk, writing by the moonlight shining in. I don't want to risk turning the lamp on, Daddy seeing. The light is on in the garage, and he's working away.

But not on a body. In fact, I'm not really sure what he's doing. Cleaning up maybe? Reorganizing? I'm not certain. I'm dying to know, but I can't sneak out without him knowing. It snowed early this year, the few inches piled around. It's clean and fresh, and if I walked out back, he'd see my footprints. I couldn't have that.

Plus, he didn't leave in the truck like he usually does. He isn't out for his typical game. Maybe he's just working on improvements to the game. I can't wait until I can sneak down and take a peek at what he's accomplishing in there. I wonder if it will make the killing game more fun or maybe just easier. I'm not sure.

Or maybe the news scared him.

We were watching the news at 6:00 like we usually do. But tonight, Daddy turned up the volume when a story came on about a girl with long black hair.

Her name was Belinda Cartright. She is 26 and is missing from a city about forty miles away, Droveport. The news described her as being a drifter. Apparently, her family back in Nevada had traced her to Droveport, Pennsylvania, but no one has seen her for over a month. She never came back to check out of the motel room she's renting.

The newscaster quickly moved on to a story about a puppy after the picture flashed. Daddy rubbed his chin. I glanced at him from my peripherals. It looked like he was thinking hard. At first, there was a smirk, but then it shifted to something else. I'm not sure what Daddy was thinking.

But I'm pretty sure I know why he was so interested in the story. The picture of Belinda—it sat familiar in a way. I think she was in the garage a while ago. I think that's who the last black-haired lady in the game was, the one last month. My heart fluttered a bit. They're looking for her. Could they trace her back to Daddy? What would happen to him if they figured it out?

But then my fears were assuaged. Daddy's smart. Cunning. Skilled. He'll never get caught. *Never*. And if he did, well, I'd be his alibi. We learned about that in social studies. I'll have to do some thinking on how to make his alibi airtight.

But Stacie wouldn't. Stacie could tell everyone how Daddy was gone. Could that hurt his case? We should've got her to the garage when we had a chance. Anger bubbles. Daddy was so stupid having her come over. So, so stupid. He really needs to let me help him so I can tell him when he has stupid ideas. I could really, really help him be better, safer at the game. I'm a good observer, and I'm good at spotting things most people miss. Why doesn't Daddy see how helpful I could be to him?

Belinda's family will probably stop looking after a while. If she's a drifter, well, who's to say she didn't just move on out of town, like Stacie did?

It's funny because looking at Belinda's picture, she looks kind of like Stacie. Why did Belinda get picked for the game and not Stacie? Was it a moment of weakness? Did Stacie just manage to get away in time? Or was she too risky for some reason? I love thinking about what goes through his mind when he chooses, when he kills. It's like a really intense, live game of chess, but I don't quite have the rules all worked out. It's like a puzzle trying to figure out how and why and when.

Daddy's still working, still perfecting his latest project in the garage. I bet the next woman he picks is in for a rude awakening. I bet she's going to be better than ever. I bet he's getting better and better, and whatever he's making will make the masterpiece even more fun to watch.

I'm itching with anticipation. Just itching. And not just my neck. All over.

Who says you learn everything at school? I learn a whole heck of a lot more studying Daddy. Maybe he should've been a teacher.

Stay Safe,
Ruby

Fingers shake as she glances out the window.
The rain drops pelt against the glass, and the day is murky.
She is tired and worn. She is scared.

Where does he go? When will he come back?
And what will happen to them all?
Will their lips stay glued, frozen like dandelions in December?
Or will the tiny, wispy seeds float away and mingle with the frost,
Waiting to thaw in the spring,
For everyone to revel in their sparkling, glistening dew?

She saw a rabbit once, alone in a field.
Who waited for it to come home?
Who will wait for her?

She is alone and cold, but something else is building in her.
Hunger. Starvation. Joy.
She just needs him.
But they need him, too.

Part VI

2017

15 years old

September 2, 2017
8:57 p.m.
Dear Diary,

Daddy is Jack. That's what I've come to figure out in Mr. Pearson's English class. And being Jack isn't exactly a good thing. I mean, sure we all have a little Jack in us. That was William Golding's point. We all have that savage side that thirsts for pig's blood. But I'm beginning to understand that Daddy's pull towards Jack is stronger than most.

I asked Daddy at the dinner table tonight if he'd ever read *Lord of the Flies*. He shrugged, said he didn't remember it. Fascinating. Mr. Pearson's right, I suppose. We sometimes don't see ourselves as we really are. If Daddy did read the book, he doesn't even remember Jack or connect what he does with him.

I stayed after class today to talk to Mr. Pearson. I wanted to discuss my assessment of Daddy. Wouldn't that be a fascinating essay? I didn't, of course. I love Mr. Pearson. His slicked back hair, his tie knotted perfectly, every button on his shirt done up. He's a bit quirky and knows a lot of different facts. He has some interesting ticks, too. Like how he has to tap his hand on the desk after every two sentences—I've counted—and how he always has a mint in his mouth. Always.

But he's smart, he loves literature, and he loves poetry. Best of all, he doesn't make me present to the class. He seems to understand that I'm on the fringes of the class. He doesn't try to make it better or force me to socialize. He lets me be, lets me be different on the edges where, in truth, I flourish. Even better, he tells Clarissa off when she smart mouths me. I don't think he likes Clarissa at all, which is an added bonus if you ask me.

Yes, she's of course in my class again. You'd think the overtly sexy party girl would be too busy flirting with her football team boy toys to get good enough grades for Honors English. But somehow she pulls it off. Maybe it has something to do with the fact that her Daddy is on the school board. I don't know. But I never get rid of her and those red lips and nails. I swear, it's like she knows red is my favorite color so she tries to ruin it by wearing it all the time. I've sort of gotten used to her constant antics, I guess. Stealing my stuff. Saying horrible things about me. Calling me retarded. Tripping me, slamming into me, the list goes on and on. I almost don't notice.

Almost.

Except when she says stuff about Daddy. Then I notice. My hands start to tremble, and I have to chant to myself to stay strong and calm and flexible. Still, there are many days when I picture her, blood trickling down as her eyes stare blankly ahead. I picture what she'd look like in that grassy field, where her lips would be red from blood instead of lipstick.

I've had to stay strong and quiet and just deal with her for so many years— but not anymore. Mr. Pearson notices what she does, and he makes sure she gets in trouble. There's no sweet smile or charming words that get her out of it, either. He's immune to her in all the best ways, which makes him even more of a favorite teacher to me.

So tenth grade isn't so bad. I've actually started to like school, if only for Mr. Pearson's fifth period English class. I love hearing his ideas on the works we're reading. I love hearing his feedback on my poetry. He never says it's too dark or asks where it comes from. He just tells me what he likes and what could be better. I appreciate that. It feels good to have someone get my work, to get me.

As much as I like Mr. Pearson, though, I know I like Daddy more. I can't betray his trust, can't tell Mr. Pearson about him. In truth, there's not much to tell these days. Daddy seems to be done with the killing game. The last time he brought a lady back to the garage was almost three years ago. *Three years.* What made him stop? I'm not sure. Maybe he's just done with it, like how I outgrew my red boots and didn't want another pair. Sometimes we just change. We stop feeling what we used to feel, stop loving what we used to love, no matter how hard we fight against it. Change is hard, but sometimes staying the same is impossible.

Sometimes I think I imagined it all. Sometimes, I think maybe I hallucinated the whole game, that maybe I am crazy or retarded like so many seem to think. Did it really happen the way I remember?

I know that it did. Deep down, I know. You don't just make up those images. You also don't just forget something so epic, so glorious. I don't know what snapped in Daddy to make him stop. He's tried to stay away, or at least I thought he did. For three years. I think Belinda Cartright's news story scared him at first. I thought he was worried about getting caught. Maybe he was. Or maybe it had something to do with Mama, about his promise to not disappear.

Maybe Daddy just thought I needed him. And I did. I still do.

The past years haven't been easy, as you know. Even though Daddy has set aside the garage, there's been something palpable in him, something scary. It bubbles to the surface once in a while. I see it when he's sharpening the knife in the kitchen, the metal on metal sound singeing the edges of my awareness. I see it in the way he looks at certain women that pass us in a store, an almost undeniable, uncontrollable surge of hunger that is reflected in his trembling hands. I see it in his months of quietness, of remoteness, of aloofness.

He's worked so hard to suppress it, but he's losing the fight. I guess the dark need in Daddy eventually won out.

Maybe, though, in those three years, the thirst for the killing game was just somewhere else. It was in his dreams as he worked on the garage, on making it better, stronger, more intoxicating. Because it's been quite a remodel. To outsiders, it might not look that different. It looks like the well-oiled garage of a man who works in construction, who loves building.

There are new tables and straps. New saws. And even a lounge area. But the lounge area isn't for kicking back, for watching television and drinking beer. It's something much darker, if I know Daddy at all. There's something else, too. Daddy's hands have been shaking again, the tell-tale sign that I'm about to see what the garage is really for, what secret weapons he's stored, and what hidden lusts he's going to quench. Maybe tonight.

I should be scared or appalled or nervous. But I'm not. If I'm being honest, which I always am with you, Diary, I'm thankful. I need a release for all of this anger, besides my poetry. I need somewhere to let loose, to let go of some of the rage I feel for the girls at school. Daddy's not the only one with a darkness surging within. Because each year that passes, each month that things are hard at school, my anger intensifies. Each year that passes, I understand more and more what the garage is all about. And each year, I realize more and more that I'm not so different from the man I call Daddy.

Daddy's killing game helps with the feelings that grow within me, even though I'm just experiencing it from a distance.

I don't know how he's stayed away this long, and I'd be lying if I said I didn't miss it. I can close my eyes and envision the swirls of red, the beautiful paintings I would do anything to mimic, to recreate, to put on display under a spotlight in my room.

But it's a relief, too. It's a relief not having to worry about the worst thing—Daddy getting caught. I know what could happen to him. His killing game might be fun to watch, but it's life or death, too—Daddy's life or his death. If something happened to him, I don't think I could go on. I know I couldn't go on, and even Mr. Pearson's English class couldn't give me a reason to stay.

These past years may have been empty of the killing game, but Daddy's still been going through a lot. There's a brooding, mysterious quiet surrounding him, even more than usual. He's not the smiling, social person in public anymore. He's squirrely, wiry, antsy. He rarely sits still. It's like this weird force is driving him, like he's on some kind of mission. Or maybe he thinks if he keeps busy, he won't have time to play the game. Why is he stopping? Why does he feel the need to quit? Did something happen? Did he almost get caught?

All these years, and I still don't know the answer.

All these years, and he doesn't know I know.

Apparently, I'm a good secret keeper. I can even keep secrets from Daddy.

He does spend a lot of time in the garage still, but it's a different kind of time. He's always building something in there, organizing, reorganizing. I tried to peek in once. He shuddered when he heard my voice.

"Ruby, what are you doing in here? It's dirty. You don't want to get dirty."

I guess he realizes I'm older now and it's harder to use the "it's dangerous" excuse.

"Nothing, Daddy. What are you doing?" I stood at the door, trying to calm the excitement rising within. It felt good to be on the hallowed ground.

"Just tidying. Listen, I love you, but this is my workspace, okay? It's my sanctuary, just like your room is yours."

"Okay, Daddy," I replied soberly, trying not to let the disappointment be too transparent.

When would he let me in? When would he let me be a true part of his life?

It's frustrating. I wish I could talk to Mr. Pearson about it.

I just can't stop thinking about Jack from the story, and how Daddy is just like Jack. Smooth and cunning when he needs to be but driven by a blackness that the other boys only get a taste of. Jack owns the blackness, though, consumes it. It's admirable, in a sense, the way he takes on the evil, the Lord of the Flies, and wins, in some ways. But in class, we talked about how Jack is the villain.

Is Daddy the villain in our story? Is his life not what I thought it was?

I've been thinking a lot about it lately. I've been considering my life, too. What will happen to me when school is over? Will I become like Daddy? Will it be my turn?

I shudder at the thought—but not because it scares me. I shudder because a big piece of me is utterly convinced I would be really good at it.

Maybe even better than Daddy.

Stay Safe,

Ruby

October 2, 2017
1:27 a.m.
Dear Diary,

The killing game drought is over. It's begun again.

What prompted it? After three years? I don't know. I don't know at all. Maybe he couldn't fight the hunger for the red. I understand that. I've missed the pretty patterns, too.

Or maybe the final piece of Daddy snapped in half because he's started back to the same killing game with a new form of passion. It's the same as I remember, but it's also different. Darker. Hungrier. More wickedly wild. And more satisfying to watch.

It felt like old times, hearing the truck pull in, waiting for Daddy to get in position, and then sneaking downstairs. I'm smarter now, though, older. Wiser. I know I can be sneakier. I also know I have to be better. Because I'm older now—there would be no talking my way out of it.

If Daddy caught me, what would he say?

However, it's worth the risk. It's definitely worth the risk.

I wandered behind the garage, the familiar hole still in place. Thankfully, Daddy's remodelling of the garage left it for me. It's like fate, or like maybe, just maybe, Daddy subconsciously wants me to have a window into his world. I'd like to think that in my naïve mind even though I know it's not the case. More likely, it's just an oversight. Regardless, I'm thankful. It gives me a viewpoint into his inferno of rage, one that bubbles faintly within me. My heart beats wildly in anticipation, as if I'm at a concert waiting for the main act to come on stage.

But I hate concerts. I hate crowds. This is my greatest show, and Daddy is the rockstar I'm waiting to get an autograph from.

I peeked through the hole as Daddy prepared his area. But I did a doubletake when I looked in. Things were different. Very different indeed.

Stay Safe,
Ruby

October 2, 2017

8:57 p.m.

Dear Diary,

I'm sorry I stopped writing last night—well, actually this morning, to be correct. I just couldn't quite find the words. My hands were shaking with . . . something. Confusion? Excitement? Anxiety? I'm not sure. But Daddy's show in the garage was overpowering, something I had to sort through so I could tell it just right. I had to stew over the scenes so I could find the perfect words to describe the utter magnificence.

He's back, Diary. He's back, and he's better. The killing game has, dare I say, been perfected.

Last night, when I peered in and saw that for the very first time, the lady Daddy brought home wasn't dead, I was stunned. What was this? This wasn't how he did it, was it? He always brought them home dead, quiet, their eyes staring deadpan as he worked. But this was different.

My heart was jolted as I watched. She had blonde hair. It was pulled back into a messy ponytail. Or maybe the ponytail just got messy from Daddy. She wore a tight, super short metallic dress. It was shining, an olive green color with a fish-scale like texture. It was so short I was sure her private bits were about ready to spill out. Duct tape covered her mouth, the silvery texture a nice accessory to her dress, to her smoked eyeshadow.

But her blue eyes told a different story. Her blue eyes were ravaged with fear and terror. They didn't sparkle like her outfit. Her arms and legs were tied, and all I could hear were the mumbled words of the lady silenced by my father. He roughly tossed her on the sofa in the garage's lounge area. I couldn't believe it. I couldn't believe I would finally get to see how my father did it. Of course, this was all uncharted territory. Maybe he wasn't sure how he would do it. Maybe this wasn't how he used to do it at all. I didn't move a muscle, rocking gently as I peeked through the hole. Daddy's fingers caressed her face as he mounted her, straddling her on the sofa.

"Beautiful skin. Porcelain. So soft," he whispered, his fingers running over her cheek. His voice was quiet, calm. It sounded like a different voice altogether.

"Her skin was porcelain and soft, too. But she had a freckle right here," he added, touching a point on her cheek. I squinted, trying to figure out who Daddy was talking about. His voice didn't sound like his own. It was smooth and softer than usual. It's like he wasn't Daddy at all—except I know the truth. This is the real Daddy. Daytime Daddy is the façade, not this one.

"But porcelain, beautiful skin doesn't last forever. Does it?" he continued, and his words turned icier. I could feel the lady's terror from my spot. I breathed it in, trying to swish it in my mouth, in my lungs. I wanted to feel that intense fear, that intense power my father felt. It was riveting. I kept staring.

Daddy's fingers slowly meandered down to the woman's neck. He reached in the couch with the other hand, pulling out what looked like a rope. The woman's hushed words became muffled screams. It was odd to hear them like that. Both loud and quiet at the same time. I liked the muted sound, as if we'd taken the world and turned it down a few notches. If only all the world could be like that. Daddy tied the rope around and around her neck, pulling wildly on the ends. The blonde kicked her feet, trying to struggle to get Daddy off, but he was too strong and she didn't have a chance with her limbs tied. I watched him pull tighter and tighter, staring into her eyes the whole time. Peacefully, calmly, like he didn't have a care in the world. I watched as her kicks became less, and then finally stopped.

I watched as he propped her down flat on the couch, her still body not fighting back. I heard him rip the tape off her mouth. He planted a kiss on her lips. It was a long, fervent kiss that made me blush. Thankfully, though, it was over soon. He flopped back and rested on the couch for a moment. His happiness was palpable, contagious even. The darkness had lifted. But now the real work began.

First, the picture of her dangling body, just like old times.

Then, Daddy carried the lady to the table, as I remembered from before. However, there were some significant differences. For one, the table was bigger, with special holes that dropped into buckets laden with garbage bags. I watched as he worked, the familiar tools and some new ones appearing. Daddy's new setup was more efficient. There was less mess, less need for bleach to clean the floor. But I missed the splatters. I missed the red paintings that marked each woman as an individual. How would I recall this one? There was no distinct pattern like with Belinda or the black-haired lady or all of the others, each one's blood splatter like a fingerprint in my mind. I supposed I would have to imagine her face when the life left her.

Would it be this way every time? Would he always strangle them on the couch?

If it were me, I'd do it the same every time. I don't like change, after all. The same would be easier. You could get good at it. But Daddy likes change, at least with some things. Or maybe after all these years, Daddy just forgot how he does things. I don't know. Other than his job and me and the house, he likes variety. He doesn't eat the same thing for dinner. He doesn't watch the same show. He doesn't even wear the same clothes every day.

Except for the pictures of the bodies in the same, hanging position. That never changes. I wonder why.

I've heard more rumors that Mama killed herself that way, with a noose. I overheard the school librarian mumbling once to the custodian that yes, I was the girl whose mom hanged herself in the family garage. I've heard lunch ladies and the postman and all sorts of people say things when they thought I wasn't listening. The town likes to whisper about Mama—and it makes me realize that I'm the only one in the dark.

I wonder if that's why Daddy does it. I wonder if it's a way to commemorate Mama, to pay homage. I'd like to think so. I think it's sweet that he loves her so much, even after all those years. I wish I loved her too, but I didn't know her like he did.

I wonder if he'll eventually move on from this way of doing the killing game, though. Will he have to up the game again? And if so, how? He needs to be careful. I guess that he still takes precautions. He works late at night, when he thinks I'm sleeping. He locks the door. He even has a new door on the garage, one without windows. Plus, we still live so far from anyone; there's no risk of anyone showing up.

Still, what could he possibly do next? How could he change it up without getting caught? He's been telling me for years now that I need to be flexible, that life is about changing and growing. Will he continue to evolve in the game? Will he continue to grow in how he snuffs out lives? Even though it scares me, I'd like to think so. I'd like to see other methods, see which one is my favorite.

The blonde-haired woman has joined the silent choir of women in the field. I watched Daddy walk off last night to finish the job. I wonder if the squirrel's skeleton is still out there. Probably not. I doubt I buried it deep enough.

This evening, I watched the news carefully to see if I saw her, but there was no story. No one's missed her. Daddy's smart like that, I've come to decide. Other than Belinda, he's careful to pick women no one would miss. At least that's what I assume. It would make sense to pick drifters or women who work at night in scandalous clothes, who see lots of men. Daddy's brilliant that way.

It makes me think—if I went missing, would anyone miss me? Other than Daddy?

Mr. Pearson would. I wonder what he'd think of this. He loves Emily Dickinson's poetry. I wonder if her dad had a similar killing game because she sure knows a lot about Death.

It makes me feel hopeful. I've learned so much out here. I have so much to write about. Maybe Mr. Pearson's right. Maybe I could be a poet someday.

Because Emily Dickinson sure doesn't go into detail like I could.

Stay Safe,

Ruby

October 9, 2017
7:57 p.m.
Dear Diary,

I stayed after class today to talk to Mr. Pearson. I have lunch after his class, so I stay and talk sometimes. It's better than eating in the cafeteria where it's obnoxiously loud and everyone throws things. Plus, I like talking to him because he makes it easy to have a conversation. He cleans the board or his desk while we chat, and it makes me feel safe.

We talk about the books we're reading. Mostly, we talk about writing. He's a writer, too, but he writes political stuff. I think that sounds dull. Not enough room for expression like poetry. He asked me today where I like to write. I told him there's a field by my house with gorgeous trees, where it's peaceful. I didn't tell him about the company I keep there. Even just mentioning the field felt like a betrayal. I don't know why. It's not like he could know. No one knows. Just me.

Mr. Pearson said my poetry has the ability to touch people, to wake them up. I'm not sure how or why or what that means, but I like the idea. It's appealing to think that maybe my words could connect with someone. It makes me think about what I want to do, after I graduate. I don't often think about that. But Mr. Pearson makes me feel like I could be something, do something. He makes me feel like the rage, the anger I pour into my poetry could do some good in this world. It makes me think about Daddy and his life. What if he had a teacher like Mr. Pearson? Would he do things differently?

I know that what Daddy is doing isn't right, not in the eyes of others. It's why we keep it secret. I know the women must deserve what they get, though. They must. I also know I don't feel sorry for them. I don't feel bad for them at all, in reality. And I don't feel like Daddy is doing something wrong, even if I should or if everyone else would. It's who he is. It's what's always been done. Waffles on Saturday morning, the news at 6—and Daddy's game in the garage. It's just a family ritual we have, just like every other family I know. Some Daddys play golf on the weekends or drink with their friends on Fridays. Mine has the garage game. Why would I feel bad about it?

Then again, I sometimes struggle with what Mr. Pearson calls empathy. I struggle to put myself into another person's shoes like Atticus says to in *To*

Kill a Mockingbird. How can I really know what's in their hearts, their heads, unless I'm actually them? It doesn't make sense. I guess the closest I come is imagining what Daddy is feeling. Because sometimes, if I'm being honest, I feel it too. So I guess that's sort of cheating—not really empathy.

Despite all that, Mr. Pearson makes me feel like maybe I can keep it wrapped up. Maybe I won't need an outlet like Daddy has to keep it calm. Still, the more I watch, the more I wonder, the more I crave to feel those bones beneath my fingers, to pull that rope oh-so-tight. The more I desperately want to make paintings on the garage floor of my very own.

Would Daddy be proud of me? Of course he would. No matter what path I choose, he'd be proud. I'm his little girl, always will be. They say apples don't fall far from the tree—which I think is stupid, because yes, sometimes they do. We went apple picking once when I was little, maybe four or five, and I remember how far some of them fell from the tree. Usually the bruised ones that no one wanted.

I'm glad that even though I'm bruised, Daddy keeps me close. And vice versa. Two bruised apples huddled underneath the tree in the field, keeping each other close and safe while the other apples are preserved. But no one else can pick them. Only us.

I wonder if Mama knew about the garage game. I wonder if she ever helped. Some of the kids at school work at their families' businesses. Maybe this is the Marlowe family business. It's just we can't tell anyone about it, and we don't make money.

I'm off to the tree now, Diary, to write more poetry. Yesterday was the eighth, always a bad day for Daddy. He was sulky and in the bourbon. I suspect he'll be in the bourbon later today, too. Mr. Pearson wants me to try to write a happy poem for tomorrow, something inspirational. I'll try, but that's usually not what's on my heart . . . and poetry should come from the heart, no matter how blackened or cracked. Right?

Stay Safe,
Ruby

October 30, 2017
8:57 p.m.
Dear Diary,

The rules of the game are changing.

First, Daddy's taken another lady into his garage. It usually doesn't happen this close together. He often spaces them out. Sometimes years apart. Remember how it was three years apart? Now, it's so close together. It doesn't usually happen this quick. At least, it hasn't happened like this for a while.

Second, he didn't kill her right away like last time.

It took much, much longer. Like a cat playing with a fly and slowly pulling off its wings, he played with her for a long, long time. I watched from my spot, the chilly fall wind blowing my red hair out from underneath my hat. I wasn't sure what I was seeing, what he was doing at first. I don't always get a perfect view, and the way he positioned her on the couch, it was harder to see. Still, I couldn't look away.

Brunette this time. Short, bobbed brunette hair. Dark, dark eye makeup. I think dark eyes. She was wearing very tight jeans and a crop top in pink. And, of course, tape sealed her mouth shut. Rope bound her hands and feet like some crude accessories. Daddy carried her in. This one was a screamer. Even with the duct tape in place, it was shrill and annoying. I wanted Daddy to kill her quickly to shut her up—I couldn't stand the piercing cries. Once, there was a bird nest outside of my window and the baby birds chirped and squeaked all day until Daddy moved the nest because I couldn't relax. I wished Daddy could see this was the same, the brunette's screams relentless.

Eventually, he must've gotten worried. I saw him looking towards the house. Maybe he was afraid I would hear. Finally, mercifully, he whacked her in the head with something and her cries stopped. But I don't think she was dead. Maybe she was. I don't know.

Daddy whistled now, something he rarely did. His horrid melody echoed in an off-tune cacophony that could make Beethoven roll in his grave. He sauntered about, a lift in his step as he gathered the necessary tools. He hanged her and took his photograph. Her neck lolled, the hallmark of death. I was sure of it.

Daddy got the saw from the wall after he moved her to the chopping table. The saw took her hand off, blood spewing as her delicate fingers, what I imagined to be soft hands, fell into the bucket. Her nails had been long and shiny red. They mixed wonderfully with the red spewing from her arm.

I wondered what it would've been like if she hadn't been dead yet, if Daddy had been able to wait until this moment. I chilled at the thought, but the kind of chills that one simultaneously dreads and enjoys. I wondered if Daddy was thinking about that too. When he walked to get a new tool, I could see him smiling. Daddy took the saw to her other arm. He was facing me. It made me sad I couldn't see her face, but it was okay because I could see his.

His face was alive and dancing. Enthusiasm painted itself in the deep lines that had grown on his forehead. Softness curled his lips into a slight smile, like the time I had made him a Father's Day card in kindergarten with a pizza on the front even though I hated pizza then. I could see that this game, that his killing game, brought joy to him in a way that I both couldn't understand but also could.

You see, I think for him, the act of deconstructing the women, of taking the life from them, it's his version of what I do here. It's an outpouring of emotions—of darkness, of anger, of hurt, of regret. While I pour out in words, in black and white, he pours out in flesh and red. He pours out in borrowing emotions from others and seeing them through, in suffocating the feelings right out of them and, in turn, in himself.

It's not that different, when you think of it that way.

The red dripped everywhere. It even splattered a little as Daddy wildly worked. I engrained the splotches in my mind, indelibly sealing them in my mental scrapbook of Daddy's works. It's too bad no one gets to see this side of him. He is a prodigy in his own right. Which makes me wonder: was he always good at this? When did he start his training? Was it before me? Before Mama? I wish I could ask.

For as much as I know about him, there are still so many mysteries to my father as well. I watched my favorite part, the dessert to my main entrée—the cleaning. I breathed in deeply, trying to waft the bleach smell over to where I was. It would never, ever get old. I could watch him every single night if he played. I closed my eyes, intoxicated by the scent, as I wrapped my jacket tighter around me to fight out the cold air.

When Daddy loaded her up, ready to add her to the collection in the field, I smiled.

I'll be near you again soon, nameless lady, I thought. Maybe I'll write a poem about her and the shiny nails. Or maybe I'll write about the annoying, muffled screams.

Or maybe I'll just write about the red. I never get sick of that, either, after all.

Stay Safe,
Ruby

November 5, 2017
7:57 p.m.
Dear Diary,

I didn't mean to find it, Diary. I think Daddy would be mad I have it. I'm so scared. But I'm going to tuck it away with you and all my other diaries for safekeeping.

It's really all Clarissa and Chloe's fault. I know, it's been a while since you've heard about them. I got stuck working with them in history class for a stupid group project. Mr. Denson made us work in groups, and he assigned me to work with them. I almost cried. But then I remembered to be flexible like Daddy told me to. So I tried to breathe and just make the best of it.

However, in the middle of it, Clarissa started running her big fat mouth about Mama again. Telling me how sad it is that I don't know anything about her. And I got to thinking that Clarissa was right. I hated to admit it, but she was spot on. There's so much I don't know. So while Daddy made a quick errand to the store for some milk, I stayed home. And I did something I shouldn't have.

I went in the attic.

The attic doesn't have rules like the garage, but mostly because Daddy knows I won't go up there. Too claustrophobic up there. Too tight. The stairs are creepy, and I hate the dusty smell. But I've seen some movies where the attic is where people store all their memory books and mementos. I thought maybe I could find something of Mama's. I don't know why I didn't think about it before. I thought, though, that maybe up there, I could find something of Mama's that could prove Clarissa wrong, that could teach me about the red-haired woman who is a complete stranger to me.

I crawled up, shoving down the fear and the feeling screaming at me to turn around because I hoped that I would find something to answer the burning questions within me.

And boy did I.

Daddy has a box. I found it way, way, way in the back corner, underneath an old tablecloth. I don't even really know how I came across it, but I did. Maybe Mama wanted me to find it. Then again, I don't believe in ghosts and all that nonsense. It must have just been dumb luck. I never understood how luck could be smart or dumb, but that's how the saying goes as Grandma likes to remind me. I scavenged through the box hurriedly, knowing I didn't have

131

much time. The store is a bit of a drive since we live so far out, but Daddy wouldn't be gone long. He liked to get in and out of the store, just grab what he needed. I flipped through some items, my fingers feeling all of the textures and assessing them. There was a slippery silk dress in there, the fabric cool to the touch. A metal jewelry box cradled a few rings, its design making it prickly and cold. At the bottom were some photos, scattered about. My eyes danced over images of Mama and Daddy, and even a few of me as a little girl.

Then, Diary, at the very bottom, there was a black leather book.

And guess what? It was a Diary, just like you. My heart pounded at the sight. It was like spotting a familiar friend out in public. There was one difference between Mama's Diary and you. Mama only wrote two pages. I wonder if she didn't like writing after all. And I know diaries are secret, but I couldn't help myself. It was like a window into Mama I'd been searching for.

I read the words. My hands started shaking.

I read them again, and again, and again.

I felt the sobs coming. I was shocked by what she wrote. Mostly, though, I was devastated by the fact that even after reading them, after uncovering the window into Mama . . . I realized that I understood even less than before.

I read the words again. I read them one more time. Then, with shaking hands, I closed the box. I worked really hard to make it look like I wasn't there, but I took the diary. I had to take it with me. Those words, Diary, they're lodged in my head. They're swirling over and over and over until I'm dizzy. A part of me wishes I could forget them. A part of me hates Clarissa even more. If she hadn't said that today, I wouldn't have gone up in the attic. And maybe then I wouldn't have these complex, horrid words pounding in my head.

Daddy came home and I was in my room. He asked what was wrong. I shook my head. He must've assumed I was having a bad day. But he has no idea.

Actually, he does have an idea. He does. He's known all along.

I love Daddy still. I'll do anything for him. But suddenly, I realize that Mama's not the only one I know so little about. Because all this time, Daddy's been keeping more secrets than I could've ever imagined. He's been keeping Mama's secrets. And that hurts worse than anything. Worse than anything.

Stay Safe,
Ruby

November 16, 2017
7:57 p.m.
Dear Diary,

I don't know if it's Mama's writing that's done it or if I'm just tired, but I almost messed up. In Daddy's words when he's really mad, I almost fucked up today.

It could've been so bad.

Mr. Pearson was talking in class today about the horrible news. Apparently, a lady named Lucinda Barley went missing last month, around October 28th. It turns out, she's his neighbor's cousin, and Mr. Pearson said his neighbor is really upset. Lucinda was a bartender working about forty minutes from here in a town called West Hill. She lived alone and didn't check in much with family. I guess she had a reputation for picking up and going on adventures. The bar didn't even report her missing until last week.

Mr. Pearson was talking about how awful it was, how distraught his neighbor is. It made me feel really bad. Super bad. Mr. Pearson recently taught *Crime and Punishment,* and we talked about the idea of guilt in the book. It's been a hard concept for me to understand, but now I think I get it. Because here's the thing, Diary. Mr. Pearson showed us the news story today. He likes to talk about current events. He likes to build what he calls empathy. Plus, he says everything relates to English and he hopes by sharing Lucinda's picture, maybe she can be found.

My classmates were sleepy, only half paying attention as the brunette's picture flashed on the screen. But I jolted right up in my seat. My hands were shaking, and I couldn't look for very long.

Because I've seen Lucinda before, Diary.

In the garage.

And now I feel guilty. Because I want to tell Mr. Pearson so his neighbor doesn't have to worry. But then I feel guilty for wanting to tell—because what would happen to Daddy?

Mr. Pearson says if something happened, the person will get caught. I had to fight the urge to run out of the room. I don't want to look guilty. I don't want Mr. Pearson knowing I have any connection. Because if anyone figures it out, Daddy will be taken away. He will suffer. I can't let that happen. I have to stay strong in order for us to stay safe. I know that, Diary. But it was so hard.

Lately, I've been wondering if the killing game is worth it. Is it worth risking our family for? Does Daddy think about that, about how much he is risking? Does he even care?

I wonder if Mama would be upset if she could see us now. I bet she would be. Her diary still keeps playing on repeat in my head if I let it. I push the words aside. I don't want to think about them or Lucinda or Mr. Pearson's neighbor or Daddy going away. I don't. I just want to put on my red boots and splash in puddles like when I was little. I want to be young again. I want to do it all over. I want to go back to when the garage felt like just a fun game. I want to go back to when I thought the women were just sleeping and Daddy was invincible, could never be taken away from me. I want to go back to before the Diary I found, back to when Mama was just a giant, peaceful mystery.

Maybe I would do it differently if I went back. Maybe I'd ask Daddy to stop. Maybe I'd ask to leave. Maybe I'd tell him I knew so he'd have no choice but to quit.

Maybe I could have changed it all.

Maybe if I wasn't who I am, Mama could've stayed and Daddy would be different.

So many maybes. But maybes don't always come true, obviously. Life is what it is. That's what Grandma always says. She came over tonight. It's like she can sniff out danger—or maybe she just gets bored and wants to annoy us. But Daddy didn't throw her out.

We sat and watched the news. Grandma talked about Lucinda. I saw Daddy's eye twitch, but Grandma didn't. She's clueless. Then again, maybe she's not. I don't know what to trust or believe anymore. All I know is I can't let this all crash around me. I can't lose him. Because I love him. I do love him.

And sometimes love makes us do delusional things. Sometimes it makes us go to the extreme. Sometimes it makes us turn a blind eye . . . or blind another's eye for it.

Stay Safe,
Ruby

November 20, 2017
7:57 p.m.
Dear Diary,

I've never thought much about what life after high school will be like. I don't like change, and in truth, it scares me. But sometimes, Mr. Pearson talks about it with the class and even with me after class. Sometimes, he makes me wonder: could my life be different, and could that be a good thing?

Of course, Mr. Pearson doesn't know the truth about my life. He can't know. I would never betray Daddy like that. Still, I sometimes think about what it might be like if Mr. Pearson was my dad instead.

Stupid girl. What a horrible person I am. I hate that I even wrote that. I should scratch it out of the paper. How could I ever betray Daddy like that? He's so good to me. He loves me. I love him.

Still, if I'm being honest, sometimes I wonder: if Daddy didn't have his secret life, could things be different? Could I be different? Could the future, my future, be different? And do I even want that? I always have a lot of questions, and Mr. Pearson says it's good to be inquisitive. He encourages us to be filled with wonder. But these questions, they're hard and they make me uncomfortable. I don't like thinking about these kind of what ifs.

I think sometimes I scare Mr. Pearson. I mean, I think I scare a lot of people. But I think lately, he's been looking at me a little bit more warily. He talked to me the other day about how my poetry seems to be getting darker, how sometimes he worries about me. He also told me he knows about Mama. He meant the suicide. I think Mr. Pearson worries I might do that, too. But for me, the worries are different. I wanted to tell Mr. Pearson that I would never do that like my Mama did. I could never leave Daddy, not by choice. I know it would kill him.

I wouldn't follow in Mama's footsteps—but I might follow Daddy's.

Is that such a bad thing? Daddy is happy and respected. He has a good life, right? And he's so talented at what he does.

Nevertheless, it's also a lonely life, I think. Keeping that secret keeps him alienated, even from me a lot of the time. No one ever completely gets through those walls. I've lived my life keeping my own walls up, believing that's what I want. Sometimes, though, talking to Mr. Pearson about literature and connections in the books we read, I wonder if that's not quite true. I wonder if we all need to let our walls down completely with at least one other person.

135

We all need to feel accepted and understood. We need to have honesty and openness. And if we don't have that, what do we really have?

A tiny piece of me worries that I'll follow in Daddy's footsteps and find myself walled off completely, forever, from everyone, even Daddy. Sure, I'm used to being alone. But the killing game is a different, darker kind of alone. It's more isolating, more permanent. Once you start the game, I know there's no going back. It's like a hunger that's been unleashed and Daddy just can't seem to fight it, no matter how hard he tries. Look at how hard he tried. Years and years away, yet it still called him back in. It's like a drug addiction of a deeper variety. It's like the blackness within him is always wanting more.

I know what you're thinking. Why not choose a different life then? We all make choices, that's what Mr. Pearson says. Do Daddy's choices have to define mine?

Mr. Pearson talks to me about so many possibilities. About going to college for writing, about building a poetry career that inspires others. That sounds nice. But I don't know. I can't picture leaving Daddy all alone. Who would look out for him? Who would help make sure he doesn't get caught?

And there's something, else.

Sometimes, when I see the way my hands shake or feel the rage surging within when Clarissa is rude to me, I wonder if it goes beyond just protecting Daddy. I sometimes wonder if it's in my blood to enjoy the killing game, too. Like that time with Stacie, when I lost all control. Even though it felt like I couldn't stop even if I wanted to, I knew it was also a desire, a thirst within me that drove me to draw the blood. I enjoyed it. I craved it, even.

It's a scary thought to be hungry for something you don't quite understand—and that society never could. I wonder if someday the urge will be too strong, though, and I will paint my own masterpieces on the floor of the garage.

I don't know. It's so confusing, and it's been putting me in a bad mood. I've been having so many overwhelming moments now. I ran out of the school the other day in the middle of biology, only because the thoughts were pounding into my head. It's like the Robert Frost poem, where I have two roads to travel down.

One leads to an unknown destination, one that Mr. Pearson thinks could be great—but also would be a betrayal of Daddy, at least in my mind.

One would lead me down the path towards a life like Daddy's, which could be fulfilling in its own way. But will I feel that way later? It's hard to imagine a life different than my own. It's really hard, and I don't even know if that's what I would want. I feel pressure mounting about it all. But the worst of it?

There's been another thought creeping in, a tiny little inclination towards another, densely covered path.

What if I told someone about Daddy?

I shudder at the mere thought of it. It would be the ultimate disloyalty. My blood runs cold at the thought. I could never do that . . . could I? I could never turn in the man who has stood by me, who has done everything for me. I could never risk losing him. I could never risk going to a foster family or sending him to prison. I could never shred his happiness like that or stop him from doing what he loves. That would be so wrong, even more wrong than what happens in the garage or the lies we tell. Wouldn't it?

But a tiny little part of me wonders: If I told on Daddy, would Mr. Pearson step in? Would he take care of me? Would he help me onto a different path? Could Mr. Pearson love me the way Daddy loves me?

I don't know. It's scary to think about. I love Daddy. I love him.

I do.

I do.

I do.

I do.

I do.

I do.

I do.

I just don't know what life holds for me or where I should go next. And I hate that feeling of being lost. I hate it. Hate it. Hate it.

Stay Safe,

Ruby

December 8, 2017
2:57 p.m.
Dear Diary,

It's been a really bad day. That's why I'm writing early. I'm in my room, stewing. I thought maybe writing would help calm me down because otherwise, I'm going to snap.

I almost betrayed him.

Almost.

I almost chose Mr. Pearson over Daddy. What was I thinking? I'm so glad I didn't. Here's the thing, Diary. Daddy isn't what he seems, not to other people. They don't know all his secrets, all his talents, all his darkness like I do. But I've learned today that everyone, everyone, everyone has secrets. No one is who they seem. And for all of his dark tendencies, Daddy has one thing they don't.

Love. Love for me, above all else. How could I be so stupid to not give that in return? How could I be worrying about Mr. Pearson, wondering what it would be like to be his daughter when I have the perfect dad? To think I almost let his talk about inspirational writing and college get to me. I was a fool. A damn fool.

I went into school today and there was a substitute in English class. Again. Fifth day. I thought maybe Mr. Pearson was sick or something. But then Clarissa started talking before class started about where Mr. Pearson really is.

He's gone. Like gone for good. Word has it he got arrested for doing some pretty bad things, naked things, with a former student. She is in eleventh grade now, but she was in tenth grade when it happened. She liked poetry, just like me.

Everyone was talking about how Mr. Pearson is a slimy jerk who takes advantage of stupid girls. They talked about how he preys on girls who crave attention, makes them believe they're special so he can do things with them. I couldn't take it. I didn't even tell the sub where I was going. I just ran out of the room, out of the building, out of town. I ran and ran until I got to a tiny café, where I sat until the principal found me.

Daddy came and picked me up. He didn't ask questions on the way home. Maybe the principal told him what was going on. I don't know.

When we finally pulled into the driveway, though, Daddy looked at me. "Ruby, listen. I know he was your favorite teacher. I'm sorry he's not what he seemed." And then he let me stomp up to my room.

Here's the thing—I don't know why I thought he was different. I know people aren't what they seem. Not just because of Daddy, but because I've always spent my life on the edges. Observing, never a true part of anything. Watching, but never doing. I've learned from my position on the outer edges of my peers that everyone is wearing a mask. I guess I just wanted to believe Mr. Pearson when he said he saw something in me, that he thought I had options. Everyone likes to feel like they have options, like they could be something special. He made me believe for the first time in my life that at some point down the road, people might notice me. People might not laugh at Ruby or pity Ruby or talk about how frustrating Ruby is. They'd see me, if not me personally, then my writing.

But that's all gone now. Mr. Pearson's gone. I hate school again. I hate myself. How could I be so stupid?

I'm mostly frustrated that I fell for Mr. Pearson's garbage. I thought about turning Daddy in. Just writing that makes me squirm. How could I do that? He is everything to me. Everything. He needs me. How could I abandon him?

Daddy's never turned his back on me. Never. Sure, you could argue he leaves me in the evenings. But that's only because he thinks I'm sleeping safely in my bed, that he won't be missed. He's always here when I need him. Like today. He left work to come get me because I just couldn't be at school. He's there, patiently waiting for me to cool off, when something triggers me. He listens to me work through my memories that are all jumbled when I'm trying to figure out how to ask him something I can't quite put into words. He's there to tell people where to go when they're rude to me in public. He never runs away when I embarrass him—which I know I do. He never gets mad when I'm going through one of my repetitions or throwing a fit because the chicken tenders aren't the perfect texture.

He's there for me through all of my demons. The older I get, the more I recognize those parts of my personality for what they sometimes are. He loves me unconditionally. There's nothing I could do that would make him stop.

And what do I give him in return?

I almost think about turning him in for working out his own demons in the garage. Stupid girl. Stupid Ruby.

I want to cry or vomit or both. I want to run to Daddy and tell him his secret is safe, that I'll help him keep it safe. But I can't do that. I know I need to stay strong. I need to learn a lesson from this. I hate that I'm using Grandma's phrase. She tells me that when I get frustrated and break a glass or spill something on my shirt or trip over something when I'm not paying attention. Stupid Grandma thinks those are lesson-worthy moments.

No, Grandma. This is a lesson to learn.

No one is actually on your side. No one. Most of us go through life alone, not really knowing the people we think we know.

I'm lucky, though, because I have such a special Daddy who loves me forever. Whom I can trust unconditionally. He'll never go away—not if I'm careful. I'll make sure of it. He would never leave me like Mr. Pearson did.

So I'll keep writing my poetry—but I'll write the words I want to write. Who needs inspirational writing when the truth can shine through the darkness just as well if not better?

I'll keep an eye on Daddy, too, and make sure he doesn't make any mistakes. When you're that close to your work, it's easy to overlook something. I'll be his editor of sorts, like Mr. Pearson was for me. I'll watch his work and improve it when there's a crack that could get him in trouble. I'll stay vigilant and keep my focus on Daddy, so that I can help him if I ever need to.

I'll stay on the fringes, where I belong, so I don't risk losing what matters most.

Stay Safe,
Ruby

THE DIARY OF A SERIAL KILLER'S DAUGHTER

Her veins were whole
Her blood stayed in
The razor blade didn't cut her tongue
Until he wanted it to.

A cold, dark night
With sludge dripping from the stars
And black blood tinging the red, cold and thin.
Her lips bulged and her tongue broke forth
But no sounds to be heard, no silence either
Only the spilling of
Not-so-innocent truth
Into the red.

Part VII

2018

16 years old

February 3, 2018
7:57 p.m.
Dear Diary,

We visited Mama's grave today for her birthday. She's buried in a little cemetery in town. It's near the church where Daddy married her. We go every year on her birthday. I think Daddy goes other times, too.

I used to sit and trace the letters, the numbers on the tiny stone in the ground, wondering where Mama was. Now that I know she's here, I understand that it's more than just a stone in the ground with her name on it. It's where she is, has been, since that October day she killed herself. I wonder what it was like for Daddy to see her coffin lowered into the ground, to see them bury her six feet under. I wonder what it was like from Mama's perspective, to be lowered into her final spot in the damp, cold earth. Could she see us gathered around? Was she afraid?

I think back to those diary pages, the ones I came across. I think about the words she wrote and about what a dark place she was in. Most of all, I think about how close I came to being six feet under, too. It's odd to think about, so I try not to think about it too much.

What would Daddy have done?

Would he have hanged himself, too? I don't know. I wish I could ask him.

Standing at the grave today, Daddy looked sadder than usual. I thought he was going to cry. I don't understand why he's struggling so much again. It's like things are shifting in him, like the older I get, the more he slips. I'm worried. It makes me angry that Mr. Pearson tried to talk me into going away to college. I could never leave Daddy, that much is obvious now.

Daddy stood at the grave as the sun was setting. I kicked at a chunk of snow under my boots as Daddy set down the yellow rose he bought at the corner grocery store. One sad rose. That's all Mama gets now. It's pitiful, really. The women in the field at least have glorious, rambling trees and beautiful wildflowers in the spring. Mama just gets a sad, dying rose once in a while and all of these gross tombstones for company. I feel sorry for her.

But I'm also not sad for her. I'm glad she's here. Because if she hadn't died when she did, things could have been so, so different. For all of us. And I don't think it would have been a good different like I used to think when I was young and naïve.

Daddy and I stood for a long time, the silence dancing between us comfortably like it always does. This time, though, the hairs on my neck prickled. I scratched at them. Something felt different, tenser.

Finally, after a long time, Daddy whispered into the whipping winter wind, barely audible, "I'm sorry."

I was confused at first. I thought he was talking to me. But his eyes were lasered in on the gravestone.

"Why are you sorry? Mama killed herself." The words spewed out before I could stop them. I wanted to shove them back down my throat, my red mittens actually moving upward to try to do just that. It was too late, though. Sometimes it's too late.

Daddy rubbed his hand through his hair before turning to me. I think he had forgotten I was there. He looked embarrassed.

"It's complicated Ruby. There's a lot you don't know about her. It doesn't matter now, though. I love you."

And yet, there is a lot I know about her, if diaries are to be believed after all.

I knew the time had passed, nevertheless, to ask Daddy to explain. The case was closed. I needed to let it go. But his words mingled with the icy air, stabbing into me with a newfound clarity and confusion at the same time. Like a paradox, something Mr. Pearson taught us at school before he disappeared.

Mama was an enigma, a paradox in her own right. I think I'm better off not knowing her. But Daddy is an enigma, too. And even though the diary from the attic painted a clearer picture of Mama than I'd ever had, I still don't know the woman. I don't owe her anything.

Daddy does, though. He loved her unconditionally. Maybe he still does love her. I realize that now. I recognize that when you love someone, you'd give anything for them. Daddy just couldn't give Mama enough to make her stay. What does that feel like? I hope I never have to find out.

It still doesn't quite answer all my questions, though. It doesn't help me understand how it all played out. How am I still here? Why did Mama leave me behind? Maybe Grandma's been correct this whole time about who Mama was and who she wasn't—a sad realization in its own right.

Could it all be my fault? I complicated things. Mama never wanted to be a mom, not to someone like me. That much is becoming clearer.

And then a thought struck me.

Is that why Daddy is sorry? Did he choose me over Mama? And what did that choice mean for her? Questions swirled and zigzagged, mixing in and out with memories, with things that didn't happen—or things that maybe did. I stared at the stone in the ground, the ice-cold stone, and then turned and walked away. Mama didn't deserve our warmth. Mr. Pearson didn't deserve my warmth.

No one deserves anything except Daddy. That's become clear now. At least one thing is certain in life. At least one thing.

Stay Safe,
Ruby

March 1, 2018
7:57 p.m.
Dear Diary,

In school today, we learned about the hanging tree, the one in Salem where the witches were executed. Daddy has his own hanging tree at his disposal, right in the field with all of the beautifully dead women.

Today, I thought he was going to use the hanging tree—on me. But there would be no memorial for me, I realized. There would be no one to miss me or a creepy statue to show the world I had been here. There would just be my little book of poems and you, Diary, to tell my story. What story would that be? Suddenly, today, I realized how little I've done. I'm not really leaving my mark in life, not like Daddy. Of course, is he really leaving a mark? Like my poetry, no one recognizes his masterpieces, his skills. Are talents held in secret really talents at all? Are masterpieces truly magnificent if no one gets to appreciate them? These were the questions I thought about when I locked myself in my room after dinner to escape Daddy's rage.

I haven't seen him this angry, not at me. Not ever—at least not like this. I don't understand what's happening. I feel horrible for making him so mad. Did Mama ever make him this mad? I bet she did. I bet those diary pages made him mad when he read them.

I did something bad tonight, it's true. Daddy was out in his garage working on something—tidying, he told me. I know the truth. He's probably preparing it, making sure it's just right for the next round of the game.

I was bored and didn't feel like walking or writing today. So I decided to do something I shouldn't have. I really shouldn't have. I went into Daddy's office. It's in his bedroom. I don't usually go in there. Daddy says bedrooms are private. It's not dangerous or locked like the garage. But it's private. I respect his privacy just like he respects mine. It's an unspoken rule between us, one I violated today. Why did I do it? What's been driving me? It's like the unspeakable force usurping Daddy is getting its fangs into me as well.

His bedroom is downstairs, in the back corner of the house. It's good because sometimes Daddy snores when he sleeps, which would bother me. But I don't really hear it from my room, so that makes me happy. When the fan isn't keeping me up or the wind or the crickets, I don't hear him. I can sleep peacefully.

I wandered back, though. I don't know why. Maybe I've just been curious if he has more of Mama's words hidden in there. Maybe I wonder if I can get to know more about her if I find them. But I decided to do some digging, to see what I could find. A girl has a right to know these things, even if her mother was a monster, right? I need to know. I have to figure out if I'm going to become like her, which would be worse than becoming Daddy. At least Daddy has technique, has skill. At least Daddy never left me.

I was looking at his bookshelves when I saw them. How hadn't I noticed them? Books on so many interesting things.

Torture devices.

Poison.

Ted Bundy and Gacy and serial killers of all varieties. It was so interesting. I ran my hands over the titles, books we don't have in our school library. I pulled one down, the one on serial killers. It had a worn cover and looked quite dilapidated, shoved in the far corner of a middle shelf.

When I went to open the pages, a photograph fell out.

A picture of the black-bobbed hair woman. A familiar face from the past staring back up at me. I couldn't stop studying the picture, like it was the Holy Grail.

Beautiful. Shiny. Stunning. Like no portrait I've ever seen. Museum-worthy.

I'd almost forgotten how beautiful she was. I tucked the picture back in after a long moment, after I'd convinced myself it was now carved in my memory. I thought about taking it, about adding it to my collection. But they are in his collection. I couldn't take what's not mine. He might need them.

I slid the book back, pulling out the poison book instead. I've never learned too much about poison. I wonder if Daddy's ever used it? I glanced through the pages, shaking it. No photographs in this one. I was so caught up in the pages that I must not have heard the door, must not have heard the footsteps. I hear everything. How could I be so careless?

Before I could even think about what was going on, I was on the ground, the book out of my hands. The wind was knocked out of me as my back hit the ground. One moment I was reading about cyanide, the next I was staring up at Daddy's red, red face.

"What the fuck is this, Ruby? What the fuck?" His face was red, but not my favorite color of red. This was an ugly red, an angry red. A deadly red.

147

"S-sorry Daddy. S-sorry." I choked and sputtered on the words, terror causing my stomach to drop. I had to fix it. How could I fix it?

He slammed the book on the desk, his hands shaking visibly. He paced back and forth.

"What did you touch? What did you take?" He didn't offer to help me up. My stomach roiled with tension, with fear. He looked like he was going to snap. I pictured the saw in the garage biting into my flesh. What would it feel like? Would I pass out before the pain became unbearable? Would he paint me beautifully on the floor like the others? Which part of the field would he bury me in? Would he take a museum-worthy photograph of me, too? Which book would he keep mine in?

"S-sorry, Daddy. Just that one."

"Just this one?" he asked, picking it up, shoving it in my face.

I nodded.

"You swear to me?"

"Y-yes." A lie. A white lie, I told myself. To protect a relationship. If Daddy killed me, who would save him if he needed help, an alibi? I needed to stay where I was. I didn't care about me. I cared about him.

"Don't fucking lie to me, Ruby."

"I-I don't lie," I lied. Who was I becoming? My head started to spin, my thoughts grabbing onto the lies I just told. I squeezed my fists, trying to sit up. He put a foot on my chest and shoved me back down. I felt myself gasping for breath.

"Stay the fuck out of my stuff, Ruby. You hear me? It's important."

Tears fell from my eyes. "I'm sorry, sorry, sorry, sorry." I couldn't stop the sorries. They poured out like water from a fast-flowing pitcher, like the droplets in our leaky faucet in the upstairs bathroom. Daddy took his foot off my chest, his hands grabbing his hair and pulling like he was going to yank it out. He walked himself to the corner, banging his head on the wall as a guttural scream of agony escaped from his lips. It sounded like a wounded animal, and I hated it more than the words he'd spewed at me. I hated to hear Daddy weak and aggravated and upset. I missed the strong, stoic man I knew and loved. I hated that I'd lied to him. Most of all, I hated myself for causing his anger.

"Daddy, please," I said. He turned and looked at me. And it's like the words triggered him, incited him to return to the Daddy I always knew.

"Jesus, Ruby, I'm sorry. Fuck. I'm such a fuck-up. I'm sorry." He held out his hand, and my eyes landed on his wrist. The red bracelet, dirty and faded now, still sat on his wrist. All these years later, he still had that bracelet. He wears it often, even though it's fraying and ready to fall apart. I should make him a new one.

I took Daddy's hand, my racing heartbeat calming at the touch of his fingers on mine. Warm. Strong. Daddy's hands, for once, were a comfort.

I wanted him to pull me into him, something I never liked. I yearned for him to assure me it was okay, that he loved me. I wanted to tell him that I knew what the books were actually for, that it was fine. He didn't need to protect me. I knew everything there was to know, and I loved him for it.

I didn't want him to worry. Clearly, he was fretting about protecting me from the garage game. I'd let him feel like he was doing his job. I would let Daddy be the strong one keeping me safe. Like he couldn't keep Mama safe. He always, though, kept me safe. He always does. I'll return the favor. Always. No matter what it costs.

"You need to ask before you take my stuff, okay? It's just, this stuff is dark."

I nodded.

"I wanted to go into criminal law once," Daddy said. I wondered if it was true, or if he was trying to save our relationship. I just nodded, the white lie a wispy cloud fogging up the space between us. I could almost see it floating in the air, becoming thicker and thicker as it shoved us apart.

"That's why I have them. But they're gory and full of monsters, Ruby. The world is full of evil. You shouldn't face it if you don't need to. You're safe here. Always safe."

"I know, Daddy." And I did. I knew I was safe with him, safest of all.

"I'd do anything to protect you."

"I know, Daddy." *And I'd do anything to protect you,* I thought.

He walked me out of the bedroom, and I announced I was going to go write. Daddy nodded. I've been up here since then. Daddy seems to have calmed down, but there's still a detectable, malicious friction brewing. I can sense it like a smog in the air. I can almost see its blackness oozing on his skin, floating out of the pupils in his mystifying eyes.

I brought him back today. He didn't hurt me. What happens, however, if I can't bring him back? What happens if the monster inside of him wins?

I'll be in the field. That's what. If he knows what I know, he'll have no choice in his mind. He'll have to protect me from the monster in my world—himself.

Daddy's a complicated man. That's what Mr. Pearson would say. But we've all got our troubles, our quirks, and our needs. I just need to be more careful. I need to help Daddy more with his.

Stay Safe,
Ruby

March 20, 2018
7:57 p.m.
Dear Diary,

I wish I'd read all of Daddy's poison book. I wish I'd told him what I know—so he could help me start my own game. Daddy's not the monster in my world. Nor am I.

It's Clarissa. She's the monster.

Daddy said my hair looks fine. He says it makes me look older. But I hate it. Mama's hair was long and flowing like a mermaid. So was mine. Now it's just a hacked-off boy haircut because of that bitch. And Mr. Pearson's substitute watched it all. She did nothing about it.

She watched Clarissa spit her gum into my hair. She watched her collect Paul's gum and Chloe's gum and Sarah's gum in our row and stick it in my long, red locks. She watched me yell at Clarissa and cry and slam my fists on the desk.

Mr. Pearson would have put Clarissa in her place. He would have kicked her out and told her to never come back after the first wad. But the substitute just kept her huge, ugly plane window glasses on the seating chart and mumbled all nervous-like about Chaucer. She pretended she had no idea what was going on while Clarissa giggled wildly and told me Daddy would never want to sleep with me now that I looked like a boy—or maybe he would. And the substitute did something even worse—she kicked me out of the class for swearing and yelling at Clarissa.

Daddy's furious. He's threatening a lawsuit.

At least the weasel-like principal listened. He's suspending Clarissa for ten days. But what does that matter? She's still won. I had to get my hair cut today when Daddy couldn't get the gum out. I look like a boy. I've lost Mama's beautiful, wavy hair.

Maybe it's a good thing. After all I know about Mama now, do I really want to look like her? She was weak and pathetic. She thought I needed to get away from Daddy. I'm glad she didn't win. I'm glad she killed herself so I can be here with Daddy. I don't think she was as good of a woman as he would like to think. Memory taints reality, that's what our history teacher said once. He also talks about how the victor tells the story. I think because Daddy's still here, he's painted the story of Mama being a good, loving woman. He feels sorry that she killed herself. He feels guilty. But he shouldn't. He's seen her diary. He knows what she was going to do. How could he feel anything for her but hate?

I run a hand through my ugly hair. I'm still mad. I still think Clarissa needs to pay, severely. But I'm also realizing it might be a blessing in disguise. I'm not Mama's girl. I'm Daddy's girl. I will not follow in her footsteps. I'll follow in his.

Besides, I'm sure Grandma will hate this haircut, so that makes me a little bit happy. I can't wait to hear her gasp at the sight of me and demand answers from my father. Maybe she'll make Daddy so mad that he'll have no choice but to make her next in the game.

Sometimes I think about what it would look like, her fleshy, pallid skin falling in chunks to the ground as her face is finally frozen in a permanent silence. I picture all of the lurid cuts, all of the bites into her skin of the sharp saw. It makes me grin, even in the face of all that's wrong.

Me and Daddy. That's all that matters.

What a glorious story we will write, the two victors after all.

Stay Safe,

Ruby

Invisible girl, see-through and worn.
Where are you going? When will you get there?
They don't even look through you.
They look completely around you,
Their weary eyes too drawn
by the flashing lights
behind
and beside
and in front of
you.

You are not them.
You are not shiny and shouting.
Quiet and skulking,
you slink along unnoticed.
Will they ever see you?

You watch the world move by you.
You watch her, with her
Golden locks
and perfect thighs
grabbing their attention
While you perish in the mud.

Down,
down
you float,
until only your forehead
is left out in
the cold.
Mud fills
your lungs,
and the daffodil
wilts.

It is difficult to be

invisible,
but more difficult still
to float
above them all
And not
know
where
you
are.

September 24, 2018
9:57 p.m.
Dear Diary,
He's going to get caught.

That's what I've come to realize. That's what I've come to fear. Even Sweeney Todd couldn't escape forever and eventually met his demise. Daddy's ramped up his killing—but there are no pies to hide the bodies in.

I've tried to figure out why Daddy's killing more and more. Is something in him completely snapped now? Or is it because as I get older, he feels like he doesn't need to protect me as much? Like there's not as much of a risk? Or maybe he's just gotten brazen, gotten arrogant. Or, I am afraid to even write this . . . maybe he's just lost it completely. I don't know.

Sometimes there's a new lady in the garage every week. Usually on weekends now. He still leaves late at night, when he thinks I'm sleeping. He's grown complacent, grown comfortable. He figures his daughter is none the wiser, that she'll never uncover his truth. It makes me shake with anger sometimes that he thinks I'm that naïve. Hasn't he spent his whole life teaching me that I'm different but smart? Is this a white lie he tells to save our relationship? Because if he really thought I was smart, wouldn't he realize that I know?

Stop it, Ruby. Stop it. Stop doubting Daddy. He loves you. He thinks you're smart. This isn't about you. Besides, it's a good thing he doesn't know. That means you're a good secret keeper. It's important to keep his secret so you can help him. This is about keeping him safe, not about you.

I can't blame Daddy for what he does. I don't think he knows the women he kills, not really. How could he? Daddy doesn't go out that much. I think they're random. Well, that's not true. I think they're carefully chosen as to not be missed. Prostitutes, drifters, women who are on the edges of society. Women like me, who have no friends, who would go unnoticed if they disappear.

I know, too, that the hanging ritual must be a homage to Mama. Why would he want to do that, though? After what she did, what she almost did? It ticks me off sometimes that he still reveres her. It makes me feel like he's disloyal to me after all. I shove the journal pages I have memorized aside, though. It's complicated. I know that's what Daddy says. But is it?

Mama killed herself.

She left me behind, even knowing things might be difficult for me.

Mama, as I've come to realize, never loved me.

It's okay. I don't feel sorry for myself. I never needed her love, in truth. I'm better without it. Daddy's done a fine job of making me feel loved, safe. I just hope he doesn't blow it now. Because no matter how old I get, I still need him. Doesn't he realize that? Why is he risking it all?

The world's a lonely place, isn't it? It's an unforgiving, daunting place filled with lies and pain. Everyone is out for something for themselves, and no one can be trusted. Even after all this time, I'm still dealing with the same problems at school, the same bullying and cruelties. It's okay, though. I've grown used to it. People are afraid of different. That's what Daddy says. And how do they deal with that fear? They abuse. They take advantage. They mock. They belittle. I've come to learn that the world is full of monsters of the worst variety, and Daddy isn't even close to being one of them.

Daddy tells me it's okay, that after high school, I won't have to see these people again. He tells me I can live the life I choose. But I don't think that's quite true. I know I can't leave him, not now, not ever. I can't leave him all alone. What if he needs me? What if he gets caught? He needs me to help protect him, even if he won't admit it.

I've got to go, Diary. Daddy's coming to say goodnight. His hands are shaking. I think he's going out tonight to take out some frustrations, to set some things straight in the world.

Because when I was young I didn't understand Daddy's game, but now I do.

Darkness prevails in the world. Daddy needs a way to set things right, to get out some of the rage. We all need an outlet. And even if those women might not deserve it—which I'm betting they do—we all need a scapegoat to pay for the sins of others. We all need someone to take the blame.

We all need some way to set the universe even, to let the darkness balance out.

Stay Safe,

Ruby

September 25, 2018
7:57 p.m.
Dear Diary,

I didn't really want company, but the boy didn't ask.

He just sat down at my lunch table and started talking to me a mile a minute in his Southern drawl—which I find irritating, I might add.

Apparently, Aaron is from Tennessee and just moved here last week. His dad's job in construction transferred him here. He used to live in Georgia when he was really young. That's where he was born. He's an only child. He likes cars and wants to be a mechanic or maybe a lawyer because he also likes to argue things. He loves pizza, and pizza only. He packed his lunch so he could bring pizza. And he loves history. He could rattle off all of the presidents in order and tell me what date they were sworn in.

Not that I asked any of this, of course. Aaron took it upon himself to tell me all of that and more within four seconds of sitting down. It was a ceaseless chant I couldn't make stop. Still, it was like a train wreck—I couldn't look away, no matter how much I knew I should.

Aaron, I think, will be the death of me.

For all those years I wanted, needed a friend, I now realize that the grass really isn't always greener on the other side as Grandma likes to say incessantly. I spent my lunch staring at the table, hoping if I ignored him properly, he would go away.

There were two good things about the boy with pale skin and a motor mouth, though.

He didn't ask me any questions. I like that he was fine with my silence even though he isn't fine with his silence, apparently.

He has red hair. Really nice, coppery red hair. I like that.

Aaron walked me to my classes—not that I asked him too. I don't know why he picked me. I doubt it will last, though. Eventually, he'll learn from the other kids that Ruby Marlowe in her bright red sneakers or bright red boots is to be avoided at all costs because she is social suicide—I learned that term from Clarissa last week. But my days, like it or not, might not be so empty, at least for a little while. At least until he gets a bit wiser.

I think that could be good, but it could also be bad. I need to stay focused. Daddy's been moodier, darker than usual. I think he's going out again tonight. And if Aaron doesn't go away, it could be a risk. Letting anyone close is a

157

risk now, I realize. It's been a blessing, maybe from the universe, that I've been secluded all these years. Less interaction with others equates to less chances for me to blow Daddy's cover.

He's what matters. Truly.

Still, there was something about that coppery hair, the way it fell in his face while he talked with his hands. There's a lightness about him, a bright aura that is stunningly intriguing. Maybe when you're surrounded by darkness for so long, the antithesis of it is unignorable. Of course I've learned that you never really know what one's true colors are, not from a distance. Still, the way he talks with his hands and the way he smiles—it's like there's a light shining from within. While Daddy seems to have darkness inside that he has to quell, Aaron seems to have lightness that won't stay put.

Maybe I should put sunglasses on to block him out. Still, the warmth I felt today—it was confusing. It was a little terrifying.

It was a little exciting.

Who knew presidents and cars could be so interesting?

Clarissa doesn't seem so happy that the new boy sat with me. On the school bus today—Daddy still takes me in the morning, but I ride bus in the afternoons. I need to be flexible, after all—she tripped me and called me a slut. Told me the new boy would wise up soon. I ignored her, taking my seat in the back. Thank God she's one of the first bus stops.

I'm the last, but I don't mind. It gives me time to think. Plus, there's a long walk from the bus stop up the lane, through the wooded path, and to the house. The solitude is wonderful, though. It lets me think.

And today, what did I think about?

Aaron. The redheaded boy named Aaron who sat with me—me!—and not Clarissa.

The redheaded boy sat with me.

Stay Safe,

Ruby

October 2, 2018
9:57 p.m.
Dear Diary

Aaron hasn't gone away. Still. How many days has it been? I'll have to flip back through your pages to see. But I know it's been a while.

I've learned more about Aaron. Like that his father actually works with Daddy. It's weird to think about people other than me knowing Daddy. I don't know how I feel about that. It seems ridiculous I haven't thought about it before, but I really haven't. I guess my isolation makes me think that Daddy is isolated, too. Of course, the truth is, no matter what Aaron's father thinks he knows, he doesn't know the whole story. Not even close. What would Aaron think if he knew? Would he still sit with me at lunch? Something tells me he wouldn't be so apt to sit with me and tell me all about his life. It doesn't matter though—it's a moot point. He'll never find out. I'll make sure of it. It's sort of a shame, really, that no one will get to know just how ingenious Daddy is. It makes me a bit sad for him. He's an artist in hiding, a prodigy who never gets to show off his brains.

But I see them. I see you, Daddy. I know what you're capable of.

Daddy actually went out last night. I decided to sneak down and watch, for old time's sake. I have the garage dance memorized, of course. It hasn't changed, not since the remodel. There's still the strangling, the noose, the photograph. The butchering, the blood, the cleaning. Last night, I was feeling especially intrigued, though.

The woman had red hair. Bright, coppery red hair like Aaron's. Like mine. I especially am intrigued when it's a redhead. I don't know why. Maybe it's because Daddy seems more passionate, too, when it's a redhead. He takes his time more. He stands and stares at the noose a little longer. His hands shake a little more, too. I like that.

I even followed him to the field last night. Quiet as a mouse, as always. I watched for a long time. Daddy's so used to the routine, he doesn't seem as nervous anymore. I think he figures if I haven't noticed by now, I never will. He's comfortable in his habits, which I understand. So many people value variety, but there's so much to be said for predictability. It's safe, just like I like it.

Daddy has his dance down to a science, has the killing game mastered. It's peaceful now. There's no hurrying, no looking over his shoulder like when I was younger. There's just him and his work, and me the silent, adoring spectator.

It's interesting, I thought last night when I crawled into bed. Never boys. Never men. Always women. I suppose it makes sense. I know there's an attraction involved in his work; the women he picks are always gorgeous, plump, and lustworthy. Maybe that's why he never brings live women home, into our house. Grandma was asking him the other week if he ever gets lonely, mentioning that men have needs. He grew angry and brushed her off, said he didn't need anyone. I guess in a way it's true. Daddy finds his own women and satisfies himself on his own terms.

Last night, though, watching, I wondered if I were to follow in his footsteps, would I choose women, too? Like Daddy? No. It didn't feel right. I thought about Aaron, resting on the table in the garage. I thought about what it would be like to watch the blood drip to the floor. There, there. That seems better.

Boys it would be. Boys for me.

If I were to follow in his footsteps, of course. For now, I'm content watching. Watching Daddy. He's the master. I can't compete with him. We all have a role to play. We learned that in science class today when we were talking about ecosystems. We all have a part to play. Protector. Secret keeper. That's my role. That's me.

And that's why when Aaron asked if he could come over and study for our science test tonight, I shook my head no. I don't have people over, I said.

"Ever?" he asked.

"Ever." The word was pointed and attacking. I didn't want him thinking there was room to budge or that I would be flexible.

He said that was weird. I didn't reply, nor did it bother me. I'm used to being called weird, immune to it even. Besides, I know it's not weird. It's necessary. Guests mean unwarranted risks. Because invited guests sometimes become uninvited guests. And if that ever happened at the wrong time . . .

Daddy's careful of course. That's why his work is late. That's why the garage is locked. But we've had some close encounters with unexpected visits from Grandma. Last week, she decided to swing by after a late round of cards with her haggard friends. Daddy's hands were shaking. I knew he had somewhere to be.

Grandma stayed and talked and talked and talked, and we couldn't even kick her out with the thinly veiled excuse of us having work and school the next morning—it was a Friday. She stayed and yapped, and Daddy brooded and shook. It was a bad mix. For a while, I thought maybe Grandma's flappy lips would be silenced. I imagined what the noose would look like around her jiggly, loose neck. It made me laugh out loud. Grandma thought I was laughing at her dumb joke about a bar and a horse.

Still, Grandma's big fat nose sticking in our business is tiresome and worrisome enough. I won't add any extra worry to Daddy's shoulders with guests and visitors to concern him with. I'll let him think he's safe. Because he is.

He will be as long as I'm around.

Stay Safe,

Ruby

October 5, 2018
9:57 p.m.
Dear Diary,

That redhaired boy is dangerous. He needs to disappear. He needs to rest in the field with the others. I can't take it anymore.

He came over unannounced. Can you believe it?

Daddy and I finished dinner and we were watching television. A redheaded prostitute is missing in Dunnsville, which is about twenty miles from here. I recognized the photograph. Daddy stared with intrigue at the television. I saw his smirk when the news lady said there were no leads.

There never would be. They didn't stand a chance. My Daddy is too brilliant. I was getting ready to head upstairs to grab my journal. I was planning on going to the field to do my writing, to spend some time by the fresh mound of earth that hides the newest woman. But before I could, the doorbell rang. Daddy answered it. He called me down, confusion and fear hidden behind the stoic expression on his face.

Aaron. At the door.

"What are you doing here?" I asked.

"Sorry to drop in. I just wanted to see if you wanted to go with me for a milkshake at that new place in town I was telling you about?"

I blinked. Daddy cleared his throat. Aaron flipped the red hair out of his face, his hands shoved in his pockets. He stared. I looked over at the yellow truck in the driveway, parked behind Daddy's.

My hands started to shake. I didn't want him here. No. This was wrong. What would Daddy think? I didn't want Daddy thinking I was inviting strangers over. This would worry Daddy.

"I can't." I slammed the door in his face. How did he even know where I lived? How could he possibly know? I'd mentioned what bus I rode. Maybe one of the kids had told him. The nerve of him, though, to just show up. Fury bubbled inside, masked by an outpouring of tears.

"Ruby," Daddy said, but I didn't answer. I dashed upstairs, slamming my bedroom door.

I rocked back and forth, holding the pillow. Stupid girl. Why did you let him in? Why did you let him into your life? I don't need anyone. I don't. That boy could ruin everything.

Daddy tried to talk to me. He said it was okay to have friends, but that I needed to be careful. He said that high school boys have one thing on their minds. Daddy's talk made things so much worse.

I didn't want to talk about sex with him. I didn't want to talk about Aaron. I would need to be more careful. I couldn't have some stupid redheaded boy ruining it all. We had too much to lose.

We have so much to lose.

Stay Safe,

Ruby

October 8, 2018
9:57 p.m.
Dear Diary,

Flowers are for graves. That's what I told Aaron when he brought me a handful of wildflowers today to apologize. I don't understand how flowers equate to an apology. I honestly don't know why he even wants to speak with me again.

Four minutes and thirty-eight seconds. That's how long after I slammed the door in his face on Friday that he started up his truck and left. I wonder what he was doing in those four minutes and thirty-eight seconds. Did he peek in the garage? It wouldn't matter. Daddy, thankfully, is a professional. He keeps it clean. He keeps it safe. Thank God he's such a good man.

Aaron apologized today and said he had been rude but that he hadn't meant any harm. And get this Diary—he said he likes me. Really likes me. I mean, I know he must like me as a person because he still hasn't stopped sitting with me.

Clarissa has tried to lure him away. For weeks now, she shamelessly flirts with him in the hallways. She leans on his arm, wraps her red nails around his bicep, and flashes him that pearly smile. She tells him how I'm a weirdo and how I'm a freak and all sorts of things. Despite her best efforts, Aaron never budges. From the outside, it seems that Clarissa fails to entice him, something she's not accustomed to. And when she's horrible to me in class or in gym, Aaron steps in. He protects me. It makes me, if I'm being honest, like him, too.

But I can never admit that. I get mad at myself for even thinking it. Because I can't get distracted by some silly high school boy, no matter his hair color. What would Daddy think? He's my priority. Aaron might be nice and he might bring me flowers, but Daddy needs me. Daddy has no one. I need to help him, to be there for him. How can I watch out for him if I'm off drinking milkshakes? How can I make sure he doesn't drop a rag or help cover for him with Grandma if he needs it if I'm out with Aaron? I can't be both Daddy's protector and Aaron's. I can't.

I've thought about what it might be like to let Aaron in. He's one of the only people in this world I actually enjoy being around. He makes me feel safe at school, safe from the accusatory eyes and horrible comments and Clarissa. Maybe he would be a good protector of Daddy. But that's crazy talk, wild fantasy talk. This is no fairy tale, and Aaron's no knight riding in to save the day. Knights slay dragons, after all, and Daddy is a bloodthirsty dragon of the skilled variety.

Plus, Aaron's family is different than mine. He has a mom and a dad who look quite dull. Aaron's dad works with Daddy, but he's scrawny and quiet looking. I saw him once in town when Daddy and I were getting groceries. And Aaron's mom is a bank teller. Talk about boring. They're the kind of parents who have dinner on the table at exactly six o'clock, who go to church and bowling for fun as a family. They're the kind who wouldn't understand the garage game or Daddy's moods or my differences, not at all.

If he knew about Daddy, he'd think Daddy was a bad guy. He wouldn't understand, wouldn't see it how I do. And it's not like I have the words to make him understand. I could never help him see Daddy's true goodness, the brilliant man I know and love. Aaron wouldn't understand Daddy and, thus, he couldn't fully understand me.

I think that's why the kids think I'm weird. I think Daddy is different than anyone they know. I think maybe no other kids know secrets about their parents like I do. I think it sets me apart. I'm different, like I've always been. But like Daddy says, different isn't bad. It just is.

Daddy just is who he is, too. I love him for it. Other people, though, probably couldn't. I've experienced firsthand what happens and how people treat you when you're a little bit different than them. I don't want Daddy to experience any of that if he doesn't have to.

Even though it's all complicated, I can't lie. Aaron and his flowers made me smile. I carried Aaron's flowers around all day. It felt good to have something from him. Not that I could admit it. Clarissa glared at me all day. I don't know if she likes Aaron or if she just doesn't like him liking me.

When I got home, Daddy put the flowers in water. He sighed. I could tell he was worried. He rubbed his chin a lot and crinkled his forehead as he stared at them. It probably doesn't help that today is the really tough day for Daddy, the day Mama killed herself. I thought about telling Daddy that we could put the flowers on Mama's grave, wondering if maybe that would cheer him up. I don't like the thought of sharing the flowers with Mama, but I'd do it for Daddy's sake. Before I could suggest it, though, Daddy spoke up.

"Be careful, Ruby. Sometimes people aren't as good as they seem." That was all he said. I know he worries that I'll be taken advantage of. I know sometimes I don't read people or situations well. It's part of what makes me different. I know Daddy is worried about that.

I just wish Daddy knew that I'm not as naïve as I seem. I know a lot. A whole lot more than most kids about being careful and about appearances. I know what people are capable of, what he's capable of.

I'm not scared. Because I know that deep down in me, there's a part of Daddy lurking. I can bring it to the surface if I need to. I'm smart and I'm capable and I'm a professional, just like him. No one will hurt me because I know how to hurt them back.

Don't worry, Daddy, I want to say. *You've taught your daughter well.*
Stay Safe,
Ruby

October 12, 2018
2:57 a.m.
Dear Diary,

Ever since Aaron's been around, the killing's been more intense and frequent. And for the first time, Diary, I'm truly, completely convinced Daddy's going to get caught. He's getting sloppy. Really, really sloppy.

Daddy's constantly in the garage now, at least once a week. This week it's been more. He's down there now, sawing away. I thought about going down, for old time's sake. But honestly, Diary, I'm scared. I wish I wasn't. But something's changed.

It's in the way his eyes look at the breakfast table. Usually, after a night in the garage, he's calmer. He's always a little tired and shaky, but there's still a release in his eyes. Now, though, I see something else. It's almost like an insatiable quality, an unquenchable thirst. His eyes scream out for more, even when his hands can't keep up.

The worst part of it? I think it's my fault.

Ever since Aaron's shown up, Daddy's been more intense, more frequent in his kills. He asks me more questions, and I heard him talking to Grandma the other day about how he's worried I have a boyfriend.

Grandma was thrilled. "It's a good thing. At least she won't die a helpless old maid. And if he's a nice young man, which if he's bringing her flowers, he probably is, then he could keep an eye on her. Wouldn't it be good for her to move out and have her own life? Then you could have yours back," she'd said as I listened upstairs. I had squeezed my hands, wanting to wring her neck. How dare her imply I was holding Daddy back!

"I guess," he'd said glumly. "But I worry about her. I hate the idea of not being able to keep her safe. And so help me, if that boy so much as touches her wrong . . ." Daddy had barked through gritted teeth.

It felt good that Daddy was looking out for me, but it scared me, too. I didn't want Daddy to hurt Aaron. I didn't want Aaron to end up on Daddy's table. But I also didn't want to have someone else to protect.

Daddy's been different around me. I want to shout and tell him I'm still the same Ruby, that nothing has changed. I'm not interested in a life with Aaron or even a milkshake. He doesn't need to worry. But it's October, a hard month for Daddy anyway. And I think the added pressure isn't helping. I think he's worried about what's going to happen to me—and the garage ladies are paying for his heightened anxieties. I feel bad for what I'm doing to Daddy. Sometimes I wish I'd never met Aaron. Things were easier when he wasn't around, when I was all alone.

I understand why Daddy is struggling. Change is hard. I'm probably the person who understands that best of all. Still, Daddy needs to be careful. He's going to make a mistake if he's not. Even professionals can mess up sometimes.

Daddy isn't going as far away, for one thing. I notice his truck isn't gone for very long. Plus, on the news the other night, the prostitute who was missing was from only ten minutes away. He needs to be cautious. And two nights ago, when he was in the garage and I watched, he messed up again.

This time was worse than the rag, Diary. It was a shoe.

A shoe! How could he be so clumsy, so foolish? He'd walked off and left it, the black stiletto marking the entrance to the woods. It was like a red flashing sign for someone to see. It may as well have been a yellow brick road leading everyone down to Daddy's demented version of Oz. I'd rushed out from my spot and snatched the shoe while Daddy was gone. I shoved it with the rag from before. Thank goodness I was home to take care of these things. It was just more proof that I couldn't let anyone else in, least of all Aaron. I was Daddy's, and that was that. I had a duty to him.

I just hope Daddy gets it together and slows down. Haste makes waste, that's what Grandma always says when I'm forced to help her in the kitchen making pies. I hate that saying, but I think she might be right when it comes to the recipes Daddy's following. I can't wait for October to be over because usually he slows down then and gets a hold on his emotions.

And I'm worried because it seems like the town is catching on that something isn't right, that women are disappearing in odd patterns. The news today mentioned another missing woman. The anchor said something about a suspected serial killer. It was so strange to hear Daddy called that. It scares me because if they start to put it together, to investigate—could this be the end of the game for Daddy? Could he get caught in a trap that he set for himself?

It chills me to think how close it all is to crashing down around us. I wish I could ask him to slow down, to stop. But I know that it is who he is, and I have to love him anyway. Just like he loves me.

Still, I can't afford for him to keep dropping items because pretty soon, I'll need a bigger hiding place for all of his collectibles. You know?
Stay Safe,
Ruby

October 13, 2018
9:57 p.m.
Dear Diary,

I'm starting to worry more and more about the man I call Daddy. I'm feeling like maybe I don't know him like I thought I did, like maybe he's different. Or maybe I really am naïve.

Daddy went out tonight. Again. What's he thinking? His eyes are bloodshot and he clearly needs rest. Luckily, he came back a few minutes ago—emptyhanded. He seemed angry and was shaking all over. His face was scowling as he told me he was tired and going to bed.

I was thankful. Sad that he was upset but grateful that I wouldn't have to worry about cleaning up after him, at least for tonight. Because I have other things to think about, Diary. After what I found, my mind needs time to just think.

When he left tonight, I was bored. I was thinking about that time I went in Daddy's bedroom, thinking about the books in there. I was curious about what other books he had. I was thinking about the poison book especially. Maybe, just maybe, I could study up and make my killing game a little different—if I decided to make my own killing game someday. Poison seemed fun. After all, I'm good at chemistry. I like the exactness of it all, the specific recipes and numbers. It all adds up if you do it just right. I imagined poisons to be similar, rule-following concoctions.

It was a risk to go in Daddy's room. After all, his schedule was sporadic now. He could be back in ten minutes. And his mood was dark. If he found me in there again, I was certain I would end up dead.

It was a risk that felt worth it, though, if for no other reason than for the fact that I was just so intrigued by the idea of poison making. Sure, I could Google it—but I wanted to learn from the master. Daddy's poison book was undoubtedly tried and true, and there was nothing quite like having a real book in your hands.

So I'd crept into his room, his sanctuary. I felt sort of dirty being in there, like a snake. But I just wanted to look. I just wanted to know what Daddy knew, after all. It would be okay, wouldn't it? When I got to the room and glanced at the familiar bookshelf, though, my eyes wandered. I told myself to follow the rules, to only look at the one book and then leave. I told myself Daddy would be so furious to find out I was in there again. I shivered, thinking of the last encounter we had when I was caught in his room. It was a dangerous game I was playing, and I knew it.

I couldn't discourage myself, though. My eyes fell on the drawer on the little desk. There were two drawers, scuffed and worn. For some reason, the right-hand drawer caught my eye. Maybe because Daddy was right-handed.

I squeaked the drawer open, telling myself I would just take a peek. But the drawer was so neat and orderly. It was awe-inspiring, really, even though the contents were quite dull. A few old utility bills on the right-hand side in a stack. A few expired driver's licenses of Daddy's on the left. A stack of cash peeking out from an envelope in the back of the drawer, and some empty notepads with the name of the company Daddy works for at the top.

I picked up the notepad, feeling the paper under my fingers, wanting to flip through and see if Daddy is a writer, too. And that's when I saw it. Underneath the memo pad, right there for any snooping eyes to see.

An envelope. Yellow. Unassuming.

I was intrigued.

I dug my hand in, the feel of glossy photo paper exciting me.

Just one photograph in the average-looking envelope.

I pulled it out, curious. Was it a photo of me that Daddy kept safe? Another wedding photo like the one I had in my room? I flipped it over, gasping at the sight.

At first, I almost didn't recognize the woman in the photo. Her pallid skin, her dangling body. But then, slowly, recognition clicked.

Mama, in all her glory, looked back at me. Her red hair drooped forward, covering part of her face and one of her bulging eyes. Her pink sleepshirt hung in an uninspiring fashion. It looked baggy and sad on her, like a tent. Her feet were bare, hanging well above the spotless garage floor.

The noose was wrapped around her neck, hanging from the beam I'd seen Daddy use so many times before. I stared at the final photograph of my mother, my mind racing. Why would Daddy take that photograph? Why would Daddy keep it?

I'd seen Daddy take this very photograph through the years. Over and over, he'd snap the photograph and flick his wrist to develop it as he stared into the bulging, dead faces in the killing game. But I'd never imagined Daddy had a similar photo of Mama. Why would he take that photo? Why would he want to keep it? Was it because, like me, he was fascinated by the final photograph of her? My finger traced the photograph as my mind wandered. That could be it. That could be logical.

But another thought oozed in. I tried to strangle it, to tie a noose around it. I didn't want a photograph of the thought. I wanted to forget it.

Mama's diary entries snuck in, polluting my mind. It didn't make sense. How could she write that—but then not carry through her plan? And why would Daddy take the photograph? Why would he re-enact that moment over and over? And was the photograph the only part he was re-enacting?

My Daddy is a killer. He killed Mama.

The thought wormed its way out of the apple in my brain, taunting me with its slimy, eerie texture. No. Impossible. Daddy couldn't do that. He wouldn't. Not to Mama, the woman he loved so much. She wouldn't be a part of the killing game. That would be against the rules. Wouldn't it be? No. Maybe. I don't know.

I rocked back and forth, engraving the photograph in my mind before carefully tucking it back in place, just as it was. I double and triple checked to make sure Daddy wouldn't know I had been in his room again. I thought about stealing it, so I could look at it later. I thought about hiding it better— after all, what if Grandma came snooping or someone else? He wasn't being careful enough. Still, something told me to leave it be. Something told me that Daddy revisited the photograph often, especially in October, the anniversary month of Mama's death.

Something also told me that all those "I'm sorry" statements at Mama's grave and scrawled on the photographs weren't a coincidence. The question became: Did I really think Daddy had something to be sorry about? The words of my dead Mama drifted in and out of my mind randomly.

No.

He had nothing to be sorry about. Nothing at all. Not after what she'd planned on doing.

Stay Safe,
Ruby

October 16, 2018
9:57 p.m.
Dear Diary,

We all have our obsessions. Daddy and mine happens to be death these days.

He's still busy in the garage. If he isn't killing or out looking for his next plaything, he's in there cleaning and organizing. Which leaves me with a lot of time to think. I've, of course, been thinking a lot about Mama and the state of things.

Yesterday, I got Daddy to drop me off at the library. I had some researching to do. It took me a while, but I dug up the newspapers from the archives from that date. October 10, 2004. Two days after Mama's death date.

It was vague, Mama's obituary. It talked about how she died suddenly. That was code word for suicide, or at least that's what I'd surmise. It talked about her daughter left behind. Me. Ruby. It didn't say much else. It made me wonder what my obituary will say someday. What will I have to leave behind?

But that's not important now.

I talked to Aaron today at lunch about it. I told him about how Mama killed herself. He was really sorry. His eyes looked honestly sad. I told him it was okay, that I barely knew her. But the pity on his face lasted throughout lunch. I don't like to be pitied. I almost told him the truth, told him about what I think Daddy might have done. But I still don't know that for sure. It doesn't make sense. Why would Mama write what she did and then not follow through? Why write plans and then ignore them?

Unless . . .

No. It couldn't be. Could it? Would Daddy do it, really? But wouldn't the police have found out? Why would everyone report it as a suicide or as a "suddenly" kind of death, which is the same thing? Then again, if Daddy did do it, could I blame him? Maybe he found out about Mama's plans. In that case . . .

It's all so confusing, in truth. I've been scratching my neck wildly, so much so that it's raw and bleeding. I had to wear a turtleneck today to cover the wounds.

I think Daddy's been thinking about it all lately, too. He's been muttering strange things. Strange, strange things. I heard him mumbling yesterday when he was making dinner about how sometimes you do what you need to. I heard him chattering about nooses. I heard him whispering that he loved her—but there was no one there.

Daddy's still being sloppy. It's frustrating. I want to yell at him to pay attention. I want to tell him that I still need him, that he can't get messy. I want to tell him I could do better if he would just let me help.

Dropped rags.

Missed splotches of blood in the wheelbarrow.

Stupid, reckless mistakes. He's getting too comfortable.

I'm terrified, Diary. I'm terrified he's going to get caught any day now. And then what? It would have all been for nothing. He can't protect me when he's locked up, after all.

The sad truth is that if Daddy goes away, there will be no one to write my obituary when I die. There will be no one to love me. No one. Not even Aaron—there's no way he'd stick around if he found out what Daddy did. Would he? No love is that deep, no love other than Daddy's love for me. Look what he's done for me over the years. Look at the lengths he's gone to for me.

Without Daddy, it will all fall apart. I'll be lonely, on-the-fringes Ruby all the time. Sure, there's Grandma—but that's no comfort. I might tie my own noose if I'm stuck living with her and her stale cookies, kale, and scratchy sweaters. I can't even imagine what she'd say if she found out about Daddy. Life would be a constant yammering about repentance and sin and death. In short, that would be no life at all. No life worth living at least.

Is that what drove Mama to it, if she did kill herself? Did she finally feel like it wasn't worth it? I can understand that. I can.

I picture myself swinging in the noose, floating freely. Maybe Mama had the right idea after all.

Stay Safe,
Ruby

October 18, 2018
9:57 p.m.
Dear Diary,
Red. All I can see, taste, feel is red.
I fucking hate her. She needs to fucking die.
Die.
Die.
Die.
Die.
Die.
Die.
Die.
Clarissa IS going to die for what she did today.

I don't care why the bitch did what she did. I think it's because of Aaron. I think she can't stand that she's alone and I have someone. I don't know what goes through her mind, in truth, however. I just know she's been tense with me, trying to get back at me. Today, she went too far . . .

Sorry, Diary. I had to take a break. My hands are shaking uncontrollably, a shake like Daddy's. Is this why he does what he does? Is the rage too much for him?

Sure, Clarissa's done horrible things before today. Bloody tampons in my locker. Stolen books, feet tripping me when I walk by. Verbal insults in the locker room when the teachers are gone. Social media taunts that circulate the school calling me a retard and dad fucker.

The usual. But today, things went too far. Way too far. Today, Clarissa earned herself a spot in the game, if I have my way.

Clarissa was scowling when I went in the locker room after gym class, angrier than usual. Maybe it was because Aaron asked me to the homecoming dance yesterday—even though I hate dances. Maybe it was because I heard things aren't going well at home, that they may even be losing their house. Or maybe Clarissa is just finding a darkness within, the kind of darkness Daddy and I know very well.

I don't know what happened or why, but she seemed ready to pounce. I ignored her when she called me a retard and told me to stay away from Aaron, insisting that he was too good for me. I meandered back to the bathrooms to change, as is my custom. When I came back to put my clothes in my locker, though, things took a sinister turn.

Clarissa convinced Tiffany Glasgow, the girl from the rugby team, to be on her side. Maybe this has been planned for a while, or maybe it was spur of the moment. I don't care. I don't. Clarissa's persuasive abilities with our peers are unarguable. When I was tucking my folded clothes away, Tiffany ambushed me. Her behemoth body plowed into me, and I crashed to the ground. The wind knocked out of my lungs, I found myself shocked and confused, crunched on the floor within a few seconds. Her weighty body suffocated me as something sharp scraped against my neck. I kicked and flailed, but I was no match. Tears and shock swirled within my veins as I pleaded with the universe to get me out of this mess, as I cursed the weakness in my limbs, in my body.

"Scream and you die," Tiffany warned, spit landing on my face as it escaped through her crooked teeth. I couldn't even inhale, couldn't breathe at all. I wanted so desperately to inhale, for my lungs to suck in the heavy locker-room air just for a moment. Pain bit into my chest, into my bones. A few of Clarissa's cronies crowded around, blocking any view of me from Mrs. Carlisle. There would be no savior. I was on my own, all alone, no one here to save me. Daddy couldn't save me. Tears welled, blurring my vision.

Clarissa had her phone aimed at me. She was grinning.

"Tell us the truth, and we'll let you go. Tell us your Daddy fucks you."

My face burned red, and my hands shook with anger. Why was she so obsessed with Daddy? And why would he ever fuck me? No, no, no, no, no. I wouldn't lie about Daddy, even if I ended up dying. And right then and there, I thought I was going to die. I choked and sputtered.

"Say it," Tiffany ordered, shoving the sharp object deeper into my neck. Her words were a forceful growl, like a sneering dog lunging at your throat. Pain surged within, and flashes of red exploded in my head. "Say he fucks you. We all know he does."

I shook my head. She slammed her body down on my chest even harder. My head bobbed back against the cold concrete, and a burning sensation crashed through my skull.

"Your Daddy's a fucking psycho, isn't he? He deserves to be locked up, both of you. He deserves to go away, and then what, Ruby? Then you'll be all alone, the freak abandoned by the freak."

The words sent a shiver through my spine as I stared at the evil glow in Clarissa's eye. A deep roar was building in my chest, despite the fact that I could barely breath.

I hated her in that moment, more than any other moment. I could handle the hair incident and the bloody tampons and everything else. But not this.

Not my biggest fear spoken aloud.

It didn't matter if Clarissa could make the threat happen or not. It didn't matter. Because just her saying the words, just her verbalizing the possibility of Daddy going away—it made me want to kill her. A slow, agonizing death. A red death branded by torture of the darkest kind. I would follow in Daddy's ways—and then some. I would make sure she paid for the threat. Daddy wouldn't be going anywhere.

Clarissa would.

Tiffany settled harder on my chest, her hand now on my chin, squeezing so hard I thought it might pop. I didn't have the energy to gasp for breath. Everything was going fuzzy. I was going to die, I felt sure of it. I would die here with Tiffany and Clarissa spewing lies about Daddy, and I couldn't stop them. I'd vowed to protect Daddy at all costs, but I was too weak, too small, too insignificant to stop them. Tears of frustration rolled down my cheek, jolting me to a reality I wanted to crush. I wanted to shout for help. I wanted to bellow that Daddy would never hurt me. I wanted to protect Daddy. I wanted to breath. I wanted to turn the knife and carve out Tiffany's eye, pluck it out and hold it up for all to see. I wanted to slit Clarissa's throat for what she'd said, for what she was doing. For what she'd threatened.

But as it got harder and harder to breathe, as the girls kept laughing and chanting about Daddy being disgusting, a rapist, a freak, I wanted to die. Maybe this was my way out, my way to the peaceful field. Maybe I could let the red spill, let the breath stop all together. Maybe I could just disappear into the solitude of the wildflowers, the trees, of the red that Daddy had made.

But then I thought of Daddy and how hard it would be for him, losing Mama and me.

I thought of all that he'd done to save me, protect me over the years.

I thought about how I needed to protect him from the ugly, filthy lies the girls were saying.

I needed to protect myself.

So I reached over and did the only thing I could. I bit Tiffany's arm, hard and fast. Blood squirted out, dribbling on my face. It was beautiful. I could taste red, feel the stickiness on my tongue. Red. Red. Red.

The bell rang. The girls scattered as Mrs. Carlisle's voice echoed for the locker room to clear out. Tiffany kicked me in the ribs and then walked on. I scurried away, gasping for breath but relieved the girls' plan wasn't very well thought out—this time. But what would be next? Clarissa wasn't one to back down. She was a rabid dog lunging for the throat, hungry for it. If she didn't get what she wanted, she'd come back for seconds.

And I was terrified that even though her claims were ridiculous, she'd stir just enough drama to potentially ruin it all for Daddy. Daddy had secrets he didn't need uncovered, and Clarissa's stupid threats were hitting way, way, way too close to the field for my comfort.

I wouldn't let her take Daddy away. I wouldn't let her risk it all.

Mrs. Carlisle asked if I was okay, her face alarmed. I didn't stop to answer questions. I ran past her. I didn't want to explain. I didn't want her hearing about Clarissa's dirty question, about what she said about Daddy. I didn't want to utter the threats she made about Daddy disappearing. I didn't want to talk to anyone, not even Aaron. I was terrified of what he would think if he heard what Clarissa said. Would he believe it? And if he kept talking to me, would she hurt him next?

I need to protect Daddy, Diary. From Clarissa's disgusting words. I need to protect myself. I keep thinking about how it felt, being crushed by Tiffany, being asked those questions that made me squirm, that made me enraged, that made me want to hurt them all.

I think about what it felt like to hear Clarissa threaten to take away the one thing I can't live without—him.

They made me want to splatter red all about the locker room, a masterpiece tinged by the bitch's blood, the shadows created from my deep need for revenge.

My head is still pounding, the memories of Tiffany crushing my chest obliterating my spirit. No wonder Daddy keeps the killing game a secret. People are too anxious to ruin everything good. Well, I won't let it happen. I won't. You see, I have a little secret, Diary, one Daddy wouldn't even like.

I know what I need to do. My hands are shaking, quaking with the knowledge.

She'll pay. She'll suffer for what she did. More than that, she'll suffer for what she said.

All afternoon, the ideas, the images, the red swirled in my head.

So when Daddy stepped out, I knew I had to act fast.

We have a lot of knives in the utensil drawer, Diary. A lot of very sharp knives. Daddy hasn't been cooking much, and even if he does cook, he's too tired to notice the lovely, silver knife I've stolen. I've tucked it inside my boot. Daddy bought me new red boots at my request a few weeks ago. What perfect luck. What solid timing. The old red boots are back but with a new twist.

I reach down now, touching the cool, crisp handle. I swear, the knife is just waiting to kiss Clarissa's skin, to dig deep into her flesh and splatter the red all about.

I grasp the handle, imagining what it will feel like when it dives into her stomach, across her throat. My hands are shaking, but I picture the steady strokes, the heavy cuts I'll make as I watch her shriek and squirm and beg for mercy.

But there won't be mercy. She doesn't deserve it. The bitch doesn't deserve it at all.

I stroke the handle seven times. Wait your turn, I silently implore it. Wait until the time is just right. It wouldn't do to rush. It needs to be beautiful, a splendid masterpiece. Just like Daddy's taught me, even though he doesn't know it.

I've learned from the master. Soon, it will be my time to work.

I'm ready to let my own brilliance shine—and ready to make her fucking pay.

She'll fucking pay.

Stay Safe,

Ruby

October 19, 2018
6:57 p.m.
Dear Diary,

I'm a good secret keeper . . . but today, I've learned Aaron isn't.

Daddy came to get me from school today. Really early, almost as soon as I got there. He found out about what happened yesterday in the locker room.

At first, I was confused. How did Daddy find out? I hadn't told anyone, not a teacher or principal or Daddy. I didn't need to. I wasn't afraid of Clarissa anymore. I had my plan, the knife in my right boot. Loaded and ready for anytime I needed it. I felt safer. I wished I had done that earlier. But I hadn't needed to use them today. Daddy had come to my rescue before I'd even known I'd needed rescued, like he always does.

"Why didn't you tell me?" he asked as he drove me home. The knife felt hot and cold at the same time, making its presence known in my boot. My heart raced as I thought about how mad Daddy would be if he knew.

"What?" I asked, playing dumb. I thought it must be about the knife in my boot. How did he find out? Why was he acting so calm? The calmness scared me even more. Daddy always looked subdued and peaceful in the garage, too. It wasn't a good sign.

"About Clarissa. About everything that happened. Ruby, you need to tell me these things."

I almost sighed audibly. The knife felt safe again.

But then I realized that he knew what happened. How did he find out? I hadn't told anyone. How did he know? I felt my cheeks warm with embarrassment. I didn't want Daddy knowing what Clarissa had said.

"Sorry, Daddy. Sorry."

"Ruby, it's okay. You didn't do anything wrong. But those bitches did. Those bitches are going to pay. I'm making sure of it. If I have to get a lawyer and sue, I will. I'm not letting you in that school until that principal sorts this out and punishes those two. Until he kicks them out, you're not going back."

"Sorry," I said again, not sure what to say. I knew Daddy was lying. He didn't handle things with lawyers. He handled them with saws and trash bags and wheelbarrows.

My mind whirled. Clarissa and Tiffany were going to be in trouble. They wouldn't be at school anymore if Daddy could make it happen—and he never broke promises. This would be good . . . wouldn't it? My stomach churned. I could put back the knife if they were gone. I could stop worrying about protecting myself. Couldn't I?

Something told me that Clarissa wouldn't give up that easily. In truth, I liked the feeling of the knife in my boot, ready at a moment's notice.

"How did you find out?" I asked, curiosity getting to me.

"That boy from school turned them in, that Aaron kid. I guess he saw some videos they posted on social media. But don't worry about it. It's being taken care of. I just didn't want to risk leaving you there with those incompetent teachers until they straightened this all out. We're going to take a couple of days off, you know? Let this all cool down."

"Okay," I said, scratching my neck.

Aaron did this. If he saw the video—what would he think? Would he stop talking to me?

I scratched and scratched, feeling skin flakes loosen and float into the air. I shook my head, squeezing my eyes shut. *It doesn't matter,* I told myself. *I don't need him.* Aaron's too nosy. And he's probably what started this whole mess anyway.

But now it's early evening, and I'm sitting here writing in you to try to get my thoughts straight, Diary. Here's the thing though—I can't stop worrying.

Worrying about what Clarissa will do if she gets expelled.

Worrying about Aaron getting hurt.

Worrying that Daddy heard the awful things those kids said.

Worrying that Daddy will end up being taken away from me.

And most of all? I can't admit this to anyone, but I'm really worried that Aaron is going to stop talking to me. Because now that I have someone at school, now that I have someone to sit with and listen to at lunch, I've realized how nice it is. How good it is to have someone by your side. The way his eyes light up when he talks about presidents or about law. The way his red hair falls in his face and he swoops it back with a confident hand. The way he walks close enough for me to feel his presence but far enough away that our skin isn't kissing. It's like someone finally gets me, understands what I need—someone besides just Daddy. How can I lose that?

I'm thankful that Daddy is fighting for me and that it's the weekend. I don't want to hear the kids' comments about the video or have people harass me. I want peace and quiet, time to write poetry and just think. But I also hate that for the next few days, I have to wonder where things with Aaron stand.

Daddy's watching TV. His hands are shaky and he looks angry. I hope the principal takes care of this whole situation for Clarissa's sake. Because if he doesn't, I think for the first time, there might be a familiar face in the garage game.

I can't say I would mind. I don't know what the other ladies did to end up in Daddy's game, but I know Clarissa is one who has done plenty to deserve a worse death than Daddy gives. In fact, she doesn't even deserve the garage game, the beauty in the dance of it. She doesn't deserve the peaceful field under the beautiful tree with the gorgeous women.

She deserves much, much worse. My neck itches at the thought.

Tonight, when Daddy is sleeping, I have an important job to do. I need to take the knife back to the kitchen so Daddy doesn't notice. Partially, I'm returning it because I'm not as afraid. Not with the principal knowing about the situation and with Aaron there to keep an eye out.

But there's another reason, Diary. Another reason I'm putting it back.

My hands are feeling itchy. They've been wanting to grab that knife all day. They've wanted to track down Clarissa's house and bury it deep in her—for saying those things about Daddy. For spreading bad lies.

And most of all, they've been starving for a reason to paint a bloody masterpiece of their very own.

Stay Safe,
Ruby

THE DIARY OF A SERIAL KILLER'S DAUGHTER

A trembling voice
Rattles through her skin
Her fingers are tempted
With the divine hunger

Cool metal,
Silky and scorching,
Calls to her
Dying brain.

Piercing,
Cutting,
Stabbing,
Stroking.
Death's dance
Has a rhythm
Of its own.

Red smears
Decay into black.
A dark soul
Tinged by a
Scarlet goodbye.

October 22, 2018
7:57 p.m.
Dear Diary,

The weekend dragged by like a wayward train that gets lost on its own tracks. I couldn't stop thinking about Aaron and the mess at school. I couldn't stop wondering what would happen to Clarissa. I couldn't stop studying Daddy, the hatred in his eyes palpable from across the room. He hates Clarissa. I don't blame him. I do, too. I haven't seen what Daddy does to people he hates—but I have a really good idea that it isn't pretty.

I thought Daddy would go out this weekend the way he was shaking all over. He didn't, though, staying and stewing in his venomous animosity instead. I wonder if he was afraid to leave me with all that's happened. I did notice him on his computer a lot. When I would come over, he would turn the screen. I wonder if Clarissa's video has made its rounds despite the principal's promise to Daddy that it was taken down.

I go back to school tomorrow. Daddy told me I could take another day off, but honestly, I'm bored. I thought being alone at home with Daddy would be great. But I miss school. Correction. I miss Aaron. It's weird how he inserted himself into my life and now he's become sort of important.

Not as important as Daddy. Obviously. But I realize that he does make things better.

I just hope he'll talk to me. I hope he's not believing the video. I hope he hasn't realized what he should have long ago—talking to me is trouble. It's suicide. He should probably stop.

What makes him talk to me anyway? I often wonder. There are so many other people. Why me?

There are a lot of mysteries in life. How Grandma is still alive and no one has murdered her—she stopped by yesterday, having heard rumors about the video from her blabbering friends. She brought a rhubarb pie for us. Disgusting. She stayed and forced Daddy to make her coffee and talked on and on about how in her day, there weren't such horrific occurrences because they didn't have technology. She then proceeded to ramble about a woman at Bingo, her arthritis, and other things Daddy and I couldn't care less about. She always has impeccably bad timing. But Grandma's mindless chatter isn't the biggest mystery in my life, not at all.

There's the mystery surrounding Mama. I haven't forgotten about it despite all of the other chaos.

There's the mystery surrounding the women I write poetry with in the field.

But above all, lately, I've been thinking about the mystery with Aaron. What drives him to talk to me?

Grandma always says if something seems to be too good to be true, it is.

Maybe Aaron is too good to be true. Maybe he's just like the rest of them. I hope not. Because if that were the case, I don't know what I'd do. I think the pent-up anger I keep swallowing would spew out. I think I might be uncontrollable with sadness and hurt and rage, all rolled into one. I think that would be a dangerous concoction.

Sometimes I think that's what's going on with Daddy. Sadness and hurt and rage. I think it's Mama's fault. I don't think she was as good of a woman as Daddy claims. From what I've read in the paper, everyone thought she was perfect. But they haven't read the things I have. They haven't seen those lines from her Diary.

There is something severely wrong with me, in truth.

Anyone would say sure, to commit suicide, something has to be wrong. That's not normal behavior. What is normal, anyway? I could argue. Regardless, I think about the other lines. The other words Mama wrote. I don't think suicidal tendencies were the only thing wrong with her. I think there was something else.

Me.

That hurts, to be honest. Which I try to be these days except when it's necessary to lie.

It just makes me think. And I'd never say this to anyone else, Diary. But if even Mama thought there was something wrong with me, if even Mama was driven to extreme lengths to escape me, how could anyone else love me? How could Daddy? How could Aaron?

Maybe I'm a hopeless case. Maybe, like Mama, my life is a shitshow.

Maybe I should've let Tiffany Glasgow crush me. Maybe Daddy would bury me in the field and it wouldn't be so bad after all. And, this is the hardest part to admit. Maybe, just maybe, even Daddy would be better off without me.

Stay Safe,

Ruby

October 23, 2018
8:57 p.m.
Dear Diary,

Thinks are looking up. I almost want to scratch out the darkness from the past few entries. But I can't. I know they're a part of my story. I can't just pretend those thoughts didn't exist. That wouldn't be truthful. But today, I'm seeing things much more clearly. Things aren't so bad. They're fine, actually.

For one, Aaron did talk to me. And as much as I hate to admit that I was clinging to the hope that he would, I know now that I'm relieved. He sat with me at lunch, and things weren't even awkward. He filled me in on the mundane occurrences in the school on Friday and about his weekend—he's in mock trial, and they had a competition. He didn't even bring up Clarissa or the video. I thought about just leaving it go like the typical Ruby would. Keeping my lips sealed, pretending none of it happened. But I knew that I couldn't. I knew this was different, that Aaron was different.

So I'd asked him. "The video . . ." I murmured. It wasn't what I'd wanted to say, what I'd rehearsed in my head. But they were the only words I could get out.

"Ruby, we don't need to talk about it. Those girls are awful. I'm sorry you had to go through that."

"It's not true," I managed to murmur as I eyed my chicken tenders on my plate, pushing them around aimlessly with the plastic fork.

"I know," he said, reaching his hand towards mine but stopping it right on the table near mine. He let his pinkie float over and lightly brush against mine. I looked up at him, into those eyes that exuded kindness and joy and understanding.

"Thank you," I whispered, my chest heaving with nervous tension and the inhalations I couldn't slow down. And then Aaron did the best thing. He moved on, talking about a book he read on Woodrow Wilson last night and about presidential debates and all sorts of things I don't care about.

It didn't matter though. Listening as he yammered on about his life, his average, not-so-grand life, I was entranced. And for a moment, I realized that it could all be okay. That there was life beyond the moment with Clarissa, beyond the confusion of the garage and the itch in my hand. Aaron quieted the urges I'd felt to hold that knife, to create a blood-stained masterpiece. Aaron made me think about other choices, possibilities.

And most of all, Aaron didn't make me feel like thinking about it was a betrayal of Daddy. For a moment, I could picture something I'd never dared to imagine—a life beyond our home, a life beyond my bedroom, a life beyond Daddy.

A life with the redhead who loved presidents, politics, and talking about cars.

A life with the redhead who knew my limits and respected them.

A life with the redhead who could make me feel like it might all turn out okay, that I wasn't a monster, and that I wasn't that different after all.

I was allowed to skip gym class and go to study hall instead. I decided to go anyway. Maybe it was my good mood brought on by Aaron or maybe it was my good mood brought on by the fact that Clarissa was suspended for ten days. Tiffany Glasgow had been expelled.

Regardless, nothing seems so bad, Diary. Even Daddy's resuming his schedule as normal. He's out right now, told me he'd be back in a few hours. I think he's out scoping, his shaking hands telling me what's coming.

But I know it will be okay. Daddy's smart. He looks more focused.

And to be honest, I could use a good killing game round to boost my mood even more.

Stay Safe,
Ruby

October 24, 2018
7:57 p.m.
Dear Diary,

Aaron offered to drive me home from school today, but I said no. I need to ease into this whole vision of us thing. I need to go slow. Plus, I actually enjoy riding the bus now that Clarissa is suspended. I sit in the backseat staring out the window. Daddy got me headphones so I can listen to classical music and relax. It's my time to think, to let my mind dance over the day's events.

Plus, if I ride the bus home, there's the long walk home by myself. It's a serene walk through the wooded lane to our house, and it cleanses my soul from the harsh realities of the school building. It makes me feel better breathing in the fresh air and being lost with my thoughts in nature.

Things today, though, were different.

I don't know if it's all the thinking about Mama or that I'm on edge because of the Clarissa incident and the fact that Daddy's killing game has me nervous he'll get caught. Or maybe it's because I let my mind flirt with the possibility of letting Aaron in, of seeing where things go with him. I'm just a ball of nerves, of anxiety, and of fear.

I was walking up the lane, and I got a chill. My eyes darted around, but there was no one. I don't know what it was, but I got this eerie suspicion that someone was nearby. A branch crackled to my right halfway up the lane. I stopped, wishing the knife was in my boot. My breathing intensified as I listened. There was nothing.

I shook my head. What an idiot. It was just my overwrought imagination playing tricks. I really needed to get a grip.

I shook it off, Diary, and Daddy and I had a decent night. We settled into our routine. He wasn't shaking today, and everything just seemed normal.

Normal. Calm. Peaceful.

Is this how most families are?

Aaron said maybe sometime I could come over for dinner. I don't know. I don't like eating certain foods, I hate meeting new people, and I guess a part of me is still reserved with him.

Grandma's words keep echoing. If something seems too good to be true . . .

189

And it's not just Aaron. It's me. Maybe I'm afraid that Aaron will realize I'm too good to be true. Maybe if he saw me, the real me, he wouldn't be so interested.

Maybe if he saw the words flowing through my head, the stories I could tell, maybe he'd be something else entirely.

Stay Safe,

Ruby

October 26, 2018
9:57 p.m.
Dear Diary,

Diary, it's my turn to play. I know now that it is absolutely my turn.

My side is throbbing. I re-examine the bruises, the marks that I've kept hidden.

They're a reminder that Clarissa unknowingly took things to the next level, but I wasn't ready.

I didn't tell Daddy about the marks, about the hurt. I had simply headed inside to the bathroom to take care of it myself, doing my best to hide the limp, the pain I felt with every inhale. I tried to be strong like I hadn't been earlier. I didn't want Daddy thinking he'd raised a weak girl. He's the master. I need to be worthy of the game.

I couldn't tell him the truth. Luckily, he's distracted anyway, by his insatiable addiction to the game. At least I know he'll be going out again, letting me exact my revenge soon.

I couldn't tell him what really happened—because if he found out, he would kill her. He would slice her throat, slaughter her like a deceased cow, and chuck her into the forest like the roadkill she is. There's nothing wrong with that. I would like to see her at my father's mercy. But, well, there is just one slight issue.

I want to be the one to make her pay. I need to be the one to feel her perfect little body writhe underneath my fingertips, to watch her red pour out into a tumultuous display of evil and beauty mixed together as a final goodbye.

It's finally, undoubtedly my time.

Gone are the dreams of a new life I thought I could choose. Gone are the whimsical, fantastical images of Aaron and me starting a new life beyond these walls, beyond the killing game. My heart pangs a little at the thought of what might have been if life was different, if people were different, if I was different.

Different in a good way.

But I'm not. I'm different in a bad way, as Clarissa has made known.

And now it's my turn to take up the family business, to pick up the reins, and take care of things myself.

My hands shake, not with the fear they shook with yesterday afternoon.

They shake with a hunger, a passion, a desire to make her pay.

I think back to yesterday, how naïve and innocent I was walking home from the bus stop, down the winding pathway. I think about how shocked I was as I approached the house and saw Clarissa running at me from the direction of the field. Daddy's field. My field.

I think about the rage that usurped all rational thought. What was she doing there? What did she find? This was my field, Daddy's field. I would kill her before I let her hurt him. I needed to protect him.

But I didn't get the chance. Before I could process what was happening or react, Clarissa grabbed my hair. She threw me to the ground, the air once again leaving my lungs as pain shot through me. Flashes of the locker room came to my head, but I knew this was different. There was no protection, however weak it might've been, of the four school walls.

There was no protection for Daddy's secret, which was the worst thing of all.

There was just Clarissa, kicking me in the ribs over and over and over again. The pain was unbearable, my breath unattainable. I shrieked and shielded myself, wanting nothing more than to put an end to it. To put an end to Clarissa. All the while, my mind raced with the possibilities of what Clarissa had found. With Daddy's secret threatened.

Clarissa screamed like a wild beast about how I'd ruined her life. How she'd make me pay, and how if I didn't stay away from Aaron, worse things would come. The whole time I gasped for air, the only thing I worried about was: Had she been in our field? Had she seen our secrets?

"How did you find me?" I croaked out.

"What do you mean? Everyone knows where the freak lives. And everyone knows that you walk home alone."

I remember back to the other day, when I had that eerie sensation of being watched. How long has she been watching me? Us? How much has she seen?

Clarissa just stared at me with smugness oozing.

"You fucking bitch. You're going to pay for what you've done."

Clarissa kicked me once more, her foot's contact with my side making me cry out in pain this time.

"This isn't finished," Clarissa mouthed. "I'll be back, and I'll kill you if I have to. Stay the fuck away from Aaron."

And with those words, I knew what was at stake. I could deal with the physical pain. I could deal with the bullying. But I couldn't deal with her threat. I couldn't let her risk everything Daddy had worked so hard for.

Daddy's been in the garage more frequently. The cops are on the lookout for a serial killer, trying to piece together clues. And Clarissa has now come onto our property, has inserted herself into a secret she can't be privy to. I can't risk her coming back and seeing what Daddy's done. I can't ruin everything that Daddy's worked so hard for.

I can't let Clarissa ruin it all. I'll do what I have to do to save him, just like he did for me.

When she left, I dragged myself to my feet and limped inside. Daddy still wasn't home. He was running late. For once, I was glad.

After cleaning myself up, I lay in bed, thinking about all that had happened. Thinking about Clarissa and her threats. Thinking about Mama and the diary. Thinking about her red hair cascading down her back in the picture. Thinking about all the women decaying in the ground. And most of all, I lay there thinking about the animalistic thirst in me to kill, to dismember, and to bury.

Thinking about how the bloodlust rising inside of me is so exciting, so enthralling.

I'll do it all like he taught me. Just like Daddy taught me.

Clarissa took things to a new level today. She'd branded me with the bruises, had tried to scare me with threats. She didn't deserve to do that. Daddy is the master of the game. I'm his understudy. Not her.

But soon, soon I'll scar her with the promise of death. I'll watch all of her red spill out, a splash of her that I get to control.

I'll paint her wonderfully. I'll paint her skilfully.

I get to paint her finally.

Things change in an instant. That's what Grandma always said when I was younger, when I was stuck in bed with a cold. That's what she would chant as she brought me tea and soups I didn't want and tried to placate me with promises of health coming back. I never believed her then, but I do understand the verity in her words.

Things really can change quickly—and we have to be ready. Because sometimes people need to pay. Sometimes you have to seek your own justice. Sometimes you have to use your own skills and talents to exact the revenge you deserve.

Stay Safe,
Ruby

October 28, 2018
8:57 p.m.
Dear Diary,

It's become an obsession, waiting, waiting for Clarissa. It makes me feel alive with excitement, the prospect that anytime, the killing game could begin. A different killing game this time—my very own.

I've had dreams the past two nights of how it will work out.

The knife chomping into her alabaster skin, the sticky red dripping down as her eyes stare at me, begging for a mercy that will not come. The look on her face as she fades away, her last sight me. The power of sucking out her soul and crushing her permanently.

The way the red will ooze and splatter in the field.

The way I get to pick her final resting spot in the field, a secret only I'll get to keep.

The knowledge that I killed her, finally—and that she deserved the searing, burning pain of the knife chewing her skin.

I've toyed with the details and pictured how it will all play out. I've watched the master for long enough. I've put in my time. My hands have practically memorized the dance, can perform the act as if on cue. Now I just have to make sure the setup is right so my fingers get the chance to feel the knife usurp Clarissa's life. I want to paint my own masterpiece. I want to be the master of the game.

But the thing is—I can't plan it, not completely. I don't know when she'll come back or if Tiffany will be with her. And where will Daddy fit in? I have to keep it secret. Hopefully he'll be out, and I'll be able to play at my leisure. I'll be able to take my time with my masterpiece. He's taught me well, after all. It's so complicated, though. I wish I knew more about how Daddy lures in his victims. I wish I could ask him.

I've thought about bringing him into it. I've thought about killing her and then letting him help me dispose of her. A true father-daughter team. Would that quiet his shaking hands?

I wonder what it will feel like, that first kill. I wonder what it will feel like to watch Clarissa bleed out in front of me, to watch her imploring eyes still for the final time. I wonder what it will be like to finally witness her at my mercy—and mercy I will not have.

She threatened to come back, and I should be nervous. Because at any time, she could show up and see what Daddy is really like. She could ruin it all, blow the whistle on this whole operation. I should be terrified, but I'm not. I'm anxious, thrilled even. My chance will present itself. I just have to be smart. I know I can stop her. I know I can finally show Daddy how much he means by protecting his secret.

I've stocked myself from the few tools Daddy stores in the basement. He went out for a while last night, so I had time to go in and swipe a few tools I'll be needing. I found a saw, pliers, some gloves, and grabbed two knives from the kitchen—one for under my pillow and one for in my boot. I keep them at the ready. I hope he doesn't notice they're missing. But there's no choice now. I have to be prepared.

How hard will it be to bury her? I wish I could use the garage like I've seen Daddy do. That would be so much simpler. The system is in place. I wish I could just do that. But I'll have to make my own way. Even the understudy has to add their own flair to the process, to the art. It's time to add my own style.

So many questions swirl. I've been preparing for this my whole life, but I know I'm still an amateur.

"You're very quiet lately," Daddy mentioned tonight at dinner. "Everything okay? You seem withdrawn, occupied," he said. "More than usual, I mean."

I grinned, offering him my sweet, Ruby smile. "Fine, Daddy. Just tired."

I felt bad lying. But sometimes we have to tell small lies to protect relationships. This lie, though was different. I see now why Daddy likes keeping his hobby secret, other than the obvious reasons, of course. I see the exhilaration one gets from always being one step away from being caught. It keeps you on your toes, keeps you at your best. Keeps you thinking and moving and alive. So alive.

It's funny how killing amplifies those feelings. Not that I know yet.

I've been struggling, though, thinking about Aaron. That red hair and those kind eyes that light up at me. It's so hard to think about him, knowing that life I imagined for a minute can never be. It's hard to think about what I'm giving up. A piece of me sits here and wonders: is it too late? Could I make another choice?

I scratch my neck, imagining what it would be like to go for milkshakes with Aaron, to take a walk with him and write poetry while he reads his history books. A part of me wonders what it would be like to have our own house with routines and habits.

But then the knife feels cold and itchy against my skin as it slides in my boot.

My neck gets itchy again.

Some things just can't be. Some things just cannot be.

Focus, Ruby. Don't lose focus. You need to be ready in case she comes tonight. And you need to plan for if she doesn't . . .because you can't let her ruin everything. You can't let her ruin Daddy.

You owe him that much. You owe Aaron nothing.

You have to protect the ones you love.

Daddy protected me from Mama. I know that now. I understand now why the killing game started. It wasn't a sadistic hunger or a need to kill. It was Daddy looking out for me. He always looked out for me, even when I didn't know it.

I owe it to him to carry on that legacy.

We're not killers. We're protectors.

And I'll protect him no matter what.

I need to go now. I have a note to write. The most important note of my life, one that I have to get sent safely on its way. It will be easy, I know. I just need to get off at the first bus stop, drop the note in just the right place.

It's risky. I could get caught, I suppose. But it's worth the risk. And the long, long walk.

Besides, if she comes for me early—I'll be ready. I'm always ready now.

Stay Safe,

Ruby

Shining glory,
Redness drawn.
Revenge is
Seeking its
True victim.

Savage mercy
Hear her roar.
Life's release
Is never sure.

Stupid girl,
You should've known.
You hurt me,
But the pain's your own.

October 30, 2018
11:57 p.m.
Dear Diary,

I'm sorry, Diary. My hands are shaking this as I write it. I'm so excited. So proud.

I'm not weak, and Clarissa knows that now. I'm an artist, a brilliant artist. Just like Daddy.

I stayed home from school today. I told a lie—a lie to protect our relationship. I told Daddy I wasn't feeling well and that I needed to stay home. It was risky. He usually offered to stay. But I thought I could sell it.

I told him I was tired and needed to sleep and would be fine. I assured him I was too old to need him at home watching over me for a stupid virus and that I was capable. I begged him to trust me. I promised to call him or Grandma—as if—when I needed something. I made him promise not to send her with her disgusting soup. He obliged.

He came home at lunch to check on me. I stayed in bed, thinking over the plan, over the knife resting in my boot, over what I was about to do. I convinced him I was fine, feeling better. He told me the words I was hoping to hear—since I was feeling better, he had to stay late at work for a meeting.

I didn't think he had a meeting. I think it was a lie. But I lied too, so I can't be very mad.

So Daddy was taken care of and the plan was perfectly in motion. I could barely calm my shaking hands as I observed the minutes tick by on my watch, lighting it up over and over as they dragged on.

She came for me alone just like last time. It was as if the universe was raining down blessings upon me. It was like the universe was anxious for me to step into my role, like it really was my time. Waiting in the woods, I thought about Aaron. A pang of hunger, of guilt, slapped into me. What would he think?

There was no time to wonder, though. This was about me and Daddy. Always me and Daddy. There wasn't room for anyone else, and there wasn't room to risk a bitch like Clarissa ruining everything Daddy had worked so hard to build.

Stupid girl. Stupid fool. She came alone because I'd told her to—or, rather, the note she thought Aaron dropped in her mailbox yesterday did. I'd been brilliant, dropping it in the familiar mailbox after the bus was long gone. For once, I was glad she'd ridden my bus so I knew exactly where the note needed to go. I'd addressed the letter, made it look like a formal one. I just hoped she got it in time.

Indeed, she did. Thank goodness, she did.

For all of Clarissa's looks and charisma, she was also very dumb. She was easy to manipulate, to trick. She came to the bus stop and walked down the lane, lured by the promise that Aaron was pissed off at me and wanted to get revenge. I'm a good writer, after all, Diary. I know Aaron's voice. I know what it would look like in print. I also know how stupid desperate girls are, how their bleeding hearts will believe anything at all, especially when they're longing to cause someone else pain.

She turned off our lane and walked towards the field, where I wrote was our place, mine and Aaron's. Waiting to exact her revenge on the girl she thought was weak. Waiting to finish me once and for all, to claim the boy she thought I'd tried to steal from her. I stood and watched from behind the tree, savoring how Clarissa was standing the place that she would unknowingly remain forever.

Diary, it was wonderful. I came out from behind the tree with a quiet confidence.

"Who are you waiting for?" I asked, my voice sugary sweet with a touch of the menacing quality I couldn't manage to cover.

She was stunned for a moment as I stood, staring at the shocked look on her face. I saw that she was afraid, that she was weak. I studied the girl who would soon be mine to claim.

Clarissa charged at me, anger seething as she realized she'd been fooled. But I was ready. I was strong. I'd already grabbed the knife from my boot. It was new and sharp. It was perfect as it hadn't yet been used, and it was in my excited hands. I looked into her eyes as my hand swiped masterfully, the knife performing the beautiful brushstroke it was made for.

And the red spilled. Oh, did the red spill as the knife bit into the delicate skin of her throat, slicing it as the shock on her face registered in my mind.

I was strong. She was weak.

She was dying.

She knew it.

She sunk to the ground, and euphoria took over. It was addicting, enthralling, a rush. Over and over, the knife plunged and sliced, bit and chomped. Each cut was more perfect than the last, each swipe a masterful addition to the beautiful painting I created right there in the field.

Right there, in the field where Daddy works, the blood spilled and splashed. I concentrated, searing every second in my memory so I could immortalize it forever.

I stabbed over and over and over. Seven times. Then seventeen times. And then, even I lost count. My hand grew tired, so I stabbed with two. The knife plunged deeper and deeper. I looked down to see that my hands were trembling, but not from fear or rage. From sheer elation. I looked at my watch. 3:47 p.m.

I understand why Daddy plays the game now.

It felt wonderful to know I sucked that life energy from her and made the world a better place. That must be what Daddy's doing, too. It was amazing that I was there the moment it faded away, when she faded away. It was gorgeous to see the red, all the red flowing against her pale, perfect skin.

And the blood. Oh, the blood didn't disappoint.

I sank to the ground, onto my knees, staring up at the cloudy sky as Clarissa lay on her back in the field, her body limp and mangled. The ugliness on her inside was now visible on the outside. She didn't look so beautiful now. She didn't look so scary now.

I needed to sit with her, to languish in the moment. I sat and stared and memorized and studied. I wanted to relish in my work longer, but I knew I had to move fast. Daddy would be home, and I didn't want him knowing what had happened. This was for him, but I didn't want him knowing I had to protect him. Clarissa was a problem I solved. I needed to handle it. It wasn't his problem to fix. And, I suppose I realized how amazing it was to have a secret, a dark, heavy secret. There was power in that. There was also safety. Because if anyone found out . . .

I longed to use the garage, to use the tools I had watched the master use year after year. But I knew I didn't have time. Daddy would be home in exactly one hour and four minutes. That wouldn't be enough time to make my masterpiece in privacy. I wanted to take my time, after all. I was just an observer. I knew I wasn't as adept as Daddy yet. I needed practice, after all.

Hauling Clarissa's dead body to the shed for later was the best option. I'd hidden some tools in there that I'd need later. It wasn't ideal, but it was private. With any luck, Daddy would go out, giving me time to work. If not, my plan was to slip outside while he was sleeping and finish the job then. I'd get it done, enjoy the task, and then bury Clarissa. She'd never be found. I'd never be found. Daddy and I will live out our legacy, our dark, dark legacy, and no one will be any wiser. Clarissa will just be added to the list of girls who disappear, who vanish, who run away. No one will find her—and maybe, in truth, no one will miss her. That's a sad thought, but I don't linger on it.

I dragged Clarissa, finding a strength within. I'm no weak girl. I knew I could handle the task. Plus, Clarissa's habit of barely eating anything to stay skinny is helpful. Thank goodness she was so vain. Her head flopped on the ground as I dragged her through the field, over rocks, past the trees. I kept peeking back, making sure none of her pieces were left behind. When I got to the end of the tree line, I paused, making sure Daddy's truck wasn't home. Making sure stupid Grandma hasn't shown up. Wouldn't that be just my luck? And her body is much fatter than Clarissa's. It wouldn't do to have to drag her dead heap of skin to the shed, too.

The coast was clear. I was safe. Sweating, I stopped to itch my neck before sliding her towards the shed.

Once inside, I checked my watch. 4:16 p.m. I examined the limp body. That's when I saw them. Her signature red nails. Ruby red nails. Gorgeous. I knew then what I'd have to do. It wouldn't be pretty, but it was necessary, I knew. It would be my photograph, my ritual.

My ritual. I was already thinking as if I'd . . .

No. I couldn't think about that. One step at a time. I'd done what I needed to do. I could stop now.

Couldn't I?

I took off my clothes that were spattered with blood, masterpieces in their own right. I wished I could frame them. They were artwork, after all. But I knew I couldn't. I left them with Clarissa, to be taken care of later. Naked, I shut the shed door, wandering back to the house to clean up, to get rid of the dirt and red on my own skin, and to steady my shaking, hungry hands.

When Daddy came home, I made my way through dinner. Glancing over my plate of chicken nuggets, I noticed Daddy's hands were shaking, too. Something must've been in the air. It was like he could sense what had been done, could taste the killing game floating about. After dinner, he said the words I'd longed to hear.

"Ruby, I have to go out again. I'll be gone for a while because we have to go to a site pretty far away. Will you be okay?"

"Fine, Daddy," I reassured, holding back the smirk that was spreading to my face.

"Okay, then. Stay safe," he said.

"I will," I promised, as I scratched my neck, waiting to hear the truck pull away so I could finish my work.

I started with the nails, thankful I'd put pliers in the shed. It was almost like a higher power was at work in the universe. Daddy never really uses pliers. But I had an itchy feeling when I saw them in the basement the other day. I had to grab them. Once the nails were safely removed, I began my real work. I was clumsy. It was different doing than watching. I liked watching Daddy's graceful movements. I knew I wasn't as good, as pretty, or as skilled. It was painful to admit maybe I wasn't quite a prodigy.

Still, I'd learned so much from watching. I'd learned from the best teacher. I made quick work of the body, an insatiable appetite stirring within as I sawed and chopped and watched the blood spray. It was beautiful in its own right. I wondered if Daddy felt this way when he worked on his first killing game.

I bagged and bleached and sweated. I cleaned and scrubbed and scrubbed and scoured. I ensured that no traces of her were left, other than the nails that had been set to the side.

I dragged the garbage bags through the woods.

But when I got to the woods, I realized I didn't have a shovel. I didn't have the energy to dig, and in truth, I wasn't crazy about burying her with Daddy's women. She didn't deserve that kind of treatment. She didn't deserve to be there with his masterpieces.

Looking around, I debated. I couldn't have Daddy find her. I couldn't risk him knowing because I needed to protect him. I needed to be careful.

So I dragged the bags farther, farther into the woods. Past the point I'd ever seen Daddy work. I found some leaves and some branches and some tall, tall weeds. I threw her bags there, covering them with brush and branches, scattering them about. No one would be the wiser. No one came out here. No one would find her here. She'd decompose like the rotten wench she was, alone and forgotten like she deserved to be.

Heading back to the shed, I scattered some dirt and leaves on the pools of blood in the field. It looked like rain, so if I was lucky, the pools of water falling would wash away the red that stained the grass. Daddy wouldn't notice, would he? He'd assume an animal had been attacked. He'd never suspect his sweet, innocent Ruby had anything to do with it.

I smiled at the thought.

The perfect cover. The perfect smile. The perfect protection.

Different Ruby.

Retarded Ruby.

Quiet Ruby.

Weird Ruby.

But when you were different and retarded and quiet and weird, you couldn't kill, could you?

They'd never expect the greatness I'd achieved.

They'd never, ever expect it.

I went back to the shed to get the nails. Ruby red nails. Red like my hair. Ruby red like my name. What a fitting end to the story.

I knew exactly where I'd tuck them, exactly where I'd put them so I could remind myself of the power I have at my fingertips.

I'm not weak or stupid or quiet or different.

I'm brilliant.

Stay Safe,

Ruby

October 31, 2018
9:57 p.m.
Dear Diary,

The thoughts of what I've done swirl in my head, making me feel crazed with excitement, with anticipation, and with a hint of fear. I'd be lying if I didn't say I was afraid.

Afraid the secret will come out.

Afraid Daddy will get caught.

Afraid it will all come crashing down.

Tonight, on the news, there was another plea for a missing girl. Not Clarissa, though. A lady. A familiar lady that Daddy couldn't stop staring at.

The news mentioned that she was last seen in a tavern, Tavern 7 to be exact. They also noted that with the rising number of missing women, the police are certain there's something dark going on in our sleepy town. Rumors of a serial killer are resurfacing with more certainty.

My blood turned cold. Daddy. The serial killer they're all looking for. And me, the serial killer's daughter who has just committed her first murder, too.

Daddy didn't even flinch when they mentioned it. I think he even grinned a little bit. Maybe this is part of the game for him, the part that's been missing for so long. Does he want them to piece things together, to figure out how brilliant he's been? I understand that sentiment now. I know we'd never want to get caught, but there's also this tiny piece that hates keeping it all silent. It's like I want to shout to the kids at school: remember me? The girl you see as weak? Well, look what I've actually done. *Fear me.*

Grandma swung by this evening. Barf. She was going on and on about how it chills her blood that so many are going missing, especially that girl my age—her friend from Bingo is neighbors with Clarissa and heard that they were looking for her. I felt my stomach churn a little bit as I thought about those fingernails tucked away with you. Grandma eyed me cautiously. I didn't say a word.

"Aren't you concerned, Ruby? She was your classmate." Grandma clucked her tongue like an crazed chicken. I giggled, remembering a video on the funny videos show that had a chicken.

"Honestly, what's wrong with you?"

At that, my neck snapped to the left, my head turning to face her. I glared at her, imagining her neck squeezed by the noose in the garage, in the shed. It didn't matter.

"Mother, stop it," Daddy said, standing up from his chair.

"A girl's missing and she has no empathy. My God, what would people think?"

Let them think what they want, Grandma. Because they'd be right.

If only she knew.

Stay Safe,

Ruby

THE DIARY OF A SERIAL KILLER'S DAUGHTER

November 2, 2018
7:57 p.m.
Dear Diary,

It's so, so hard to hold back the trembling, the urge to scream. I force myself to steady my shaking hands at school, and to paint on a sad face when they mention her name. In reality, I want to just forget, to feel nothing.

I want to forget about the fact that I killed Clarissa, that I threw her in the field, and that any moment, it could all crumble down around me. I was supposed to protect him. I thought killing her would protect him. What if it did the exact opposite?

The town knows now—Clarissa's missing. But they are under the false impression that she might come back. That she's just an aggravated runaway who has had enough of the town. They don't know. How could they?

It's fine, I reassure myself. Daddy's never been caught. They'll never tie me to Clarissa, will they? There's no way. I'm Daddy's daughter. Smart and sneaky. Capable. They'll never know what I'm truly capable of.

The police have been to the school. At first, the sight of them in the office stabbed into my gut. But I reminded myself to stay calm. Marlowes didn't get caught. I'd been clever. No one would ever suspect a thing. They questioned and searched the school, asking everyone who had talked to Clarissa for information. Clarissa's parents even were on the news, begging for information and asking Clarissa to come home. The tears looked real to me. That sank in a little bit. I thought of Daddy and what he would feel like if I was missing.

But the thought didn't last long. Because there's another feeling besides guilt that has taken over my body if I'm being completely honest. And I'm always honest with you, Diary. Even more than I am with myself.

Behind the pangs of guilt and the fear, something else is bubbling within. Hunger. Thirst. Appreciation for what I've done.

My hands are shaky, my body giddy with the relief I felt when that knife plunged in. I can't deny that although I did what I felt I had to do—I liked it. I really, truly liked it.

I revisit the shed often, in my mind. It wouldn't do for Daddy to get suspicious after all. I think about that night, all those cuts, the red on the floor. I think about how exhausting yet exhilarating the work was. I think about the power I felt wielding that knife and watching her go down for the final time.

I think about what it was like to take a life, to harness the life spirit of her and to let it slip away. The thing is, Diary—I don't feel as guilty as I thought I would. Not really. I feel empowered. I feel accomplished. I feel like I'm just beginning.

No, stop. Stop it, Ruby. One was it. One was enough. You did it for Daddy. You killed Clarissa to protect Daddy and now you're finished. Leave the work to the master.

In English class, we're studying *Crime and Punishment*—again. What a coincidence, right? The thing is, the book is all about guilt and how it gets to you. How it gets you caught. I keep telling myself, though, that you can't get caught from guilt if you don't feel it in the first place. I need to keep things in perspective. Maybe the lack of empathy all those therapists tried to work out of me is actually a gift.

It's weird how anticlimactic it's all been, really. For me, the world feels like it's shifted and changed. However, things are very much the same. The same schedule, the same people. The same foods for dinner, and Daddy's same routine of going out late at night.

The same things keep going. I've kept my secret well.

Daddy's secrets are easy to keep because they're not mine. But this secret—it's aching to be told. I want so badly to tell Daddy what an amazing thing I've done, how brilliant I've been. I want him to be proud of how much he's taught me. I want him to see me following in his magnificent footsteps.

I know I can't, though. It will complicate things. I protect him. I don't want him feeling like he has to protect me. Still, a piece of me wonders if it would be so bad if he found Clarissa, if he put it together. Maybe then we could really be the father and daughter team I've always dreamed of.

My pencil box is sitting on my desk, Diary. I keep it close by. It's like I can still feel that day breathing through the box. There's a cloth bag inside, a tiny cloth bag that a pair of sunglasses came in. It's cinched shut. I'm careful with the box. I know it's a risk to carry it. I know I should tuck it safely in my hiding spot. But I can't. Maybe it's just that I like having a piece of her there, reminding me of how strong I am. Maybe I like carrying it into gym class and remembering all the hell she put me through.

Maybe it just helps me feel like I've won.

I think, Diary, I have.

Stay Safe,

Ruby

November 5, 2018
7:57 p.m.
Dear Diary,
It started with the phrase I didn't want to hear, not from him.
"You're different."
The words that have plagued me my whole life. They are practically scratched underneath the surface of my skin, an indelible black mar. I feel the scar burn in my stomach and fill the space between us.

In fairness, I know what Aaron meant at lunch today when he coldly spewed the phrase. Because, it's true. I am different now. I'm not the same girl I was a few weeks ago. It's crazy how one choice, one stroke of the knife, can change it all. My hands shake now, and my heart trembles with the knowledge of my purpose. Gone are the days I thought there was another option. Stupid girl. This was the life destined for you. How didn't you see it?

I still sit with Aaron at lunch. In truth, he still sits with me. I'd be okay without him now. I still love his dimpled cheeks and his red hair and the passion he speaks with. But things are different. He's right. I'm different. I know where my priorities are. I know I'm strong enough to be alone, that I don't need him.

Nevertheless, hearing the words pissed me off. I thought about the knife in my boot, the pieces of Clarissa in the box that sat inches from Aaron. Stupid boy. So naïve. He had no idea how powerful I was.

In fairness, I hadn't either.

But I *am* different. It's hard for me to pretend to care about things I used to pretend to care about. Aaron talks about cars and presidents like he always has, but my mind is somewhere else. Dancing over the moments of that day, thinking about Clarissa's final breaths. Thinking about how skilled I was— because I've decided I was brilliant. After all, the police have no idea. They never will. I'm sure of it now. I'm as sure as Daddy is. The field is our refuge, a sanctuary never to be found. Clarissa will never be found. And even though sometimes the worry and the tiny twinges of guilt pang a little bit, mostly I've been able to shove them away.

I don't feel bad about it. I don't. I can't. I did what I needed to do, what I was always trained to do. I followed in Daddy's beautiful footsteps. Last night, though, when Daddy and I were watching the news again, her parents were on the television. Her dad was crying. My stomach wrenched with the sight. I looked at Daddy through my peripherals.

"Tough break for her parents. The girl was a bitch, but I can't imagine what they're going through," Daddy murmured.

I was floored. I told myself to stay calm and stoic, but it was so hard. I hadn't thought of it that way. I had only thought about myself and Clarissa and Daddy. But what about them?

I felt the *Crime and Punishment* style guilt threatening to usurp my relative calm and collectedness. I drowned it in my brain but excused myself to my room, my hands visibly shaking. Would Daddy think what I did was wrong? How could he, when he's taught me so well? But it sounded like even Daddy had moral lines he didn't cross. Did I go too far?

I'm up here now, Diary, the pencil box and you and the picture of Mama surrounding me. How dare Daddy say that? How can he kill all those women and yet throw these judgements at me? Anger builds.

But maybe it's not anger at Daddy. Maybe it's anger at myself. How did I think I could be so strong to not care? How did I think I could be as masterful as Daddy?

I stare at the relics around me, the symbols of a life I'm now committed to. Suddenly, I wonder if it was all worth it. I wonder if maybe I did make a mistake. Aaron thinks I'm different and what would Daddy think? And how about Clarissa's Dad? Did he deserve this?

Round and round the thoughts swirl. I can barely think. I scratch my neck until it burns, sticky and oozing with blood. Tears fall.

I'm not okay, Diary.

I'm different.

I've always been different—but this kind of different, well, it might be too different indeed.

Stay Safe,

Ruby

A nail pounds into my brain,
Stabbing into the gooey, pink surface.
Blood surges from somewhere within,
A spraying cacophony of sadness
And fear.

We all end up as dust in the field,
In the street,
In the forest,
In the ground.
It all ends.

But when the reaper comes,
Will you run? Or will you
Face him with the majestic
Pride you know?

I saw a cardinal once,
Fly from the tree.
Its wing was broken,
And it crashed to the ground,
Its neck twisting at an
Unnatural angle.

We are all cardinals,
Falling down, down, down
From the tree and succumbing
To nothingness.

When will it all fall down?

November 6, 2018
1:57 p.m.
Dear Diary,

We have a big problem. I'm not a masterpiece or a prodigy or anything of the sort. I'm not brilliant like Daddy. I'm a fucking disaster. A *disaster!* And now everyone is going to pay, everyone I love.

How could I be such an idiot?

The police found it. Well, Clarissa's parents found it. The note from Aaron—the note from me. They must have found it—because at school today, the police came and they took Aaron away.

It's over. It's done. How did I overlook it? I guess I just thought about my privacy, how my Diary and all of my treasures stay hidden. I didn't think about how Clarissa's room might not be so private. I was so desperate to get rid of the problem, the risk to Daddy, that I didn't think it through. Dammit, why didn't I think it through? Why didn't I ask Daddy for help? He wouldn't have been this stupid.

And now it's all going to come crashing down. This whole world I tried to protect is doomed—and worse than that? Aaron is wrapped up in it, too, because now the police think he might be involved in her disappearance. It seems like he was the last person to see Clarissa alive.

He wasn't back the rest of the day. I was confused at first and thought it must have been something else. When the rumors starting dancing around the school, I almost didn't believe it. But when I heard about a note that was found and how Aaron was called in for questioning, had been there all day, my stomach sank.

I knew it was true. It was all true. How could I be so dumb? I'd tied up Aaron in my plan. How would he get out of it? And even if he had an alibi that would protect him, the police would certainly end up here, wouldn't they? To investigate, since I'm mentioned in the note.

Tears whirled. I ran out of the school, ignoring the hall monitors and the principal who eventually found me by the tree, rocking and crying and banging my head.

Daddy came to get me. He assumed I was upset over Aaron—the town is small, and no one can keep a secret. Plus, the guys at Daddy's work all knew about it since Aaron's dad works with him.

"Ruby, I'm sorry." That was all he said. But what was he sorry for, Diary? That my best friend had been questioned for a murder I committed? That he hadn't taught his daughter well enough? That his daughter was an idiotic failure?

In truth, Daddy was probably sorry because he thought I was just sad over Aaron. But he doesn't know the half of it.

I thought about telling him then. I did. I thought that he might know how to fix it. But the truth is, admitting to him what I've done would be admitting that it's all going to crumble around him. If the police come searching, will they find Daddy's secrets, too? I don't want to think about what Daddy will do if he finds out the jeopardy we're in. Then again, maybe I deserve anything he dishes out. Maybe I deserve the noose, the saw, the deep hole in the overgrown field.

I deserve so much worse, in truth.

I scratch and scratch and scratch my neck. I can't stop. Over and over, my fingers carve into my neck.

I'm stupid. It's going to crash down.

Any moment it's going to be decimated like a bomb raging in the middle of a populated city. The police will be here any minute and then it all becomes a barren wasteland with no relics to remind everyone we were here.

Should I confess?

If I confess, though, it's not just me that will pay. Daddy's secret will be revealed. They'll find the women in the field, won't they?

Should I tell Daddy?

Could he help?

Should I let Aaron take the heat?

The thought makes me sick, but it's better than Daddy getting caught, isn't it?

Daddy and Aaron. I always knew I couldn't have both. I always knew it would become a choice.

What choice will I make?

Do I have to make one?

Can I keep the secret hidden? Is there another way out of this?

I'm clinging to the bloody rag, the one from so long ago. It's comforting to see the swatches of red staining the worn fabric. So many years, the rag has stayed hidden, a comfort object like a baby's blanket or favorite stuffed animal. It reminds me of the majestic quality of Daddy's work. It reminds me that secrets can, in fact, stay hidden. And now, as I cling to it, rocking back and forth, it reminds me of all there is to lose. I wish I would have watched better, learned better. I wish Daddy would have taught me better. But there's no time for regrets.

I have to make a decision. I have to figure this out.

Mama, please, please, please help me. Help me figure this out.

We're Not Safe.

And I'm fucked up. I'm so fucked up.

Ruby

November 8, 2018
5:57 p.m.
Dear Diary,

I haven't slept at all, and neither has Daddy. Things are bad. He's storming around the house. He's stomping around and terrified. I think he might kill me. I think Daddy's going to kill me or himself or both of us and it's all going to end. And for what?

They came, Diary. The police came to the house to ask questions about Clarissa and if I saw her. I had to lie, Diary. Over and over I lied. I had to lie to save not a relationship, but our lives. I had to lie to save Daddy. I don't lie very much, or at least I didn't. I don't have very much practice. But today, I lied and lied like our lives depended on it—because they do.

It seemed harmless, their questioning. When the blue and red lights pulled up, though, Daddy turned pale. My hands were shaking, and I couldn't stop scratching. I knew what it was about. Daddy didn't, though. I think he thought the worst, that his secret wasn't safe.

I tried to reassure him with my eyes that this wasn't about him, but how could I?

Focus, I told myself. *You can do this. It's not over yet. You need to try to save Daddy. Do your best. Stay calm. They don't know a thing.*

I knew that lying to them might mean condemning Aaron. But it was a price I'd have to pay. Daddy was more important. Ruby and Daddy. Always Ruby and Daddy.

Over and over, they asked questions. About where I was and Clarissa and Aaron. I did my best to tell the truth. Daddy asked if I needed a lawyer. The police assured him I wasn't a suspect. They asked Daddy about Aaron, but he barely said a word. He was pale and I could tell he was nervous, but he didn't leave my side. He was forceful with them, telling them to lay off when they got too intense.

I was shaking the whole time as I told them the words I had to say, the answers I hoped were the right ones. The whole time, pictures of Clarissa's body rolled in my head. I didn't look at the police, afraid they could see the images in my mind even though I knew they couldn't.

They talked about the note and about revenge, and Daddy told them about the whole scenario from the school. I lied over and over, telling them I hadn't seen Clarissa that day and that she never came to look for revenge. Daddy asked to see a copy of the note, and they obliged. I shuddered, not wanting to see the words I had written, the words that would mean life or death for Aaron, for Daddy, for me.

Daddy froze at the sight of the note, flashing a glance to me.

I felt his gaze burning into me. I felt the truth seeping out.

He knew. I knew that he knew. My secret was out. At least part of it.

The police then said the words we didn't want to hear.

"We need to take a look at the field, if it's okay with you."

"Not without a search warrant," Daddy responded. The police officers eyed him suspiciously.

"Don't you want to help us find out what happened to this girl, your daughter's peer?"

"Yes, but not without a search warrant. I know my rights."

Daddy was insistent. My blood chilled. I knew why he was so adamant about not letting them in the field.

"Fine. We'll be back," they murmured. Daddy got rid of them.

I sat, shaking on the sofa. I knew it was over. It was all over.

Daddy turned to me once the police had left. His hands were trembling, and, in fact, his whole body shook.

He walked over to me, staring at my face.

"What are you hiding?" he screamed, his voice so dark and grating that I jumped.

"Sorry, Daddy. Sorry." How did he know? How could he possibly know? Maybe the same way I knew, had always known who he was.

"Were you involved in this?"

I looked up. To lie? To tell the truth?

"No, Daddy," I lied. I needed to save us, to save our relationship.

"Those words. About the field. About laying a body to rest in the field. How would that boy know about our field? Did you take him there?"

So Daddy thought I'd taken Aaron to the field. It had made sense. To him, the worst-case scenario was that Aaron had been in the field, had found something about Daddy's secret.

"No," I replied, truthfully.

"Don't lie to me, Ruby." He was pacing now, like a wild animal strutting in its cell-like cage in a zoo. He wrung his hands, and he was practically frothing at the mouth. It was crashing down, and it was my fault.

Tears fell from my eyes. "I'm not lying. I didn't. I didn't. I'm sorry, Daddy."

He paced back and forth, back and forth.

I thought of the fingernails in my pencil box. I thought of them tucked in my backpack, the last piece of Clarissa unearthed. I thought about telling him. He would understand. He would completely understand, wouldn't he? But I couldn't bring myself to tell him. Not that I was ashamed of following in his footsteps. He had taught me well. I had done well with that part. I messed up with the note, but I'd done the important part well. No matter what happened, I knew that I'd done him proud in that respect.

I was afraid to tell him, though, that I knew his secrets, that all this time he had failed miserably at one thing—at keeping his killing hidden from me. Dad felt invincible in that garage, and I wanted him to keep feeling that way.

I needed to tell him, though. I needed him to know we were in it together. That I would do what I could to protect him to the end.

The words flashed in my mind. The final words from Mama's diary pages I found so long ago.

I leave with her and never come back.

I kill us both.

Either way, I think it's safe to say this.

Things will never be the same.

Neither of Mama's options came to fruition. Did she choose another path? No. I didn't think so. I think somewhere, deep down, I've known all along. I thought of the women hanging in the garage, the photographs. The words. And suddenly, I spewed the words I'd been needing to all along, the lie that he'd told to save our relationship but that had tainted the trust between us. If he'd told the truth, how different would our lives be?

"I know what you did to Mama. It wasn't suicide. I know you killed her. You killed her." The words flew out of my mouth before I could stop them. Before I could call them back. Stupid, Ruby. Stupid, stupid Ruby. This wasn't the time. It wasn't the time to tell him about Mama's diary and about how I know the truth. I've known it all along. I know the truth. I know that the words in Mama's diary aren't the whole story. It played out differently. Daddy made sure of it.

Daddy froze, his face turning even whiter and drawn. There was a long, long moment where I thought maybe it would all end there. I thought maybe like Mama, my diary would be all that was left to tell the story of who I was—and in her case, it was a false story, or at least not the whole truth.

But Daddy snapped out of it, pinned me up against the wall. His arm trembled, and his eyes burned with fury.

"You're right," he yelled, frothing at the mouth like a deranged fiend. "I killed her. I did it. I killed your mother."

"Why?" I asked, but I knew. I had always known.

He let up on the pressure on me, backing away. His arms were still trembling, and he was both looking at me and not. His eyes were faraway, in some other life that he didn't get a chance to live. A life where his daughter was normal and his wife was still alive. A life where his secret was safe and he could be his truest self. A life where he didn't fuck it all up, and neither did I.

But that life wasn't the truth, especially not now. His eyes seemed glassed over, like he realized that vision wasn't to be. When he finally spoke, it was like he was possessed, the Daddy I knew only a vessel for the words.

"I'm dark, Ruby. I'm twisted. I've always been. There's always been something within, something that I couldn't push down. Your mother knew that. She figured it out. And I think she was scared for you. But I would never hurt you," he murmured. He had completely backed away now, but I was frozen against the wall.

"I know, Daddy," I whispered. And I did. Even at his worst, even at his darkest, I knew that was true. He would never hurt me. He loved me. He was a good father.

"But she wanted to take you away. I found her diary. I could tell she was slipping away," he said, pacing around the room now. He looked older, suddenly, lost. He was changed, transported back to another time.

"She was going to hurt you Ruby or take you away. Her diary said she was getting ready for that. And I loved you. I always loved you. I always will."

I nodded, and he continued.

"I couldn't let her do that. I couldn't. I just snapped, Ruby. I did what I had to do. You were sleeping, and I waited for her. I waited for her in the bedroom with that rope. I did what I needed to do to save you." Tears rolled down his face. I rarely had seen him cry.

"It's okay, Daddy," I added after a long moment.

219

Daddy turned to me then, his face stoic. "But Ruby, it isn't. I did what I had to do. But I didn't have to enjoy it."

I stared, wordless. Silent at his admission. The lie had been broken, and now the truth was finally freely flowing between us.

"I enjoyed killing her. It was a high, like the strongest kind of addiction. I felt so alive when I took her life from her. The feel of the rope tightening around her neck as I strangled the energy out of her. The look of her body when I staged her in the garage. Writing the fake suicide note. It was such a fucking rush. I became addicted. Ruby, I'm sorry. I'm sorry you have to hear this. I'm sorry I'm not who you think I am. But I'm not sorry for killing her, or at least I wasn't in the moment. I did what I had to do, both to protect you and to do what I thought would get this darkness out of my system."

Daddy was crumpled into himself, his eyes defiant but his lip quivering. For the first time in my life, I saw the weakness in him. It was hidden behind the stoic eyes, the harsh words. It was there, though. Darkness was his true power, but Mama was his hidden weakness. What happened to her, the truth her death unlocked, was Daddy's complete undoing, even if he didn't realize it.

My eyes studied him. I noticed the bracelet, the red one I'd made him so many years ago. It was tied on his wrist today, a sign of a time so long ago when everything was different yet nothing was different, too.

I stared at him. It didn't work, I thought. Killing Mama didn't get the darkness out. It incited an unquenchable thirst. I knew, though, it wasn't his fault. Daddy's confession changed nothing. Nothing at all. I didn't know Mama, didn't love her. I love Daddy.

And I also know it's not all his fault. Not really. I know who I am. I know what she thought of me. I crossed the floor then, doing something I'd never done in sixteen years of life.

I wrapped my arms around him.

"I'm sorry, Daddy. I'm the one who is sorry. It's not your fault. It's not. It's mine."

He pulled back. "Of course it isn't."

"It is. My condition. Mama didn't love me. I pushed her to what she was going to do, and she pushed you. I caused all of it." I thought of the diary entry, the words. Mama didn't love me. I did this. I created this mess. Daddy just was the one who had to finish it.

"She was sick, Ruby. She had something wrong with her. It isn't your fault. Your Mama loved you, even if she didn't realize it. But I knew I could love you more. I thought I could. I thought I could calm the demons in me. But I was wrong. Fuck, I was wrong." His words are mixed with the threat of tears. It's all so messy. I look down at my watch, the glow of it flashing at me. It usually reassures me. Today, it doesn't. Nothing is glowing.

I looked at him and thought about mentioning the others. Maybe I could finally tell him. I could tell him what I knew. I could finally be a full, complete part of Daddy's world. I was already, wasn't I? I'd done it, too. Now we could be a team.

But Daddy spoke first. "I love you Ruby. I'll do anything to protect you."

And I know he will. I know we will. Things are such a mess. But now one of the secrets is out. Still, Daddy's not the only one with secrets—I have one of my own.

Does he know? Does he know on some level? I think about his dark eyes and how even though mine are blue, his eyes reflect mine right back. I see myself in them. Does he see me, the real me? Does he know?

And will he really have to protect me? I hope not. I hope my secret stays buried, just like the rest of Daddy's. We've come too far to get caught now, and the dead aren't speaking. I have to make sure I don't, either. Maybe it's not too late. Maybe things can be salvaged.

Maybe, if we're lucky, it'll all just disappear. Can Daddy make it disappear? Daddy says he needs to think, to make a plan.

He's brilliant. He can save this, can't he?

But what about Aaron? Will he be another casualty?

We should have put him in the killing game when we had the chance.

Stay Safe,

Ruby

Nov 8' 2018
6:57 p.m.
Diary,
This is goodbye.
For good.

I thought about taking you, but Daddy says we need to start over. That we have to leave this all behind. Our bags are packed, and we're heading out. We've got to get away, he said. We can't get wrapped up in this. He doesn't want the secret about Mama to come out, and he doesn't want me being involved in the investigation. He's told me it's time we start over, away from this town.

I didn't tell him that I know the truth of why we really have to leave.

There are too many bodies in the field. There's one body he doesn't know about. So many women left to tell the wrong story about us. We can't make them understand, so we have to escape while we can.

It'll really just be Daddy and Ruby, a grand adventure.

I want to tell him what I know, but then again, a part of me wants to leave his legacy unscathed. I owe that to him, to allow him to have that piece of himself. If I tell him what I know, will he see me differently? Mama's death was for me—it was a sign of love. The other women were for him. I don't want him to think he's selfish or to think less of himself. Even now, I know I need to protect his secret.

I'm scared, Diary. I'm terrified of leaving the familiar house and the familiar routine. I'm sad about leaving behind the garage.

But Daddy taught me to be strong and flexible when I need to. We're protective of each other, and we have to stick together now.

Just Daddy and Ruby, off to see the world. I don't know where we'll end up. But at least we'll be together. Always together. It's sad I won't get to say goodbye to Aaron. I wish he knew how much I love his red hair and how I hope it all works out for him. But I can't worry about that now.

My bags are packed. I took the photo of Mama and my red boots and some favorite clothes. Daddy said to pack light. He said we need to get going. I told him I just needed ten minutes to finish up here.

I wanted to say goodbye to you, Diary, and all the Diaries before you. It makes me sad to leave you, but maybe someday, my story will be able to be told. I won't be Ruby the retard, the different, the quiet. I'll be Ruby the girl with a story, the girl who wrote real, raw poetry. The girl the world will remember and fear. Maybe the kids will realize I was different in a good way all along.

I've left Clarissa's nails with you. I don't need them anymore. I know there are new collections for me to start, new options out there. I wonder if maybe someone will find them and it will bring Clarissa's daddy closure to have a piece of her left. I'd like to think that it will make up for what I've done to him, just a little bit. Clarissa was an awful girl, but I bet her Daddy is sad he couldn't protect her.

I have to go now, Diary. Daddy yelled that it's time to leave. I'll miss you. But maybe I'll start a new Diary with new poems. Maybe I'll find a different voice or a different style. The possibilities are endless.

Still, I know some things won't change. Daddy's hands are still shaking—and so are mine. There's a familiar hunger growing. The killing game might have to change, but I don't think it will go away. I think about all the possibilities waiting out there—all the people and places we can visit. I need to ask Daddy if he grabbed the camera. For documenting it all.

So, Diary, I hope you Stay Safe. Thanks for always being there for me.
Goodbye,
Ruby

P.S.-I'm leaving Mama's diary with you. I dug it out of the attic when Daddy said we were going to be leaving. He was busy downstairs, so I don't think he noticed. I thought about taking it with me, but I don't want to remember Mama like that. I want to start fresh, which means starting fresh with Mama, too. I think Daddy said we're going to stop at her grave before we leave. I'm going to tell her that I forgive her. I understand that life is, truly, fucked up sometimes. We all just do the best we can. Goodbye for real now, Diary. Stay safe and true.

The Diary of Caroline Marlowe
October 6, 2004
Dear Diary,

He came home with blood on his hands again.

To the untrained eye, it was almost imperceptible. But with everything else that's been going on, I was looking for it. Paying attention.

I've known for a while that something's not right.

He tries to pretend to be a loving father, a good husband. But I see the way his hands shake all the time. I see that darkness in his eyes. I feel the way he squeezes my neck when we're having sex, feel the hunger for more in his hands as they constrict.

I hear his lame stories about where he was so late and why there's dirt on his hands. I've watched him walk the path into the woods and heard about downed trees and all sorts of things.

Still, it can't be, can it?

Maybe everyone's right. Maybe the depression isn't under control like I thought. Maybe the treatment from the doctors isn't working. If I tell them my suspicions, who will believe me? I've done my time in the special wing of the hospital. I really don't want to be committed again. And if I throw these accusations out, he'll make sure I end up back there.

Ruby's not gotten any better, either, which is certainly grating on my nerves. So many things the other kids do at the park, in the stores, at parties that she doesn't. Something's very wrong. I can see it. Everyone says give her time. I don't need time to recognize the signs.

His mother isn't helping things, either. Always accusing me of being a bad mother, a bad wife. Her son is an angel in her eyes. I wonder what she'd say if she could see him now.

I should be scared. I am. But I'm more scared, I suppose, of being right and having to figure a way out of this mess than I am scared of him right now.

I'm just so tired. So tired of everything.

Be True,
Caroline

The Diary of Caroline Marlowe
October 7, 2004
Life is a fucking mess. I don't even know why I'm writing this.

I was never cut out to be a mother. I told him I wanted to terminate the pregnancy when I found out, but he wouldn't have it. He said we'd make it work. We'd be a family. I agreed.

But that was before I found out I was married to a fucking psychopath. It was before I gave birth to a daughter who has now been showing signs of severe developmental issues. The doctors say they have an idea of what it is, but we can't be certain until she ages a bit. I don't need a fucking doctor or a therapist to tell me that there's something wrong with my daughter. I also don't need to find the body to know that my husband is most definitely a killer, and that I could be next.

Life is a shitshow. My mother was right. She always said that.

I don't know a way out of this. I could take off on my own, but I don't feel right doing that. It's not that I have a strong mothering instinct, that's for sure. Then again, who could blame me? It's not like my daughter's normal or easy to love. Still, there must be some kind of undeniable chemistry or natural tendency. Because no matter how badly I want to, I can't leave knowing she'll be stuck with her psychopath of a father. Even I can't do that.

So what to do?

There is something wrong with him. Severely wrong.

There is something severely wrong with the child.

There is something severely wrong with me, in truth.

The way I see it now, I have two options.

I leave with her and never come back.

I kill us both.

Either way, I think it's safe to say this.

Things will never be the same.

Epilogue

Never the same indeed, the Prosecutor thinks as he looks at the last pages that have been tagged in evidence. So many were never going to be the same now. Caroline, the women slaughtered. Everyone assumed she'd committed suicide. How didn't they see it? And Ruby, the daughter. How could he have done this to her? What father could ruin their child so badly and still sleep at night? Of course, he hadn't slept at night, not every night at least.

The Prosecutor pats his trustworthy dog, Sita, on the head as he sets aside the copy of the final piece of evidence. Stroking the majestic dog's fur, his mind struggles to focus. It's all been too much. The retired working dog rests its muzzle on him as if to comfort him. In truth, he needs it. Because, despite his smug, confident face he puts on for the media, he got no satisfaction from the case. They'll obviously win. They have more evidence than the court would know what to do with. The diary of this serial killer's daughter outlined it all. The dates. The times. His methods. All of which they could corroborate. Ruby had made their job so much easier. Thank God the girl had left the evidence out on her desk before they had left town. She'd presented it on a silver platter. Did the girl want them to know the truth? It helped that her obsession with time seemed spot on, too.

But he still wondered what would happen to Ruby. A piece of him felt sorry for her. She'd killed a girl, it was true. But could she really be blamed? Look at what she'd been raised in, who she had been raised by. She'd convinced herself she was protecting her father, the man she worshipped.

How could he not have known that his daughter was watching him the whole time? How didn't he know? And to think the monster had ruined his little girl, the child he proclaimed to love so much.

He worried the courts would try to go soft on her because of everything she'd been through. Her condition, the loss of her mother, living with a fucked-up man for a father.

Still, no life is perfect. And everyone is a product of their environment—to an extent. People still choose, in the end. And she chose the killing game. She chose to follow in her father's footsteps, even though they had evidence she thought it was wrong. She'd written it all out for them, spelled out that she was of sane mind. She knew right from wrong, despite her condition. Despite her upbringing. She felt guilt. And she'd even premeditated it all. She knew the killing game was wrong. But she wasn't only an accessory to her father's crimes—she committed her own.

It wasn't easy, though, taking the rest of her life. In truth, jail was probably the best place for her. Because once you're that marred by the sights she saw, what help is there? What hope of rehabilitation existed for Ruby?

None. Absolutely none. They were all fucked indeed.

In truth, a confession wasn't even needed. It was all right there. They of course had the evidence, too. Ruby's bloody clothes she'd left in the shed, covered in Clarissa's blood. The bodies, all perfectly buried in the field. All but Caroline Marlowe's.

To his credit, he'd tried to protect his daughter, even up to the end. He tried to take the credit for Clarissa's death, even though it was pointless. They had the evidence to convict Ruby. Still, he was willing to do that for his daughter. Just like he'd told them repeatedly, through tears, that he'd tried to stop. That he'd set the game aside for months, even years at points because he knew he needed to be there for his daughter. It was clear that even though the sick bastard was a monster, he loved his daughter in his own way. In his mind, he tried to do right by her—he just succumbed to the darkness within.

Even serial killers had some standards, it seemed.

It was a shame that she was ruined. So many chances to turn things around, to go a different path than her father. What could have changed it? Could anything have changed her? So many lives ruined by one senseless freak. Wasn't that how it always was, though?

The trial started tomorrow. A piece of him felt sorry for the girl. But then he remembered what she'd done. They would throw the book at her, He was sure of it. A girl was dead because of her. A vicious murder.

Still, he wondered sometimes if things could have been different. With a different mother, a different father, a different life. Who could she have become?

It was the age-old question so many asked. But Ruby would never know.

Nor would he.

The prosecutor shoved aside his stack of copies, all the diary entries perfectly flagged. All of the damning words prepared, all of the corroborating evidence stacked in piles.

Ruby and her father were done for. There was no doubt. It was a certain win for him—but really, in a case like this, no one won. No one won anything at all.

Spatters of dust, flickered about
Spatters of red, glimmering too
Seething and bubbling,
Her hands start to shake
Where is the justice,
When will it come?

She is the dove, speckled but white
He is the God, awaiting deliverance
Peace she will bring
But rest she will not.
All is clean
For now

October 1, 2039
3:57 p.m.
Dear Diary,

I think my poetry is lacking now. It's a shame. Of course, there's no one to tell me whether it's good or bad. But how couldn't it be worse? It's been so long since I've seen him, since I've witnessed his work. It depresses me. It angers me. But mostly, it saddens me.

I miss him. I miss him so much. Is this how he felt when Mama left?

I know it's his fault, the missing of her. He did it. He killed her. I can still hear him saying those words, pinning me up against the wall as he cleared from his chest what I'd known all along. He killed Mama.

Of course, he killed all those other women, too. All but one.

The court made him out to seem like a bad man. But I know the truth. He wasn't bad. He was good. He loved me, really loved me. He would do anything to protect me from the darkness of Mama, of the world, and even of himself. His killing game kept the nefarious side of him contained to the garage. It helped him, I think, be a better father to me. I'm forever thankful.

I often think of the night it all went down, the night we got caught. I think of all that led up to the year that changed everything—Aaron, Clarissa, and the dark urges that were stirring more and more in Daddy.

The night it all ended, we'd been watching television in the room. The police pulled up to the motel, their lights flashing outside. But it was too late. We'd been lulled into feeling safe, and we didn't see the end coming. I was writing a poem on my bed in the motel, smiling at how I'd finally written something happy. By the time the pounding was happening, it was too late. I hid in the bathroom like Daddy told me to, hoping it would all disappear. We'd made it out of town, had two glorious weeks of travelling and seeing things I'd never thought I would see. In those two weeks on the run, we didn't even need the killing game to be happy. I got to see a different side of Daddy, of me, and I got to see all the possibilities I'd never even considered for a different life.

But it all came crashing down, like life always does. They'd traced us thanks to an anonymous tip, and the serial killer of our old town was finally in handcuffs after a lengthy fight with a knife. I was so afraid Daddy would get hurt. I remember Daddy's look of fear when they yanked me out of the bathroom. The handcuffs on my wrists, the cars surrounding us. The tears from Daddy's eyes as he fought to get me back, to save me.

I think about his selfless confession about Clarissa's death—even though he didn't do it. But when he saw me, when he saw my tears, I think he knew. I think he knew that the accusations were true, and I think finally after all that time, he realized that his secret life hadn't been so secret at all. It had seeped into his daughter, into her heart and her desires.

Bruised apples never fall far, and poisonous ones don't fall any distance at all.

The look in his eyes as he saw his daughter, me, in a new light, sent chills right through me. It still does. If only I'd have told him sooner, maybe he could've saved us both.

Did he figure it out then, that his secret wasn't safe? Did he have a moment of realization then, that I'd known all along? That I'd learned from the best?

That night was terrible. I was so scared. I had no idea what to expect in prison. I missed Daddy. I hated being away from him. But there was worse to come. Like how when the police found Clarissa's body, they discovered all the others. My choice wrecked Daddy's killing game. My choice got us caught. The knowledge of that was still the worst thing that's ever wrecked into my brain.

And it was even worse. Like how my diaries were used as evidence. Like how I realized that my words, my writing helped put not just me away—but Daddy too. It must have almost killed him—the betrayal. I still shake when I think about it. I was so upset when I realized it, that I stopped writing. I stopped writing for a long, long time.

I failed him. He did nothing but protect me and I failed him. He got caught because of me. He spent the rest of his life in prison because of me. He died there—because of me.

I killed him, too. I killed the only person I ever loved, the only person who ever truly loved me back. I am alone now, all, all alone.

It would have been better if Daddy had killed me, had put me in the field. At least I wouldn't have been alone. I'd have had all those women beside me. I wish he'd have buried me next to the redheads. I liked them the best.

I found out later that it was twenty-seven. Twenty-seven women buried in the field. Twenty-seven prostitutes and drifters that he slaughtered, that they unearthed. I'm only mad that I think I missed a couple. How did I miss a couple? Maybe I was young when they happened. I don't know. But I wish I had seen them all.

I can still picture their splatters, the paintings they made on the floor. Everyone made it sound so ugly. The other prisoners, my lawyer, everyone. They tried to make Daddy a villain. If only they had been there. If only they had seen.

He'd made them masterpieces, all of the beautiful, bloody masterpieces.

I've started writing again. I know that it can't hurt anything now. I write to Daddy sometimes. I can't send the letter of course. He won't get it. But I still write and tell him how I am. I just miss him. It's hard without him. It's so hard.

But I do like it here. It's quiet. It's peaceful. I like the solitude. I've always liked being alone. I wasn't always alone, of course. When I first got here, it was overwhelming. All the women around, all the questions and harassment and all of the interactions. It was too much. I was overloaded. The fluorescent lights and the yelling and the banging and the talking. I hated it. On the third night, I tried to bash my head in on the bars when my cellmate wouldn't stop singing. Too loud. Too loud. Always too loud.

The court system apparently decided I would do better in a quieter part of the jail. Alone. It was safer for everyone.

So here I am alone, finally alone.

They tell me in five years, I could be eligible for parole. I don't know how or why that works, but I guess that's the deal the lawyer got for me. I was told it was a bad deal, that I shouldn't have spent this long here. But I don't mind. Like I said, it's quiet. And what is there to go back to? Daddy's not out there anyways. I don't know what will happen to me if I get to leave her. Grandma's dead, after all, and I don't have any friends. Maybe they'll just let me stay here. Sometimes I wonder about Aaron, and where he might be. I wonder what his life is like. I've never seen him, not since that final time at the school. I wonder if he became a lawyer. I wonder if he helps lock up people like me and Daddy.

They should have been lenient and took mercy, my lawyer said. Because of Daddy and my upbringing. Because of my condition. But this was the best I could do because Clarissa's death was premeditated. It seems a little unfair. How about all of the things she did to me premeditated? At least I know she'll never do them again to me or anyone else.

232

I feel sorry that what I did got Daddy and me in trouble. I don't feel sorry for killing her though. The guilt has subsided with time. It's faded right into place.

Some things are still bad here. They don't let me pick what to eat, so some days it's hard. I hate certain textures, still. When I think about skipping meals, though, I think of Daddy. I think of him telling me that it's good to try new things and to be flexible. I try really hard to be. I want to make him proud. I wish I had him here with me. All I have is a picture of him. A smiling picture of us. I'm wearing my red rainboots, and you can see the red bracelet I made him on his wrist. Best friends. Always. Forever. Grandma took the photo. It's an instant picture. It's the same camera Daddy used to take his pictures. Sometimes I wish I had those, too, just so I could remember those days.

Grandma brought me the photo after I was sentenced. She would visit me in the early days. She was always weeping though and saying it was her fault, that she knew something was wrong. That she knew she shouldn't have let Daddy take care of me alone. I hated that she made it about her, as always. I eventually stopped taking her visits.

It took a while until my therapist I see agreed to let me have a journal again and writing utensils. She made it part of my rehabilitation. The agreement is she has to be allowed to read this diary, though. That's the promise. I'm okay with that. There's nothing to hide now. All the secrets are out.

When she let me have the markers, I picked red. Always red. After all, it's my favorite color. Daddy's too.

Red like my hair.

Red like apples.

Red like all the blood on his hands . . . and on mine.

I don't know how many more days I have here, but when I get out, the first thing I'm going to do? I'm going to my tree to write more poetry. Because even though Daddy is long gone, I still remember. I still remember all his secrets, all the things he taught me.

So until then, Diary, I'll write and I'll keep time and I'll wait.

I'll wait until I can make it all clean again. There's nothing you can't wipe clean, after all. Daddy taught me that, and I'll never stop believing that he was brilliant.

Because he was strangely, darkly brilliant, no matter what the courts say.

Stay Safe,

Ruby

The End

Acknowledgments

First and foremost, I want to thank my amazing husband for encouraging me to finish this novel and to send it out into the world to be read. You are my rock and my biggest cheerleader. Thank you for believing in my dreams and in my stories even when I'm struggling to find my confidence. I love you.

I want to thank Jenny Heinlein for always lending a reader's ear to my stories, for reading my books early, and for being such an amazing friend.

There are so many friends and family members who have been there for me along the way on this journey. I want to thank all of you who have supported me from day one and helped me chase these dreams. I especially want to thank my parents, Ken and Lori, for teaching me that words are power. Thank you to my in-laws, Tom and Diane, for always supporting my dreams. Thank you to my Grandma Bonnie for showing up at all of my events and spreading the word about my stories. Thank you to Christie James for being such an amazing friend and co-worker. I also want to give a special shoutout to Alicia Schmouder and Kay Shuma for being there from day one supporting my books.

There are so many bookstore owners, bloggers, and readers out there who I am so thankful for. Thank you to each and every single one of you.

Thank you, reader, for taking a chance on a small-town girl with a big dream. It's still surreal to see my books in others' hands and to know other people are reading about the characters who have haunted me for so long.

And last but not least, thank you to my big buddy, Henry, for being my true best friend. I hope we have many more days of cupcakes and snuggles in front of Netflix.

About the Author

L.A. Detwiler is a USA TODAY bestselling thriller author. Her debut thriller, *The Widow Next Door,* is a USA and International Bestseller with Avon Books/HarperCollins UK. *The One Who Got Away* released in February of 2020 with One More Chapter/HarperCollins UK. She wrote her first novel, a romance, in 2015 and has written articles for various online and women's publications. She has numerous romances published under Lindsay Detwiler, including the Lines in the Sand series set in Ocean City, Maryland.

L.A. lives in her hometown in Central Pennsylvania where she also teaches high school English. She is married to her junior high sweetheart, Chad. They have five cats and a mastiff named Henry who appears in every single one of her books.

To connect with L.A. Detwiler and find out where her next book event is, check out her blog at www.ladetwiler.com, her Facebook at http://www.facebook.com/ladetwiler, or her Instagram at www.instagram.com/ladetwiler. She loves to hear from her fans as well at authorladetwiler@gmail.com.

Printed in Great Britain
by Amazon